The Haunting of Gospall

The Haunting of Gospall

Solomon Strange

First published in July 2018 by Telos Publishing, 139 Whitstable Road, Canterbury, Kent CT2 8EQ, United Kingdom

Telos Publishing values feedback if you have any comments about this book please email feedback@telos.co.uk

The Haunting of Gospall © 2018 Solomon Strange

ISBN: 978-1-84583-973-4

Cover Art: © 2018 Linzi Gold
Cover design: David J Howe

The moral right of the author has been asserted.

British Library Cataloguing in Publication Data. A catalogue record for this book is available from the British Library.

Praise for
The Haunting of Gospall

'*The Haunting of Gospall* will continue to haunt you long after the last page. An assured, confident debut.' - Tim Lebbon, author of *Relics*

'Fascinating slice of mystery-horror, with a strong nautical flavour and some very eerie voodoo elements. An unexpected delight.' Paul Finch, author of the best-selling DS Heckenburg series

'A fast-paced descent into hell. Solomon Strange unleashes one scare after another, turning the screws without mercy right up until the devastating climax. Supernatural thrillers don't come more relentless than this.' Paul Lewis, author of *Small Ghosts*

'Crackling with invention and chills, *The Haunting of Gospall* has all the energy of a great first novel from a fresh new voice.' Steven Savile, author of *Glass Town* and *Parallel Lines*

'Beautifully written, emotive and dark. A world we all recognise and pray we may never live in.' Sam Stone, author of award winning *Vampire Gene* Series

To my wife Helen, my love, my rock, my everything.
To my children Robert and Holly, I couldn't be prouder.

We are here for the experience of life and I have been truly
blessed that you have been the best part of it.

INTRODUCTION
Steve Lockley

I've never met Solomon Strange, but we have spoken on the telephone a few times. He's clearly a fan of the horror genre, and it's easy to spot some of the touchstones in *The Haunting of Gospall*, but that's not a bad thing. It's a sign that we love the same kind of things.

Despite its title, *The Haunting of Gospall* is not a ghost story in any traditional sense. If that's what you were expecting you are in for a surprise, but it's a pleasant one. Strange merges naval history, voodoo, spiritualism and demonic possession. In a narrative that manages to weave events from the past with the present these disparate tropes are pulled together to create something that is more than the sum of its parts.

I was delighted to be approached by Solomon to help him edit the novel a couple of years ago and while we worked on several drafts this is very much Solomon's work, not mine. I'd like to think that I helped point him in what I thought was the right direction so if you enjoy this book then he deserves all the credit. If you don't, then I guess I deserve the blame. But this is not about me.

When the novel seemed to have reached the point where Solomon was ready to start shopping it around I thought that it would be the last I would hear from him until he had found a home for it; that's certainly the way it usually goes. But then I was contacted out of the blue by a mutual friend to ask my advice on what he should do with *The Haunting of Gospall* as the publishing world can move incredibly slowly.

There was always the possibility of self-publishing, and while that would have ensured that the book could be made available, there would always be the danger that it would sink without trace among the mass of books being released every week. What it needed was a publisher who might be willing and able to work with a debut author to bring out the best book they could and do more than just push it out into the world to let it find its own way. Telos Publishing was the first name to come to my mind. I had worked with them before and had no hesitation in recommending that they might be a good fit.

Sam Stone and David Howe are good people and they have pulled out all the stops to make this book available. I can't thank them enough for picking up the ball and running with it, and I'm sure that Solomon feels the same. I was also thrilled by the response of the fellow authors I approached with a request that they read the manuscript and offer a line of encouragement.

This industry is full of people who want to do their best and it's one that I'm so proud to be part of, and I'm delighted to welcome Solomon into the fold.

I really hope you enjoy this particular offering.

1

June 1809

Lieutenant William Pike woke with a jolt. In the darkness of the sleeping-cabin, his mind responded to the sound of movement above. Steadying himself with one hand on a deck-head beam he clambered from the cot, taking care not to disturb any of the other officers.

The morning was cold and dark on the deck of *Gospall.* He sucked in fresh salty air and listened to the thud of his own footsteps as he paced the war ship. Pike wiped a hand across his face in mild irritation. He'd been forced to leave his berth again because of persistent nightmares. Pike turned his head slowly, troubled by the final vestiges of the dream still playing out in his mind. *An ululation of voices echoing through a dense fog. Lurking within it were shadowy creatures that had once been human but were now relegated to this desolate purgatory. He heard their wails as they approached, their cries rising in outrage, and he had no doubt that their fury was directed at him and him alone.* Pike was breathing faster, his heart racing, even though he was now wide awake. *They encircled him; a spectral carousel of monstrous wraiths. He heard a chorus of mocking laughter, echoing eerily through the fog that had now all but filled the chamber. Their blurred faces and mist-concealed forms closed in.*

The dark dregs had lingered. Pike was a little unsteady, his body cold and clammy. These nightmares were getting worse and he had no explanation for them. He'd spoken to Mr Teague, the ship's surgeon, a couple of weeks before, and he had told him that it was probably down to the bad food disrupting his sleep. No-one could argue with that. The food was becoming less edible with each passing day. Most of the bread was edged with mould, and he had been over-indulging in his consumption of mistela, a particularly potent Spanish wine he enjoyed, perhaps a little too much on occasion. But the uneasy feeling persisted, as did the after-images of the dream.

He thought for a moment of *Larnet,* the last ship he had served on. It was considered inauspicious to dream of *ghost ships.* One of the senior officers, an intellectual man named Blake, who had made a study of the occult, had explained during dinner that the end of someone's life could be interpreted in numerous ways, but for a man of the sea, a vision of Charon, the mythological boatman, always meant death. Many of the younger officers had found his remarks amusing, but Pike knew most sea-going cultures around the world had believed that ships carried the departed to the realm of the dead. He shivered, then closed his eyes as a memory forced its way into his mind, a memory he'd tried hard to suppress. Harris, a young officer on *Larnet,* had experienced recurring dreams of a dark hooded figure standing on a small boat.

Although he was unable to see its face, it held a long staff in one hand, while the other extended out toward him with bony fingers that uncurled as if expecting payment for a journey to be undertaken across the oil-black river behind it. Pike breathed a long, tremulous sigh, his mind locked in the past. Harris had explained that during his last encounter with the figure he had felt compelled to place a sovereign into the palm of its skeletal hand. His eyes had displayed such fear, such abject horror, that Pike had placed a steadying hand on his shoulder to calm him. The young man had continued, stammering that as the wraith's fingers had closed around the coin, he had felt his life ebbing away.

Pike wiped small beads of sweat from his forehead. It was the terror in Harris's face that he couldn't forget. Harris had been found hanging from the rigging not long after that. Pike could still see the blackened skin of his bloated face, his protruding tongue and bulbous eyes that threatened to burst from their sockets. Had those bizarre dreams driven him to suicide?

Pull yourself together, man, Pike silently chided himself. He dropped his hands to his sides and quickened his step, forcing himself forward with an affected firmness. As the memory receded he tugged a round gold watch from his waistcoat, glanced at it, then quickly slipped it back.

'Soon be daybreak,' he muttered under his breath, looking up at the changing colour of the sky and the faint glow on the horizon. Still relatively young for his rank, he stood tall in his uniform; a blue jacket with gilt buttons and white breeches. Pike was well-built but not over muscular, with a tanned complexion caused by the abusive heat of a harsh foreign climate; his sun-bleached hair was drawn back and tied with a black ribbon, while his deep-set blue-grey eyes added to his youthful good looks. He loved being at sea, the feel of the wind on his back, the roll of the ship. From her counter to the elegant taper of her jib-boom to the plaque below the stern cabin window, she bore her name proudly; *Gospall* was far superior to any other ship classed as just fifth-rate. This was no ordinary ship of the line. She was new; designed to compete with and engage larger enemy ships.

She was much faster than others in the fleet and her tall mainmast made her more manoeuvrable; giving her not only an edge, but also a unique appearance. Designed as a predator, she fought in battle by evading enemy fire, then striking back quickly.

His pace slowed, and he came to a halt with thoughts of his new wife. He longed to see Rebecca again, with her fine dark eyes that smiled when she spoke. He paused, touching the gold locket beneath his shirt. It had been a small present from her, a token for his long lonely nights aboard ship. He thought of the sadness in her eyes as she had watched him leave for the East Indies. At least he'd be home soon enough.

The shadowy deck was hushed, apart from the creaking of wood and the sound of the sea. His gaze rested on a swinging lantern; the candle, all but extinguished, cast an inadequate glow. He recognised the stale smell wafting up from the crew's quarters, tobacco smoke and sweat. The men had worked hard and were exhausted. They needed rest and had received their fair share of grog. Captain Winstanly was fair and allowed his men a small ration of beer. When it was exhausted, they were allowed grog. Mixing rum and water together and adding lime not only sweetened the brew but helped fight scurvy.

Pike stood at the weather side of the quarterdeck, his blond hair ruffling in the damp breeze, remembering his first encounter with Winstanly. He wasn't at all what he'd imagined him to look like. Other Captains he had served under were menacing figures and harsh disciplinarians, whereas Winstanly was a little man in his mid-fifties. Dressed in his best frock coat with epaulettes on either shoulder, he had carried his cocked hat in his hand as he stepped onto the main deck of *Gospall* in Portsmouth. His lack of hair added character to his round, ruddy-cheeked face, and his tight-fitting uniform revealed a rounded stomach that threatened to burst the gilt buttons of his waistcoat. Winstanly was a jovial fellow; his infectious laugh had an instant, if not therapeutic quality, relaxing everyone around him. In truth, he looked more like a greengrocer than the Captain of a warship. This was one of Pike's first lessons: never judge a person by the way they look. He was to discover that Winstanly was the most intelligent seaman he would ever serve with. The man did not rule by instilling fear into the men as other officers did. He was a man of resolve, firm in his belief that there would be no floggings unless absolutely necessary, unlike on other ships where punishment at the gratings was administered with agonising regularity.

'It is important to gain the respect of the men, but you must value the crew. It is imperative that before going into battle you have mutual respect.' Winstanly had instilled in Pike a need for fair discipline and the importance of command. *'As Captain, you cannot afford the luxury of being anything less than perfect in the eyes of the crew. It is important to appear as though you have all the answers and are in complete control of any situation you may find yourself in. A Captain's life is tough, it's not easy. This is something you will find out for yourself, soon enough.'*

Pike had overcome his nervousness at the prospect of serving under such a distinguished man. Sharing the intimacy of life on board a fifth-rate he'd been able to observe his mentor at close quarters, learning continuously from one of the Navy's foremost frigate captains.

He drew in the fresh air once more, but the foul lingering taste of salt beef remained. Mixed with copious amounts of wine, it had resulted in a throbbing headache. Either his sense of taste had diminished, or the beef was beginning to taste like the carcass of a dead mule. Pike bent down, raised the lid of a barrel and scooped water from it with a ladle. He sipped, then threw what was left of it onto his face. It flowed down his forehead, trickling in smooth rivulets along the contours of his face, dripping from his jaw onto his breeches. His moist skin tingled as a light sea breeze passed over the deck of the ship. The wind had dropped, the sea was calm compared with the heavy swell of the night before when waves had washed over the decks and the sails had strained and creaked against the onslaught. It wouldn't be long before the boatswain's pipe would be blown by Samuels, a good man, in charge of the crew and sails. His mate, John Hall, a burly fine-natured sailor, assisted in rousing the men every morning. They were a good crew.

Pike shivered as he looked out over the dark sea, taking in the incipient glimmer of first light. He loved this time of the morning; it was so peaceful. The sound of a flapping sail diverted his attention. He craned his neck, staring at the rigging. To anyone other than a sailor, the maze of ropes would have looked complex and confusing, as it had been for him. *Gospall* was no ordinary ship, she was special, she'd cast a spell on him.

During evening meals around the Captain's table, Winstanly would be prompted by the Captain of the Marines and other senior officers to share his stories, and after a few glasses of wine he always obliged. At the end of his lengthy tales he often made a toast to those who had died in service. Having spent many a night in the Captain's quarters, benefitting from Winstanly's vast knowledge, he knew too well that you rarely received a second chance of promotion in the Navy. When the time came, he would be well prepared to seize the opportunity.

Life was hard as a sailor. For some reason he remembered

witnessing his first death under fire. Sammy had been the powder monkey, his job to ferry explosive charges to the gun crews below deck in the frenzy of battle. It was a dangerous job and assigned to Sammy because he was small and agile and could move quickly through the ship. Sammy had excelled in his role, manoeuvring around the men working the guns, navigating his way through the chaos of people, screams, shouts and the roar of cannon fire, so loud that the gunners' ears would sometimes bleed. In this bedlam, the wooden walls that surrounded the sailors were a death trap. In the heat of close-quarter battle, cannon balls weighing up to 32 pounds could be fired, and most injuries were caused by splinters created as the balls punched their way through the ship's hull. The impact produced showers of jagged splinters; huge shards of powder-stained wood that stabbed and slashed sailors with devastating effect.

It had been a vision of hell. He'd watched as the boy had been blown off his feet when a cannon ball struck the ship. Dazed and confused, he had saw Sammy sprawled across the floor, covered in debris with a shard of blood-drenched wood sticking out of his leg. Much of that day had been forgotten, but Pike remembered watching the surgeon go to work. This was the reality of war. Sammy had lain screaming and writhing, biting down on a folded leather belt, but the only option left to the surgeon had been to amputate the limb as quickly as possible. The cruelty of that afternoon still lingered with Pike, even to this day. Sammy had survived the operation but died two weeks later from a fever.

'Ship, ship approaching sir!' the lookout shouted, dragging Pike to the present.

'What colour does she fly?'

'I can't be sure, sir.'

With an open hand, Pike shielded his eyes from the sun and looked out to sea, turning his head slowly, watching for any signs of movement along the line of the horizon. *A trader*, he considered, *or maybe, something else.*

A light spray misted over him, speckling the lapels of his

jacket. He steadied himself against the rail, still watching. A three-masted ship was heading straight for them.

'Take up arms!' Pike bellowed. 'Quickly, take up arms!'

With the bell clanging loudly, men emerged from their quarters. Captain Winstanly slipped into his coat with its sea-tarnished epaulets, then adjusted his cocked hat as he looked toward the men at the wheel and mizzen braces.

He glanced at Pike, his eyes very much alive, and grinned. 'All hands to their stations, Mr Dawes,' he called out, 'let's take a closer look at her.' The young Third Lieutenant strode down the main deck, barking out orders. The men began to spread out on the yards; liberating the sails from their ties and rolling them down the masts, where they boomed and cracked against the fresh gusting wind. They watched with anticipation from the quarterdeck rail as the sails were quickly sheeted home.

Pike listened to the trill of calls, then the stampede of feet thundering across the deck; he looked through the rigging and heard the creaking spars and timbers as the deck tilted to the pressure of wind against tightened sail. Roused by her sudden thrust through the water, milky white spray dashed over the prow of *Gospall* in a great cataract, threatening to deluge the ship's company.

'It's French, sir,' the lookout hollered from the crow's nest.

Winstanly's fingers gripped the quarter-rail tightly and his eyes looked to the booming sails above.

'It's French,' the lookout repeated.

The Captain nodded, 'All right lad.'

'What the hell are they doing, sir?' Pike asked.

'It's a challenge, Will, and by God they've picked the wrong man to play games with.'

'It's *La Mort*, sir,' a voice called out.

'I know who and what it is,' Winstanly replied, looking through a telescope. A firmness stiffened his features. 'It's the French National Frigate *La Mort* all right. Can you speak French, Will?' he asked, forcing a smile.

'No, sir,' Pike replied, surprised by the question. 'But I do know that "mort" means "death".'

'It does indeed, Mr Pike. 'It's a bad business, this one. She destroyed a British frigate last year and crippled another. *La Mort's* a forty gunner and bigger than us. Do you think we can take her?'

Pike cleared his throat. 'Of course, sir.'

'*La Mort* eh? Let's give her a taste of death.'

Winstanly beamed a warm smile at Pike, as he handed him the telescope.

'Take a look.'

'Who's her Captain, Sir?'

'A man called Armand Ducos, an excellent military tactician by all accounts, but rather arrogant like most Frenchies.'

On deck and below, the gun captains and other older hands ensured that each division was ready for battle. Anxious scarlet-coated marines settled into place at the nettings. Some made the sign of the cross, while others scrambled aloft to man the fighting tops, armed with muskets to shoot down onto their enemy.

Painted in the darkest colours, *La Mort* was like a shadow, a phantom ship that inspired dread in those who looked upon her. Pike tore his eyes away from the formidable frigate and watched the gunner as he made his way along the deck, pausing to speak to each of the anxious gun crews. The men stood ready with their rammers and sponges. Next to them were small wooden barrels of sand that contained slow-matches, ready to be used if the flintlocks failed; it had been known to happen and could prove disastrous during battle. More sand had been sprinkled on the boards below the gangways, spread as a precaution to prevent the men slipping if water came on board in the heat of combat.

Pike raised the glass once more and felt a sour sickly feeling in his stomach. He sighed nervously as *La Mort* came into view; the large ensigns flapping from gaff to masthead, an arrogant display of French pride. He stared at the tall figure on the quarterdeck near one of three small guns. The man extended a telescope and trained it on *Gospall*, moving it carefully, until Pike could almost feel the Frenchman's contemptuous gaze upon him.

As Pike lowered the glass there was a tremendous bang, and a moment later a waterspout like whale-spewed water rose from the ocean. A second ball quickly followed, bouncing along the rippling surface.

'Is that the best they've got?' a seaman shouted amid jeers and nervous laughter.

'Steer due west,' Winstanly ordered. 'And hoist the flag.'

'Aye sir!'

From *La Mort's* most forward gun came an enormous puff of white smoke. It was swiftly followed by the ear-piercing screech of another huge ball, which this time ripped over the heads of the crew.

'Stand ready, lads,' Pike called. 'We'll return fire soon enough.'

He turned to Winstanly and handed him the telescope.

Men crouched uncomfortably, keeping close to masts, guns and anything that would offer them some form of protection against the French onslaught.

Another gun fired, its ball smashing into the hull with such force that *Gospall's* timbers shook. Some men screamed, while others glanced nervously at the trembling masts, expecting them to collapse at any moment.

In a heartbeat, a cloud of smoke rose from the enemy vessel, followed by the whine of another massive ball. It pounded the sea a few feet from the quarterdeck.

'Quick! To the pumps!' Pike shouted.

'Two points to starboard,' Winstanly called sharply.

If *La Mort* continued on her current heading she would be forced to collide with the British warship. It was an incredible strategy; a ruse Winstanly hoped would work. Ducos was faced with a dilemma: if he altered course, it would prevent a collision but would leave his stern open to *Gospall's* mighty guns.

'Bring her five points to starboard.'

'Aye aye, Captain.'

Winstanly flicked a glance at Pike, and as the big wheel began to roll, men rushed to their stations, preparing for the inevitable attack.

'Marines to the taffrail. Shoot at will,' the Captain hollered. 'More sailors to the weather braces, Mr Deacon.' The wind assisted *Gospall's* manoeuvre, and the vast array of canvas suddenly came to life, straining and cracking to its yard.

La.Mort moved swiftly, closing in on the British frigate.

'Come about, easy now. Ports open.' Winstanly's tone was composed, in stark contrast to some of the men, who looked on wide-eyed as *Gospall* charged toward the other vessel. The bowsprit moved across *La Mort's* mainmast so close that Winstanly saw several French officers on the quarterdeck.

Moments later *La Mort's* side exploded into ferocious gunfire, and thick clouds of smoke swept through the rigging like dense mist on a dark London night. *Gospall* trembled under the sheer weight of iron pounding her bows, taking out a few guns and inflicting casualties. The gun crews were now in position at the larboard side and eager to engage their adversary.

Winstanly's strategy had worked. Had *Gospall* not altered course with such haste she would have been smashed into oblivion.

Sailors staggered dazed and shocked, as others lay screaming on the blood-washed deck with pieces of human debris scattered around them.

'Lieutenant Henrick,' Pike shouted through the chaos. 'Order man, restore some order.'

The young officer acknowledged him and rushed to his duty, wiping blood and grime from his face.

The men yelled out to one another. It wasn't long before some form of normality had been restored, at least as much as could be expected under the circumstances.

Through the gunsmoke Pike saw sailors clambering up poles

like spider monkeys, moving across to dangling tangles of rigging. They worked furiously, desperately trying to repair the damage.

'Easy, lads,' Winstanly called out. He raised his sword into the air, shouting 'Long live the King,' then sliced the blade down. 'Fire!' *Gospall's* response was ear-bursting as gun after gun exploded into long fierce flames.

The French began shooting from the mizzen top, and small lead balls thudded into the quarterdeck as unseen marksmen targeted the Captain. Winstanly stood firm, unwilling to move.

Men fell to the swift crack of musket fire. The youngest midshipman, Tom, had been eager to see action but now stood rooted to the deck, watching in awe, his eyes absorbing the reality of the situation. He stared at the broadside of *La Mort* as the thunderous boom of cannon fire blazed, and a ball sped through the air and cut the boy in half.

Pike closed his eyes against the sight, then turned toward Winstanly, clasping a fist behind his back. The Captain's features stiffened. 'War, Will, bloody war.' His words were a harsh whisper.

Despite the tumult, a scarlet-coated marine's cry could be heard from the masthead, a high-pitched scream that preceded his tumbling body. Another man fell from the crosstrees; his lifeless body smashed through the nettings and hit the deck with a sickening thud.

Pike kept a watchful eye on the crew. 'Come on, lads!' he shouted, clenching his fists. Spurred on, they raced one another as they had during practice drills. The rammers worked furiously, tamping down the balls and wads, competing with one another as they had during evening contests. This time the reward wasn't for a tot of rum, it was for their lives.

Gospall's jib-boom was passing *La Mort's* stern, her name clearly visible to all on board. Pike looked on, his fists still clenched. 'Now, sir?' he asked without even looking at the Captain.

'Aye, Will, give the order.'

'Fire!' Pike roared.

McAndrews, the chief gunner, discharged one of the carronades, a short cannon of large bore but still a mighty beast. It recoiled with incredible force, to the grizzly-faced Scot's cheer.

La Mort's frame shuddered as the huge ball punched a hole in her stern. For a moment, there was an uneasy silence, then it exploded, unleashing a flaming hail of grape shot, which tore through the vessel.

Along the side of *Gospall*, all of the sleek black 12-pounders thrust back on their tackles, and almost every shot tore through *La Mort's* hull. Their swift response had a devastating effect on the French vessel; the sudden roar of *Gospall's* broadside seemed to engulf *La Mort*. She had lost her foretopmast, and amid the savage gunfire, her deck was strewn with wreckage, and shattered bodies.

Seeing the enemy ship totally disabled, Pike gripped his Captain's arm, yelling, 'They've surrendered sir,' amid the men's cheers.

As he stepped down from the quarterdeck, he looked around at the men's faces, surprised to see that so many were still alive. Winstanly placed a hand on Pike's shoulder. 'I'm very proud of you,' he said, then smiled, turning back to the rest of the exhausted crew. 'Well done, lads.'

On boarding the frigate, they found the French Captain mortally wounded. His chest had been torn apart by shrapnel and his right arm severed. Two of his Lieutenants had also been killed, along with more than a hundred other men; *La Mort's* flag was hauled down and the First Lieutenant surrendered Ducos's sword in humiliation.

At Portsmouth, every ship in the harbour cheered for *Gospall* as she returned valiantly with her prize and the flag of *La Mort*. William Pike was reunited with his wife Rebecca once more, and in July of that year Captain Winstanly was made a Knight of the Realm at St James's Palace.

2

London – Present Day

Sean Webster sat in the café, slowly sipping coffee. The small table was in a perfect location, right next to the window. Cars crawled along the busy road, and agitated drivers cursed each other under their breath. One frustrated driver in a black Mercedes gave the V sign to the car in front, then jammed his palm into the middle of the steering wheel, keeping it there for a few moments. The abusive horn did little more than blend into the mayhem of city life.

Sean shook his head. It was a real pain trying to drive through the West End, but he didn't agree with road rage mentality. His attention shifted to the large double windows of Angelo's, an exclusive hair salon opposite. He leaned forward, hands on the arms of the chair, and raised himself up, half out of his seat, hoping to catch a glimpse of his girlfriend. No joy. He slumped back into his chair with a heavy sigh.

His fingers drummed the table top. Sophie never was one to be punctual, but it wasn't her fault. The salon owner could be a right taskmaster. She rarely finished on time these days. A promotion to manageress had increased their income but had meant longer working hours. Sean ran a hand through his hair, sweeping it back off his forehead as Robbie Winters' voice flowed through the air from an overhead speaker. He listened momentarily to 'In Dreams', but the music didn't settle him at all.

Christ, she was late tonight!

Sean felt on edge but didn't know why. He scanned the collection of shops, restaurants and bars, but soon his thoughts drifted, and latent memories endeavoured to push their way back into his mind; these memories made him feel increasingly uneasy.

He'd promised his therapist that he wouldn't dwell on the past. *Christ, it was easier said than done.* How could he forget? The faint, insidious voices inside his head always reminded him of the past. *Yet … yet … there was something inexplicable about what had happened.* He shuddered, dismissing niggling thoughts in case they gave rise to more questions, then more doubts, then … *Enough.*

A flimsy mist drifted toward him, and with it the faint smell of an e-cigarette. Sean turned away from his own dishevelled reflection in the window and noticed two middle-aged women sitting at a table across from him. One of them wheezed a cough, while the other took a drag of the slender tube wedged between her fingers, then drawled on in a strong Glaswegian accent. Although it was legal, he didn't agree with vaping, but the café owner didn't seem to mind the practice. The woman drained her coffee cup and continued talking, her voice loud, grating on his nerves. The pair looked as bored as he felt. His head thumped and the sour taste in his mouth reminded him of the previous night's heavy drinking. It'd been a mistake; too much Courvoisier in too short a time had induced sleep, but with the usual side effects.

The traffic was moving faster now. He watched a few anxious people trying to cross the main road, but they were forced back onto the pavement by a steady stream of vehicles. Four teenagers ignored the flow and darted across the road with little regard for their own safety as Sophie emerged from the dark-tinted glass doors of the salon. Head bowed, she wore a light blue top tucked into figure-hugging trousers, their fashionable cut emphasising her trim figure. Sophie raised her head with a frown creasing her brow; she looked around, searching for Sean. She swept long golden strands of hair from her face, still looking confused.

'Thank God,' he mumbled to himself. 'It's about time.' Sean threw a couple of coins onto the green plastic table, then made his way out of the café and onto the street. He rubbed his temples with stretched thumb and forefinger. It didn't help; his head still pounded from the hangover. The weekend's alcohol abuse and lack of sleep were taking their toll with a vengeance.

He glanced at his wristwatch again as he waited to cross the busy road. Through gaps in the traffic and amid the bustle of people, he saw Sophie strolling along the main street with a clutch bag in hand, still looking for him.

'Oh, shit.' His eyes widened as he watched two men approaching her, their intentions unmistakable. Muggers looking for a victim; and she was their target.

'Hey!' he shouted, as they grabbed her by the arms.

Sean stepped off the kerb. Instantly a car's horn sounded angrily, forcing him to jump backwards as the vehicle sped past. He tried again and again but couldn't get across the road.

'Leave her alone,' he yelled, but his voice was lost in the commotion.

She was dragged into a narrow alleyway, leaving him with an overwhelming feeling of utter panic and uselessness.

'Oh God!'

Sickening thoughts screamed out as he waited to get across the road.

'C'mon,' he shouted at the traffic. 'just stop for a moment!'

Constantly on the move, he struggled to control his jangling nerves, but his thumping heart wouldn't allow it.

'Fuck it!' With every second vital, and without thinking of his own safety, he leapt onto the busy road, moving quickly to the sound of screeching brakes. A lorry swerved, missing him by only inches. It was chaotic; some people shouted, others mouthed obscenities, while yet more let their resentment be known by blaring horns.

It didn't matter. No-one was hurt, and Sean had reached the other side of the road uninjured. He mounted the pavement and ran toward the opening of the alleyway, breathing heavily.

Filled with apprehension, he prayed that Sophie was all right. His breaths came in short gasps as he slowed to a jog.

Frantically, he searched for any sign of his girlfriend, but couldn't see her anywhere.

'Where the hell have they taken her?' he said aloud, still

looking around. Brick walls either side of him were black, and the ground littered with old newspapers, broken bottles and used syringes.

Sean quickened his pace and heard a scream, a woman's scream, and mocking laughter.

'Oh Christ!'

He ran toward the sound, stopping when he heard muffled voices.

A street lamp cast uneven shadows; he took advantage of them, quickly slipping into the concealing darkness, and watched.

'What's in the fuckin' bag?' one of the thugs hissed at Sophie.

'Take it.'

The gaunt-faced youth snatched the bag from her hand.

'Just leave me alone …'

She shuffled backwards, almost stumbling, creating distance between herself and the man as he rummaged through her belongings for money or anything of value.

Advancing on her now was another teenager, heavy-set and grinning.

'You look real good.' His voice was deep with a Jamaican twang. He moved closer, uninterested in the contents of her bag, making his own intentions clear.

Sophie's eyes widened in horror. His hand was slowly rubbing the crotch of his jeans, stimulating himself. 'We gonna 'ave some fun.'

As he approached, she groaned in disgust.

'We gonna 'ave some real fun,' he repeated, moving closer.

Sean stepped out of the shadows.

'Don't,' he said through gritted teeth, as the big man whirled around to face him. Matted dreadlocks hung loosely around his shoulders, and a thick scar ran the length of his broad face. The man clenched his fists, slowly sucking air through his teeth.

He looked at Sophie. 'You think he's gonna help you?' The thug laughed dismissively, then turned back to Sean. 'What the fuck's it got to do with you?'

'If you touch her, then I'll touch you.'

'Back off. You think you're a tough guy or something?'

'No, just leave my girlfriend alone.'

'Ha! Your girlfriend. She's gonna do things to me that you could only dream of.'

'Let her be.'

'Or what?'

'You'll find out.'

'You no see it? You gonna die!'

'Yeah, right.'

'Boy, keep your mouth shut.'

'Make me.'

Sean drew both assailants' attention away from Sophie.

'My boy's gonna slice you,' said the first.

Sean's heart began pumping faster; the adrenaline rush had started. It was fight or flight, and he wasn't going to run. The tall, sinewy youth dropped Sophie's bag and reached into the pocket of his faded jeans. There was a clicking noise as his switchblade opened.

'Cocky bastard,' he snarled, looking at Sean.

Sean's gaze switched from one man to the other, but the menace turned his stomach. He looked into the big thug's face, trying to keep his nerve and hide his fear. The other man's eyes burned with a fierce intensity, making Sean sweat.

'I can hear your heart man, beatin' fasta and fasta,' the black man grinned, but there was no humour there.

Sean quickly twisted, turning side on, hoping this would give the thugs less of a target. He watched them both, feeling intimidated by the thug's size and the deranged look on his face. His main focus was on the one with the knife. He glanced at the thin youth's hand and saw his grip on the switchblade tighten. Time seemed to pass at an incredible pace, and Sean had just enough time to look back up before the huge Jamaican lunged at him.

He kicked out at the man's groin, and as he doubled up, brought the side of his hand down hard onto the back of his exposed neck. The black man slumped to the ground. Sean moved fast, focusing on the other thug charging toward him. He swiftly stepped to the side, avoiding the knife, and grasped the thin man's wrist, holding the weapon away from his body, then smashed the heel of his hand into the youth's face with a bone-crunching crack. The blow sent the man sprawling backwards, and the switchblade struck the cobblestones with a clatter. The man staggered for a moment, blood gushing from his nose, then collapsed onto the litter-strewn ground.

Sean felt drained. He ran to Sophie and slid an arm around her shoulders. Her whole body was trembling.

'It's over,' he said, kissing the top of her head. 'C'mon. Let's get out of here.'

He bent down, picked Sophie's bag up, then wrapped an arm around her.

As they walked toward the main street, he looked over his shoulder, checking on the two thugs. They still lay on the ground, amongst the dirt and filth.

3

Beams of sunlight crept through the partly-open curtains into the darkened bedroom.

'Get up, you'll be late for work,' Sophie said.

Sean's eyelids fluttered open. 'What time is it?' he asked, yawning louder than he had expected.

'Seven thirty,' she replied with a smile creeping across her face.

He shuffled over to the other side of the bed and kissed her cheek softly.

'Hurry up.'

He yawned again, rubbing a hand across his face.

'You'll be late.'

Sean leapt from the bed and grabbed his bathrobe. 'Won't be long, I'm just going to take a shower,' he called, hurrying into the bathroom. He closed his eyes, relishing the soothing warm water, but his thoughts soon shifted to Sophie.

The attack a week before had troubled her, but she had said she wasn't going to let it get to her long-term. But what would have happened if he'd lost the fight? Fortunately, his years of martial arts training had paid off. Hopefully the police would find the scum as soon as possible and arrest them. Sophie had broken down a couple of times, and they'd spent a few of hours giving statements at Fairhaven police station. She was determined to see these thugs caught, but he wasn't holding his breath. It was a big city and the constabulary was stretched.

'Wait a minute, it's Sunday,' he laughed. 'You devious little ...'

Sean returned to the bedroom and found Sophie sitting up in bed.

'Fooled you.'

'Am I that gullible?'

She smiled, then nodded as he moved toward her.

Later, Sean sipped black coffee from a mug clenched in both hands, while he watched TV. There was a serious tone to the newsreader's voice.

'There are unconfirmed reports that secret arms deals may have taken place between Russia and the Middle East. Fears are growing amid rumours that Iraq and Iran may have already purchased biological and nuclear weapons from renegade factions within Russia. The President of the United States of America has expressed great concern and condemned any such deals as unacceptable.'

Sean watched, stone-faced.

'What the hell are the Russians playing at?'

Sophie shrugged her shoulders. 'I wouldn't know.'

'It's no secret that Russia and China were opposed to the US's and Europe's involvement in Libya,' he said. 'But if this is true, it's just plain crazy. I can't believe they would actually trade weapons of mass destruction with these countries.'

She shrugged her shoulders again. 'Sean, they're politicians. You can't trust any of them. Look at our own government for God's sake, they're up to their eyeballs in dodgy deals.'

'But this is different, it's …'

The telephone rang.

'I'll get it,' he said, moving away from the cluttered kitchen table toward the living room.

'Hello.'

'Is this Sean Webster?'

'Yes.'

'My name is James Roocroft. I'm a close friend of your mother's. I'm afraid I have some terrible news for you. She passed away yesterday.'

He inhaled deeply, 'You're … you're …' he stammered, ' … certain it's her?'

'Who is it?' Sophie called out from the kitchen.

'She can't be …' He trailed off, bewildered and trembling.

'Sean?'

When the voice on the other end of the phone fell silent, Sean dropped the receiver. Sophie hurried into the room.

'What's happened?'

He stared through her, feeling lost to a horrible dream.

'Tell me Sean … Please … What's happened?'

'Mum's dead.' The words sounded unsteady and somehow disconnected, as though they had come from someone else's lips.

'Oh, Sean.'

'She's dead …' he repeated, staring blankly past her.

Sophie slid an arm around his shoulders, and he wept as the clock on the mantelpiece chimed.

4

An alluring blue sky hung low over the distant hills, almost touching the grassy peaks, and a peacefulness filled the air of the meadows. Worker bees droned, gathering nectar from wild flowers in the hedgerows, as grass rippled in the light breeze. Sean and Sophie sat in the car as a tractor trundled past them in the opposite direction, its machinery clunking and clanking along the country road. Overhead two skylarks soared through the air with incredible grace, then flew off toward a nearby forest. The whole area was a rich tapestry of native flora, knapweed, Lady's Bedstraw and bluebells, but Sean hardly noticed the sweet fragrance drifting in through the open car window. His attention for the moment was on the rear-view mirror. There was a distinct darkness beneath his eyes through lack of sleep and redness around his eyelids. With the news of his mum's death he'd insisted on driving to Somerset, even though Sophie had pleaded with him not to. He was in no fit state to travel all that way; he needed more time to come to terms with his mother's sudden demise. But how could he? They had been devoted to one another. There had been only the two of them throughout his childhood and they had developed an unbreakable bond.

The leather seat creaked beneath Sean as he shifted position. It had been a long, tiring drive. His muscles ached, and his eyes felt dry and scratchy with lids too heavy to keep open. The journey from London had been hectic, compounded by the dull drone of a persistent headache.

'Friggin' hell!' He swerved the Ford a little, avoiding a cat running across the road. Sean shook his head in frustration, but it didn't shift the thoughts that tormented him. *She's dead! She's actually dead!* It didn't make sense. It was crazy but, despite the fact that everyone loses their parents eventually, he couldn't believe his mother was gone. It was too sudden, and she had been far too young. He swallowed hard, but the lump was still there, along with a feeling of disbelief, so strong it threatened to overwhelm him.

In a moment he was engulfed in a barrage of emotions; sadness, grief and guilt. Why hadn't he been there for her? Perhaps he could have … He stifled a sob, trying to banish the image of his mother from his mind, sitting dead in her chair.

The Mondeo gathered speed. *She was always a healthy woman.* His hands tightened around the steering wheel. *What could have caused this heart attack?*

'Oh, Mum,' he muttered, choking back the tears.

'Sean.' Sophie glanced at him. 'Are you okay?'

Sean's eyes stung from the gathering tears.

'You haven't spoken for a while?'

He didn't want to turn and face her, didn't want to cry. He had to be strong.

'Please talk to me.'

He couldn't speak, the lump in his throat wouldn't allow it.

'Sean!' she screamed. He was oblivious to the approaching bend. She braced herself, hands flat against the dashboard, as the hedgerow grew threateningly closer.

He jerked the steering wheel to the left, stabbing the brake with his foot. Everything happened so fast. The brake pedal began resisting violently, pushing back at him, but he kept the pressure on, praying they would stop in time. His whole body tightened in anticipation of the collision. The car was thrumming, grinding loudly as the ABS took over and slowed the vehicle to a nerve-jangling halt.

He sat motionless for a few moments, his heart hammering.

'Sorry.' His voice was little more than a whisper.

'Christ! You scared me then. Want me to drive for a while?'

Sean shook his head. 'No. I promise I won't zone out again …'

'I can't take the pain away, but I'm here for you,' she said.

As Sophie studied his face, Sean knew he couldn't hide his inner turmoil from her. She always knew when something was wrong with him. Call it female intuition, or some kind of sixth sense she'd always had. Whatever it was, she wouldn't let him alone until he came out with what was bothering him.

'Talk to me. Tell me how you're feeling?' she said, as if she was reading his mind again.

'I don't know how I feel …'

'It's understandable that you're confused … and shocked.'

'It's more than that. Something's not right,' he said, even though he could not explain it.

'Perhaps you're in denial.'

'No, you don't understand.

'Sean, your mum passed away because she had a weak heart.'

'Says who? She was never ill a day in her life.'

'But …'

'I know she died from a massive heart attack, but it was so sudden, so unexpected.'

'What are you trying to say?'

'I don't know.'

'People die all the time. Sudden death is the most difficult to take.'

'I know all that. I get it … But what really caused it?'

Sophie shook her head.

'I'll find out what happened,' he said. 'Don't ask me to explain, I can't, but something's wrong.'

He looked up into Sophie's concerned eyes, and for a moment he thought he saw uncertainty and something else too: trepidation.

'Whatever happened,' Sophie said, 'you'll eventually come to terms with it …'

'I know you're trying to help, Soph … but … Look. Let's just get there in once piece, okay?'

Sophie said nothing as Sean pulled the car back onto the road, and at that moment he was relieved for the silence.

5

The grave was small, freshly dug to accommodate a tiny, frail woman. There were few mourners present; just a couple of neighbours offering their final respects, their faces reflecting inner grief. Reverend Neil Willis's shoulders stooped, diminishing his physical stature. He read from a small black prayer book, which rested in the open palms of his hands, the pages fluttering in the growing breeze.

Sean stood at the edge of the grave, head bowed and face pale. For him the whole thing seemed to be playing out in slow motion as though he were an observer to unfolding events in some nightmare. Two stone angels watched from afar with lichen-filled eyes, their sombre expression a reflection of the day itself. Behind them, willow trees loomed with full summer foliage, surrounded by an array of out-of-control shrubs and bushes, while pale-coloured vines ran freely across ancient headstones. The grey slabs stood dark and ugly, worn away by the passage of time.

Kraa … kraa … kraa …

The guttural squawking of crows threatened to drown out the balding vicar's words. The vicar peered over the rim of his small, rounded spectacles in a gesture of annoyance at the disruptive birds, as speckles of rain dampened his face and marred the glass over his eyes.

Heavy clouds hung overhead, and the sky grew darker by the minute. The dismal rain increased and the grass around them became soggy. Sean fastened his black jacket, but his clothes were already damp and the cold seeped into his already chilled bones. Around him the small gathering of people grieved, their garb as sombre as the sky itself.

Sophie slipped a hand around Sean's waist. His body was trembling from exhaustion and felt incredibly unsteady.

'Are you okay?' she asked.

Sean didn't answer. He felt so empty, so desolate. As the coffin was lowered, he swayed wearily over the deep pit, feeling near to physical collapse. Fortunately, Sophie eased him away from the open grave with the help of another mourner. Sean moved quietly, led away down the gravel path between gravestones to a waiting car.

Even the dark-suited driver of the funeral car was visibly saddened. He was James Roocroft, the friend who'd broken the news of Christine's death to Sean. He volunteered his services as driver free of charge. He tried to hold back his own tears, not wishing to upset the couple, as he manoeuvred the black limousine slowly down the lane.

Thankfully it was a short distance to Christine's home. The car slowed and eventually stopped outside the cottage. Quickly wiping away tears with a crumpled handkerchief, James turned toward Sean and Sophie.

'Can I help you inside?' he asked.

'No thanks, James, you've done more than enough,' Sophie replied.

'Not at all,' he said with a wavering smile and a sadness that was all too evident on his own face.

He made his way to the passenger side of the vehicle, breathing heavily, and opened the door. Sophie eased her way out, followed by Sean.

'Thank you.' Sean's voice was weak.

'Would you like to come in for a cup of tea or coffee?' Sophie distracted the driver from sombre thoughts.

'No thanks, I've got another call to make today,' he replied. He said his goodbyes, wished them good luck, then got back into the car.

Sean watched as the black Mercedes glided down the road and disappeared from view.

They walked slowly toward his mum's home. Bramble Cottage, with its thatched roof and white brickwork, was isolated, set into a grassy bank that swept around from the sides. A narrow gravel path wound its way to the front door.

On the bank stood an array of beautiful flowers; primroses, lilacs, peonies and bluebells, all cheerfully spread throughout the pretty garden. The windows were small, with hand painted shutters that gave the cottage a homely character.

Sean forced himself toward the front door, and Sophie followed, her feet crunching against the gravel, the sound harsh against the day.

He put the key into the lock, turning it with a trembling hand, then drew a breath to steady himself before entering. The door opened into a small cluttered living-room. He walked in and looked around, spotting a silver-framed photograph of his mum on a round teak table. Memories surged, so did anguish, and unable to suppress the grief any longer, he slumped onto the well-worn chesterfield and wept bitterly.

6

August 1810

The sun blazed its relentless heat down on the crew of *Gospall*. She moved effortlessly through the deep blue water, her reflection cast onto the ever-shifting swells of the Mediterranean Sea.

Pike shielded his eyes with an open hand, looking out to sea. In the distance he saw the *Gilbert* and the *Arden* drifting easily. 'You there, get to it!' a voice barked from the far end of the deck. Pike turned and saw Captain Tanner pointing at a petty officer.

'Aye, sir,' he replied and scuttled off.

'The new captain drives the men too hard.' The surgeon's voice was harsh in Pike's ear.

'What's troubling you, Samuel?'

'Him,' he said, pointing toward Tanner. 'Poking his nose where it doesn't belong. I'm the medical officer on this ship, so why does he see fit to interfere?'

'In what?'

'Bossing my lad around. Not only that, slapped him across the back of the head he did. I've never known the surgeon's mate treated that way before. He's a right little tyrant, Will, that's for sure. He even told me to stay off the quarter deck.'

'As ship's surgeon,' Pike said, 'you have a right to be here.'

'Aye, I do. I'm responsible for tending the sick, the injured, and for performing surgical operations, so why doesn't he trust me.'

'Why wouldn't he trust you?'

'You tell me. But he wants to see my journal of treatment every other day. Cap'n Winstanly left me to it. He was a good captain. Tanner's a bloody buffoon. Surely, you've heard the rumours? His father's Sebastian Tanner, well known in the

House of Lords, and by all accounts has the ear of the Admiralty. Politics has played its part in his position here.'

'I've heard stories.'

'They're a bit more than that. He's a bad 'un, he has a reputation for punishment. A friend of mine on the *Newark* said he insisted the bosun's mate used the heaviest knots to lash a crewman. Nearly killed him.'

'He's inexperienced,' Pike said.

'I don't trust him.'

'Samuel.' Pike's voice grew firm.

'But …'

'Careful, you'll have us both up on a charge.'

The surgeon nodded.

'Shouldn't you be below deck? The purser was complaining about having bad guts.'

'That he was. Tthere's shit all over. Why do think I'm up here?'

A smile flickered across Pike's lips. 'You'd better get to it then, before …'

'Yes, before Tanner notices I'm here.'

The grizzled-faced surgeon walked away, his coarse white hair blowing in the growing breeze.

Pike's attention shifted back to the new Captain. Tanner was a different breed from Winstanly. He was dark-haired, with a hooked nose and a chin that blended into the flabby pouch below it. His stony eyes and brooding nature troubled not just him, but the men as well.

'Lieutenant,' he called out.

Pike made his way across deck to the stout man.

'Yes, sir.'

'Another drill.'

'Captain Tanner, the men have just completed one. Is it wise to …?'

'Are you questioning my orders?'

'No sir, but the men are tired and hot. Perhaps we could do it later when the air has cooled and …'

Tanner held up a hand. 'I don't want excuses, get to it man.'

'Aye sir.'

'And while you are at it, after the drill, put the crew on clean-up duties. I want this ship spruced up. Do you hear me?'

Pike touched his hat in acknowledgment.

He missed Winstanly, his knowledge and expertise. Winstanly had known how to maintain the crew's commitment, even with some of the most uncompromising sailors among them. During evening watches, when the day had cooled, he would organise numerous team challenges, including mast climbing, combat readiness and sail drills, with extra rations of rum as reward for the most deserving team. These would be closely followed by what he had termed *jig of the sea,* a distraction of hornpipes and lively dance. Over the years, Pike had witnessed many sea-toughened rebellious brutes gradually moulded into efficient members of the Captain's crew. Soon they were well-trained and well-drilled; and it was a well-trained gunnery that gave the Navy its edge. They would endlessly practise, so they would know what to do when the time came. They would be able to do it in darkness, in terror and under hostile fire without the need to think about it. This ceaseless drilling ensured every man did his duty. Yet Winstanly could get them to do it without punishment, unlike Tanner. More importantly, the crew had respected him. He had had their loyalty, and they had known he would never betray them merely to satisfy his own political ambitions, a craving for glory to raise his standing within the Admiralty.

'Sir,' a voice bellowed from the ship's lookout.

'What is it?' Tanner cupped his hands, shouting back in reply.

'Ship approaching on larboard quarter.'

The Captain fell silent.

'What ship?' Pike called out.

'Large, sir. Maybe three masts.'

'Perhaps,' Tanner's voice suddenly weakened, 'she's one of ours?'

'If she is, she's well off station.'

'A whaler, then?' Tanner licked his dry lips. 'Or a merchant?'

Pike rushed across to the rack near the compass box and grabbed a telescope. He extended it and stood by the rail, looking out over the shimmering water. The other vessel was moving fast, and he shifted focus from her forecastle and jibs, to her topsails.

'*Le Requin*,' he shouted. 'She's a Frenchie.'

'The *Gilbert* and the *Arden* may be able to drive her off,' Tanner replied.

'They're too far away, sir.'

'But …'

'We have to engage before it's too late,' Pike called out, surprised by the Captain's hesitation.

Tanner fell to the ground and two officers rushed to his aid.

'He's not well, sir,' one of them said.

'Take him below and get our blades.'

Pike glanced toward the wheel, saw that the master and his mates were already there with extra men. Some crewmen worked frantically securing chain slings to ensure the great yards stayed in place if the rigging was damaged, and others on the nets to protect gun crews from falling spars.

One of the junior officers slipped on spray-soaked planking.

'Get that area sanded,' Pike shouted to a man near the hammock nettings.

Above his head, men settled into fighting positions, marines with their muskets preparing for battle.

'Look lively, lads,' he called out.

Footsteps pounded across deck and calls shrilled, drawing everyone up from below.

'Make sure that top men and everyone else are able to make more sail when ready,' he said to the officers that flanked him. 'The wind will be our ally. We will gain the advantage by having it astern of us.'

'Sir, are you going to rake her?' one of the officers asked.

'Yes.'

'But?'

'I know, a stern rake is more effective,' Pike interrupted, 'but that opportunity is not available to us. We will bring *Gospall* to bear on her bow. It's a smaller target to aim for, and some balls will be deflected by her curvature, but …'

'Do you think that will work, sir, or …?'

'Listen,' he cut in again. 'We just need one clean hit parallel to the axis of *Le Requin* and that ball will pass through her length, damaging her hull and sails and putting a lot of her crew out of action.'

Pike saw the anxiety in their faces.

'Remember Admiral Nelson?' he said, a firmness tempering his voice.

'Aye!' the men said in unison.

'The Battle of Trafalgar?'

'Aye!' they called out, almost cheering.

'HMS *Victory* broke the French line and raked *Bucentaure*, killing one hundred and ninety-seven and wounding eighty-five, including her captain. She was put well and truly out of the fight. Are you with me, lads?'

This time they cheered.

'Well, get to it!' He slapped one of the officers on the back.

The men rushed to their duty along the crowded deck, where sailors knelt by the guns. Every gun was primed, ready for action. Some of the new crew were jittery but that was to be expected. As long as they remained vigilant, and took care handling the guns, they would have a good chance of surviving. Loading was always dangerous, but inexperienced sailors increased the chances of a gun exploding and risked starting a fire that could destroy the ship.

'Their gun ports have opened, sir,' the lookout shouted down from the masthead.

Pike didn't respond.

'Mr Garrick, come here.'

'Sir,' the midshipman replied.

'How old are you?'

'Eleven, sir.'

'Is this the first time you have seen battle?'

'Yes, sir.'

'Well, you stay with me for now.'

Pike's jaw tightened. He thought of Tom, and couldn't help but remember the way the boy had died when they'd encountered *La Mort*.

Sails rolled down the masts, booming and cracking, and spars creaked as they tightened under the pressure of the gushing wind.

Le Requin thrust through the water, spray dashing her prow.

'She's bigger than us, sir.'

'Yes, a forty gunner.'

'We can beat her?'

'We've done it before, Mr Garrick,' Pike grinned. 'We took down *La Mort*, and she was a beast.'

Unlike *La Mort*, *Le Requin* was painted in light colours; but she was just as large and formidable.

The gun captains hollered, ensuring each division was ready for battle, and scarlet-coated marines positioned themselves, armed with muskets, as *Gospall* surged, turning in the water toward the enemy vessel.

Pike turned his attention to a gunner who was busy barking out orders. The gun crew stood ready, holding sponges and rammers, grinning nervously.

'Open ports,' Pike ordered. They opened in unison as he looked through the telescope at the French officers moving around their quarter deck.

'Stand ready, lads.'

Gospall surged due West towards *Le Requin*.

As Pike levelled the telescope again there was a puff of white smoke, and within a heart flutter a ball splashed just in front of them.

'They're trying to take down our masts.'

Another ball tore overhead as marines shot from the taffrail, taking down a French officer and several crewmen.

'Alter course,' Pike screamed through the furore as *Le Requin* returned fire with surprisingly little impact, just a couple of balls hitting below deck.

'Get down!' He grabbed the midshipman, dropping to his knees, as a huge splinter ripped across the quarter deck. He looked upwards as the French sniper tumbled from his position, screaming.

'Stay down,' he said, then rose to his feet. 'Raking manoeuvre.'

*Gospa*ll turned in a tight arc, bringing her broadside to bear on the bow of *Le Requin.*

'Fire.'

Gospall shuddered as she opened up. The sheer weight of iron that pounded the French frigate burst through her timbers, resulting in a storm of devastation.

For a moment there was smoke and screams, the cries of defeat as the French guns fell silent. Pike raised the telescope again; the *Gilbert* and the *Arden* were close now. He could see the huge ships rising and dipping in ocean swells, their ensigns flying with the same pride he felt.

After two weeks at sea, heading home with their prize, *Le Requin*, should have been a joyous occasion, but it wasn't. Tanner had seen to that.

'All hands on deck.,' the captain bellowed.

Pike and the other officers stood near the gratings as the rest of the ship's company assembled for the formal punishment ceremony. Hall, a sailor, had reputedly struck a Petty Officer after a disagreement regarding gun drills. Maybe he had done it out of frustration. The relentless preparation for combat with the enemy had taken its toll, festering into a brooding resentment toward the Petty Officer. Or perhaps it had been because he was a press gang victim. He'd been dragged kicking and screaming from a tavern and forced to join the Navy, even after showing them his American papers of protection. Pike knew about the man's background, and about the incident with the Petty Officer, but despised the ritual of flogging. It had its place, a punishment to maintain discipline on board ship, but under the present circumstances it seemed unjustified. Hall had not as much struck the officer as fallen onto him in a drunken stupor. Many of the crew had seen the sorry spectacle, but it had been Hall's misfortune that Captain Tanner had witnessed it too. Both Pike and the Petty Officer had stood in Tanner's quarters pleading for leniency. The Captain, hands clasped behind his back, had said the punishment was not up for discussion and turned to the stern windows before ordering them both to leave. The final insult had come later when they'd discovered he'd instructed the bosun's mate to use the lash with the thickest knots.

'Secure that man,' the Captain ordered. Two sailors walked Hall arm by arm to the gratings. He stood shirtless, legs astride, as his wrists were bound.

Pike noticed that the burly man's breathing was heavy. He saw sweat on his deep-lined face and could imagine his heart pounding in his chest.

The bosun's mate came to the hatchway and stepped onto the deck, rolling up the sleeves of his shirt. He carried the cat o'nine tails – nine lengths of cord, each containing several heavy knots – that he dragged along the deck.

'By God, you will learn your place this day,' Tanner said loudly.

The ginger-haired man turned his head away from Tanner, his face flat against the latticed wood. 'Little shit,' he muttered under his breath.

Some of the crew laughed.

'You impudent …' Tanner rushed forward and grabbed the cat from the bosun's mate. He swung the rope over his head as the drums rolled, and brought it down onto Hall's back.

Hall screamed as the lash bit.

'One!' the master-at-arms called out.

'Hold your tongue, man,' the Captain yelled.

Another strike tore flesh.

'Will you ever give me any more of your lip?' Tanner spat the words out through gritted teeth.

The ginger-haired man writhed in agony but said nothing.

'Answer me,' Tanner continued, face flushed red, lashing the man, his passion increasing.

Pike watched, flanked by blue-coated officers.

'How many, sir?' a lieutenant asked quietly.

'Two dozen.' Pike's eyes brushed over the young man to the crew, who remained motionless. 'It's a bad business, Mr Henson. A bad business indeed,' he said.

Hall's tongue protruded from his mouth; he held it there, biting down hard until it bled.

'You will learn respect.'

Whoo-pah … The whip cracked loudly, striking repeatedly.

'Stop,' Hall whimpered. 'Please stop.'

Tanner swung hard, and Hall screeched as a blood-speckled strip of skin was torn from his trembling body. His hands gripped the gratings, but the cat came down again and again, tearing and tugging, laying bare raw flesh as his body thrashed. Still the flogging continued.

'Stop … stop …' Hall's protests were becoming weaker, his back a crisscross of flayed flesh that hung from his frame like tattered cloth.

'Do you want more?'

Whoo-pah … *Whoo-pah* … *'Whoo-pah* … The cat came down again and again.

'He's lost control,' someone cried out.

'Captain!' Pike barked.

Tanner ignored him.

'Do you want some more?'

'Captain!' Pike shouted. 'He's passed out.'

Tanner spun around. 'Do not abuse your authority,' he replied, staring at the First Lieutenant.

Pike's blue-grey eyes met his.

'I abuse nothing sir. The man is done.'

'He's right,' the ship's surgeon said, pushing his way through the crowd. 'You won't be happy until he's dead.'

'One more word from you, Mr Teague,' the captain retorted, 'and I'll have you in irons.'

'Samuel.' Pike shook his head.

Tanner glanced around the ship. 'Let that be a lesson to all of you. I will not stand for insubordination.'

Pike heard the men behind him murmuring.

'Cut him down,' the Captain barked, as he strode off.

Two sailors loosened Hall's ties and the man fell into their arms, his face lost to a bad dream.

'Take him below deck,' Pike told them as the rest of the crew dispersed.

'Poor bastard,' Teague said.

'It's best not to rile the Captain,' Pike warned the surgeon.

'His blood's always up.'

'Nevertheless.'

'We could have done with some of that passion when we came up against *Le Requin*, instead of him resting in his cabin.'

'What are you saying?'

'You tell me, Will.'

Pike fell silent.

'You took command and handled it well. The men respect you.'

'It was my duty.'

'We are all bound by duty, but some men are driven by something else.' The surgeon looked toward the blood-smeared gratings.

'You'd better see to Hall's wounds.'

'I'll cleanse his back with salt water. It'll hurt like hell, but he should recover soon enough.'

Pike nodded.

'He'll carry those scars to the grave, Will. There's no doubting that.'

'Give him as much rum as he needs and more besides.'

As the old doctor walked away, his words chimed loud and clear in Pike's head.

'He's a bad 'un.'

7

Sean fastened the last two buttons of his shirt, looking out of the bedroom window at the forest beyond. Sleep had not been easy to find, even though it was already past nine. A mist had formed outside, and the trees appeared blurry, rooted in a ghostly landscape. He sighed, his mind searching for meaning to the thoughts tumbling through it.

'Bad dreams again?' Sophie asked.

'Not really.'

'What is it, then?'

Sean averted his eyes for a moment.

'There was more to it than a massive heart attack.'

'What are you trying to say?

He regained eye contact. 'Mum was terrified by something.'

'What?'

'Don't you get it? She was frightened to death.'

'Oh, Sean …'

'I know it sounds crazy, even to me, but I know what I know.'

'You're asking me to believe a hunch,' she said. 'It doesn't make sense. There were no signs of a forced entry or …'

'Yes, yes, I know. Nothing was stolen and there was no sign of a break-in, that's the way it seems, but …'

'But what, Sean? Listen to yourself.'

'Something's wrong. Every nerve is screaming out at me that she was …'

'Are you sure it's not just …?'

Sean laughed, a hurt laugh. 'You mean all up here?' He tapped the side of his head with his index finger.

'I don't mean that.'

'Don't you?' He fixed her with a cold stare. 'It wouldn't be the first time, would it?'

'I didn't mean it like that.'

'No?'

'You're tired, worn out. Jesus, Sean, you've just lost your mother. You're entitled to be a little confused.'

'A little confused! You think I've lost it again? I haven't.' There was no harshness to his tone, just a firm conviction. 'I'm telling you, Mum wasn't alone in this house the night she died.'

'How do you know that?'

'I just do.'

'How?'

'A couple of days ago, James came to the cottage while you were in the village shopping. Did you know that he was the one who discovered Mum's body?'

Sophie gave a half shake of her head.

'He seemed reluctant to talk about it, but you know how persuasive I can be.'

'And?'

He fell silent for a moment, gathering his thoughts.

'Over the years, Mum and James had become good friends. He would call some days just for a chat, and drop her at the village for groceries. She was trying to help him cope with the loss of his wife and he confided in her. He was feeling pretty depressed and emotionally drained that day, so he decided to pay Mum a visit. Even though it was late, well past nine, he noticed that there were no lights on in the cottage. He thought it odd, because she never went to bed before eleven. It looked like power in the cottage might be off, because he could see lights in the village beyond. Concerned, he peered through the window.

'What did he see?' she asked.

'It's not what he saw. It's what he heard.'

'I don't follow.'

'Through the darkness he heard laughter, loud, mocking laughter.'

'Jesus.'

'James forced the door open as the lights flickered back to life, and found Mum.'

'What about the intruder?'

'That's just it. He said he searched the house thoroughly but there was no-one there and the windows and doors were secure.'

'Perhaps …'

'He imagined it?' Sean interrupted.

'It was dark, and he was obviously on edge.'

'Sophie. James was frightened, there's no doubting that, but he said Mum was sitting in a chair, her eyes frozen wide as though she'd been staring at something in the corner of the room.'

'Did he see anything?'

'James said he got out of the house as quickly as he could and called for help.'

'It sounds very odd.'

'Then you believe me?'

'Honestly, I don't know what to believe. It's too soon to jump to any conclusion.'

'Then what happens now?'

'We investigate. If there was someone in the house, they were here for a reason. We need to find out why.'

It all sounded bizarre. Just how seriously could she take any of this? Yet now it seemed credible, or perhaps deep down she desperately wanted to believe in Sean.

She felt confused, but there was an awareness of something else. Like Sean, she'd felt it too, a feeling, almost tangible, that something had occurred in this house. Something … terrible.

It was a few days later before Sophie spoke to James. Reluctantly, he'd confirmed Sean's account of events. Now she stared at the beautifully-crafted Edwardian writing desk in front of her, pondering on unsettling thoughts. She remembered the psychological problems Sean had been forced to overcome. Christ, it'd been a nightmare. It had almost ripped them apart. The past needed to stay in the past; dredging it up now would achieve nothing. Besides, he was fine now. Or was he? She ran a hand across the walnut bureau that took pride of place in the living-room. Sophie lowered the front and gazed into the green baize interior.

She removed three books and a couple of discoloured newspapers.

'Look at this, Sean!'

'Yeah, coming.'

Sean wandered in from the kitchen and placed his coffee mug on the desk. He picked up one of the musty newspapers, a copy of *The Times* dated 1939. He turned the pages carefully, noticing an article highlighted in red ink.

Slaughter on the Streets of London. Three Mutilated Bodies Discovered.

He glanced down to another piece of underlined text.

Child attacked by spectre.

Then another.

Ghostly ship sighted in Grime Street.

'Really?' he said. 'A ship appearing in a street?'

'What do you make of this?' Sophie pushed back her chair and handed Sean another newspaper. It was much older than the other, dated 1914. He studied the headlines of the *Globe*.

Two bodies found in Grime Street.

There were other reports, of a strange mist and a spectral ship, all in the same vicinity.

'It doesn't make sense, Sophie. Why underline this?'

'Odd, isn't it?' she replied, noticing deep dark blemishes around his eyes. He'd not slept well; his face was pale too, and stubble shadowed his cheeks.

'Odd to say the least. Let's have a look at these books,' he said, picking them up and moving across to the sofa.

Outside the light was fading fast, and the room was feebly lit. The log fire cast a warm but inadequate glow. The first of the three books was a small, scuffed, leather-bound diary from 1939 filled with writing in a juvenile hand. It didn't contain the usual record of daily events one might have expected to find in a child's everyday life. He lingered on each page, scrutinising every entry. The disordered writings described an attack. Although gibberish at times, he was able to discern that the little girl believed she'd been attacked by a dark figure, then defended by another man dressed in a blue naval uniform. The figures had struggled with one another, before, as she put it, they evaporated. It was the ramblings of a disturbed child's mind. He wasn't convinced that he believed her.

He tilted his head back and stared at the ceiling. Whatever had happened to that child had undoubtedly left mental scars. But what did it have to do with his mum?

'Sean …' Sophie handed him the second book. It had an embossed Latin inscription: *A libri of oraculum.* The leather-bound volume was frayed along the edges and the cover almost worn away.

Carefully, he opened it to the first page. Beneath a large, intricately-designed black cross was a declaration:

'*In nomine Jesu Christi, hoc est verbum et haec veritas,*' he read. 'In the name of Jesus Christ, this is the word and the truth.'

Sophie looked at him in amazement. 'I didn't know you could read Latin.'

Sean laughed, for the first time since his mum's death. 'I can't. There's a translation here. Someone's taken a lot of time and trouble to translate every page. It must have taken forever.

'The word and truth given to me,' he read aloud.

'What does that mean?' Sophie asked.

'It appears to be a book of apocalyptic prophecies by a 16th Century Abbot named Saul. I've heard of him; he was an English version of Nostradamus. Story has it that he was burnt at the stake for being a witch.'

Although the text was faded, several passages had been underlined. He took a closer look at the translated Latin predictions.

Before the coming of the ruin of man, many shall die from plague, famine, by war, wind, fire and flood. Never was the world in such disarray.

From a lowly soldier, he shall come to have supreme command, the great liar shall obtain dominion under the crescent moon.

In the new age, great lights shall descend from the sky. Fires shall rage, many people shall be burnt with heat and great cities shall be made desolate, nothing will stop the world from dying.

He studied the final passage, which had been underlined twice, in red ink.

Before the fall of man, through the mists of time, thrice it shall come, a leprous vessel, the bringer of great evil and destruction to mankind. Heed the warning, before my prophecy is fulfilled.

'This reads like gobbledegook,' he said, looking towards Sophie.

She sat back, absorbing the predictions. 'Yeah, sounds pretty weird to me as well.'

The log fire flickered, crackling in the darkening room, its soothing glow waning fast.

Thwack …

Something struck the front door, its sound resounding around the confines of the small room.

Sophie looked over her shoulder.

'Did you hear that?'

Thwack …

Sean rose to his feet. 'Who's there?'

His question was met by a momentary silence that was every bit as startling as that which had galvanised him into action.

Thwack … thwack …

'Someone's trying to get in, Sean …'

They made their way toward the door, and Sean turned its old wrought-iron handle, pulling it hard. Slowly it creaked open and he peered into the blackness.

'Oh, shit!'

A dark shape shot past him. It flew through the doorway with a great fluttering of wings, just missing Sean by inches. It circled the room frantically as though trying to escape from an unseen predator. It smashed against the window with a dull thud, before exiting back through the front door.

Kraaa … The crow soared into the sky, its demented squawks sharp against the night.

There were more cries from night creatures in the woodland as the moon emerged from dense cloud, its hazy glow doing little to quell their nerves.

Sean caught Sophie giving him a nervous glance.

'That's odd. Crows aren't nocturnal. They roost when the sun goes down.'

'What are you trying to say, Sean?'

'Something must have disturbed it.'

'Let's go back inside,' she said.

He placed an arm around her shoulder and guided her back indoors. In truth, he had no desire to be out there any longer than necessary.

They sat back down, warming themselves in front of the log fire. The orange embers glowed, and flickering yellow flames seemed to dance around the hearth, renewed with life.

Sean turned his attention to the third book. He leaned forward with a grunt and picked it up off the floor. Although ancient, the leather-bound tome appeared to be in reasonable condition. He carefully balanced it on his knees, then flipped the first of the gilt-edged leaves over and studied its contents.

Journal of William Pike (First Lieutenant)
His Majesty's Frigate Gospall.

October 1810

We are preparing to leave the Mediterranean, a measure of which I cannot approve. This fleet has achieved great things. I lament our present orders but shall rejoice to see England again. This will be a brief respite from war. Already the shadow of conflict looms once more. America has forged an alliance with our old foe France, threatening the safety of trade routes and England herself.

I now realise how much I despise my new Captain. Edmund Tanner is a pompous upstart with little understanding of honourable warfare. Rumours abound that his father is well-

known in the House of Lords, with close friends in the Admiralty. I suspect this is how he gained command of **Gospall***, through political motives rather than military experience. I fear he has quickly passed through the ranks without the necessary hard work that befits the post he now holds. His presence on this ship dishonours the dignity of the fleet and England.*

During our last battle, Captain Tanner rested in his cabin, troubled by an ailment that confounded our surgeon. There is talk among the crew of cowardice on his part.

November 1810

Every day the poor wretches under the command of Captain Tanner are treated despicably. A few of the men have been driven mad through continual flogging and beatings. They fear him, and he seems to derive pleasure from their suffering.

His attacks on the crew have intensified. Today he beat a sailor senseless because he was slow to reply to an order. Captain Tanner is a cruel, pernicious man.

Punishment is now a common sight on the ship. I cannot approve of this barbaric treatment. It is on the whole unjustified. My patience is almost at an end. These men have performed above and beyond their duty in recent battles. They whole-heartedly deserve reward, not punishment, for their service.

Sean turned another page, wondering how this sort of thing could have been allowed to happen.

December 1810

We lost sight of the **Gilbert** *and the* **Arden** *in thick fog. By morning the rest of the fleet had disappeared in the growing mist.*

Today our navigational equipment was stolen. I can only assume it has been taken by one of the crew. Unless it is found, we will have no way of knowing where we are heading. We are totally alone, in the vastness of this mighty sea and at the mercy of any heavy-gunned enemy ships that may be in our vicinity. Punishment is harsh. Tanner flogs the men, but still they refuse to talk.

March 1811

Many months have elapsed with no sign of any vessels. Our rations are low, and the men have become agitated with the Captain. He continues to feast from what little is left in the stores, while the men slowly starve, eating stale bread and water. There is growing tension among the crew and some of the officers.
    Another man was flogged to death today.

Sean raised his head for a moment; the vision raging in his mind of the screaming sailor as each lash tore the flesh from his back. He shook his head in disbelief. Clearly, more men had been flogged to death, while others had died from malnutrition. One disobedient crewman had been dragged to the side of the ship and almost thrown overboard to the sharks while Tanner watched.

July 1811

I will not tolerate any more abuse toward the men. If mutiny be the way, so be it.
    Today the Captain raised his sword to a fellow officer. I struck Tanner, preventing him from injuring the young man. The crew have stood by me, apart from two officers. Outnumbered, they surrendered their weapons and we placed the three men in a boat and cast it adrift.
    Night after night in the clammy darkness of my sleeping quarters, I have been tortured by the possible ramifications of my actions. Although the mutiny was justified, I know that we will all hang for our part in this insurrection, if we return home. God forgive me. I did what I had to for all our sakes, but there have been times when I have questioned my actions.

Samuels and Hall approached me this evening; they returned the navigational equipment to me. The crew had kept it hidden, constantly moving it around the ship during searches to prevent Tanner from finding it.

Unable to return to England, I have plotted another course.

August 1811

We are on a heading toward the Caribbean. God willing, this course will steer us clear of any British war ships. We do not wish to battle against our own countrymen, and hope that we may take advantage of the fact that the fleet will be otherwise occupied and unaware of the mutiny.

With supplies low, we have been forced to take action. The Captain of an unaccompanied American merchant ship surrendered his vessel. Better this way than for blood to be spilled. We took only what we had to, treating all on board with dignity, and allowed the ship safe passage home afterwards.

The hand-written text became faded. Although it was barely legible, Sean could discern Pike's anguish. His emotions had been in turmoil. He had thought often of Rebecca, his young wife, and missed her terribly; he would never see her again and blamed himself because of it.

Sean thumbed through the sea-washed pages. Much of the text had been rendered illegible. Still he searched, until he was drawn to another event, unravelling more of the First Lieutenant's life.

January 1812

Last night the lookout reported seeing a small boat adrift. Fourteen men were on board, unconscious and near to death. God knows how long these poor wretches have been without food or water. We are treating them as best we can and eagerly await an account of their unfortunate circumstances.

To continue sailing **Gospall** *is madness, the risk too great. I have plotted a course for Tornave, a small island off the coast of Haiti. This will be our new home, God willing, for the remainder of our lives.*

Sean read on, but the story took a sinister turn. Some of the crew had died from malnutrition, others became seriously ill, but worse was still to come. Pike believed the men he'd rescued had begun plotting against him. Word spread that their leader was a man named Francois Santia, known to his enemies as 'the Butcher'. A former privateer turned pirate, he was brutal, sadistic and a notorious lunatic.

Being only a few days away from the island, Pike considered it unwise to confront Santia, mainly because of the deterioration of many of his crew, but also because he was unsure of the loyalty of some of the others. Had the gullible been cunningly recruited, through lies and deception, to conspire against him? He was sure that the pirate had some sinister agenda. At that time, he was unable to act, but Pike was biding his time.

I am aware that Santia has influenced some of my men and intimidated others. Sammuels has been keeping watch of his movements and reporting to me. I believe he is dangerous and dare not underestimate him.

Sean studied another entry.

We have arrived at our destination and are anchored a couple of miles from the Haitian island. At daybreak, we will go ashore in search of supplies.

Earlier, Lieutenant Baldwin managed to muster a few of the crew together. During our clandestine meeting, I gave the order for the men to be armed. This is where we will make our stand against Santia and restore order once more.

The journal ended abruptly.

Sean rose to his feet. He walked across the room and placed the journal back into the writing bureau.

'Why did she want these books? They're hardly a light read.'

'Meaning?'

'I'm not sure, but I think she was up to something.'

8

The rain had stopped, and the sun rose, cutting its way through the mists, climbing high over the treetops. Sean walked briskly down the cobblestone lane, making his way to the old church. This was always a serene time, and in recent days it had become an increasingly welcome sight. He breathed in the morning air, reflecting on sad thoughts. The loss of his mum had cut deep, and it felt as though part of him had died with her. No-one could appreciate what it was like to endure that kind of loss, unless they'd experienced it themselves. Sophie was sympathetic but didn't really understand what it felt like. How could she? It was horrible, indescribable, not being able to see or speak to your mum, or give her a hug. These things were all taken for granted. Christ, what he wouldn't give now to see her one last time and tell her how precious she was to him.

As Sean approached the gateway to the church, he fastened the top button of his leather jacket and paused to gaze up at the ancient building's steeple. The tip of the spire easily topped the highest branches of the surrounding trees. He wasn't a religious person, yet somehow this church had become a source of comfort to him.

The only sounds were birdsong and his own feet crunching on the broad gravel path as he made his way to the graveyard.

The church's double arched doors were of huge, heavy oak, studded with iron rivets. Even from where he was he could make out that they were dry and crumbling and in need of repair. It was a sombre building; the grey stonework was discoloured but, aside from a few loose roof tiles, was structurally sound.

Sean knew the doors would be locked. In the past, churches would always have been open to those needing spiritual comfort, but that was before the fear of theft had gripped churchwardens. He'd seen it for himself on the news, lead thieves targeting churches and leaving a trail of destruction behind. These historic buildings were vulnerable both inside and out. It was a real pity.

Lack of interest was evident too. In recent years congregations had dwindled as the elderly died but were rarely replaced by younger members of a community. Nevertheless, the church still held on to a meagre following. Villagers, especially pensioners, still clutched onto their faith and attended mass regularly. They were good people, and friendly enough, but you couldn't help but feel an outsider in their midst. Who could blame them for wanting to keep this idyllic little village to themselves?

At the back of the church, a narrower path took him through the grass-covered graveyard. Sean scanned the grey slabs on either side and shivered, the bitter chill penetrating every part of him. He scarcely noticed the mist that had begun weaving its way around him.

Drifting dark clouds tarnished the morning sky, and the sound of birdsong ceased.

He shuddered and felt the hairs on the back of his neck prickle at his collar.

Yes, he was in a graveyard, but he didn't believe in ghosts; they were nothing more than superstitious nonsense. Still his mind became more alert to the notion that something was here with him.

'C'mon, get it together,' he muttered, as if words alone could dismiss troublesome thoughts.

He looked over his shoulder but could see nothing. It was as though this place had developed an underlying tension; so much so that his heartbeat quickened.

Sean's resolve was waning; his steps had become faster and his breathing harsh. Every nerve was screaming at him to get the hell away from there, but this was his mum's resting place and he didn't want to be driven away by irrational thoughts. Yet unseen eyes were watching him. He sensed it. *Felt* it. Suddenly, there was movement, the rustle of leaves in the woodland about him. He stood alone, his face pale against the mist, as a black bird tore out of the forest. More rooks appeared, their wings flapping a frenzied tattoo, beating frantically across the sky.

He shivered again and heard a snapping twig. The sound drifted, echoing eerily through the icy mist. Sean cut across the grass; it was rutted, and his feet sank into the moist earth, his jeans collecting muck from the water-logged field.

Another noise! Faint laughter.

He turned sharply, with fear chiming loudly in his mind.

Someone was moving toward him. The sun came into view once more, and in the distance Sean saw a figure seeming to glide above the sodden surface of the graveyard. As the dark form drew closer he realised it resembled a man, but not quite.

He felt weak, his stomach tightening. Something was sucking the energy from him at an alarming rate. He sank to his knees as the dark clothed figure drew closer, and he caught a glimpse of its face.

Sean woke with a start. He sat upright in bed, his breath coming in sharp gasps, with the after-image of the nightmare still fresh in his mind. Even though his eyes were open, dark vestiges lingered.

It's just a nightmare, he told himself. *Just a nightmare.*

9

As he took a stroll into the village Sean quickened his pace, refusing to let the nightmare perpetuate in his thoughts. He'd come too far to allow something like this to open up a healing wound.

His breakdown had happened quickly. Sean's psychotherapist, Dr Alexander, had explained in detail that it was an experience with diverse psychological effects. Mental breakdown meant everything or nothing. Past traumatic events could trigger symptoms of a mental breakdown. And he had witnessed something truly horrific. In New England, he'd seen a Boeing 777 plunge to the ground, killing all 297 passengers on board. It was something he'd had to discuss with his psychotherapist but wasn't the root cause of his problem.

Sean stepped off the narrow pavement and crossed an old brick-built bridge with iron handrails; it hadn't changed at all. Memories returned with a clarity he relished: the joys of childhood; running across the bridge with his friends during long hot summer holidays; swimming in the slow-flowing river and swinging across it by rope. He paused midway and took in the view, scanning the flat lowlands enclosed by impossibly green hills and undulating woodland. He smiled, realising just how precious those days had been. He'd always loved this route into the village, relishing the wild yet colourful floral displays of red campion, bluebells and stitchwort, the unexpected sight of a squirrel scuttling up a tree or rabbits chasing one another through the long grass. As a small boy, his mum had brought him this way, holding his hand, chatting and laughing. He had felt so safe, so secure back then. He had thought she would always be there for him.

As he approached Wedmore, Sean glanced up at the sky, hoping for better weather. It was a dull day, with the sun shining briefly through openings in the clouds, a bonus for this time of year. October was always cold here, but the seasons didn't seem to be the same anymore. He was pleased to catch a glimpse of the sun, and the exercise would help clear his head. He continued past some thatched roof houses. Sean crossed the road, passing more cottages that oozed old-world charm, all of them with well-maintained tiny front gardens with a bright array of colourful flowers, bordered by neatly manicured hedges. The street was quiet, and the butchers and the post office had few customers inside. He stopped at the library before going inside. The single-storey structure was built of light sand-coloured stone, with tall windows that reached up to a roof of dark tiles. The arched door reminded him of a church entrance.

Inside, in the centre of the room, stood a rectangular desk, with myriad books scattered across its surface. Behind it stood a flustered-looking young woman with bobbed hair and wearing small round glasses.

'Can I help you?' she said, glancing up from a computer screen.

'Hope so,' he replied, making his way toward her. 'I was just wondering if you had any books on British naval history.'

As the woman began tapping her keyboard, he took in the room. It was bigger than he had remembered. In the corner, a silver-haired man lowered his book and regarded him with mild interest. Sean smiled at him before his attention was drawn back to the librarian.

'You're in luck.'

'Am I?'

'Yes, I've found two books, *The Complete History of Naval Battles* and *Pirates: the Savage Truth*. One of the ladies from the village specifically requested these books a few months ago.'

'Really,' he replied, dropping his gaze. Scanning the monitor, he noticed the name *Webster* and realised that it was his mum who'd requested them.

'Could I take a look at both books?'

'Of course, I'll just get them for you.'

Within a few moments she returned carrying two large volumes and gave them to him with a well-practised smile.

Sean made his way toward a table and took a seat. Head bowed, he began to flick through the larger of the two volumes. Written by Admiral J Walsey, it listed numerous naval conflicts, although Sean's attention was swiftly drawn to one battle in particular, involving a British frigate named *Gospall*. The ship's Captain was a man named Winstanly and his first officer was William Pike. In 1809 they were engaged in battle with the French National Frigate *La Mort*. *Gospall* defeated the enemy vessel and returned to Portsmouth. Both men were declared heroes of the day.

He continued reading with increasing interest. The next person to captain the ship was a man called Edmund Tanner. Very little was known about her last voyage. The frigate sailed with a flotilla and somehow, during poor weather, became lost and was never seen again.

Sean picked up the other book and turned around to see the librarian's inquisitive gaze on him; she looked back at her computer screen as his attention was drawn back to the book. He leaned forward again, scanning the index for the name Santia, then flicked to the appropriate page.

Born in Brittany, François Santia was undoubtedly one of the most bloodthirsty men to take to the sea. Known to his enemies as the Butcher, he was notorious for ferocious land raids.

Sean reflected on a harrowing account involving a disloyal sailor's execution. The young crewman had his hands bound and a rope placed around his head. Using an iron rod, Santia twisted the cord tighter and tighter, then made wagers with his cronies over how many turns it would take to kill the poor victim. It recorded that he'd died on the eleventh revolution.

Sean studied more of the text, sickened by what he found, the wickedness becoming more and more evident.

In another raid, Santia had drawn his cutlass and slashed an obstinate Spaniard's chest open. Then, after pulling his heart out, he had begun to gnaw on it, threatening other villagers with the same fate unless they told him the whereabouts of their gold. *'Santia,'* the book informed, *'had enjoyed the taste of human flesh.'*

There was more. Women and children were dragged screaming from their homes and slaughtered for pleasure. Even Santia's own men were not immune from his madness. He governed with a fist of iron, taking particular delight in meting out severe punishment to wrongdoers. One miscreant, a young lad whose crime was to steal wine from the ship's stores, was taken ashore. *'Once on the beach,'* it was recorded, *'his body was hacked to pieces and thrown limb by limb onto a raging fire.'*

What kind of man could do such things? Sean wondered. He tried to force the dreadful image from his mind, but the abhorrent vision remained, arousing fresh repulsion.

The atrocities continued; a catalogue of slaughter perpetuated by the psychotic pirate. Some victims had their eyes gouged out, others their throats cut, while many more were hung, drowned, beheaded or burnt alive.

As his reputation and passion for butchery grew, many sailors began to fear Santia. With the constant threat to the safety of various trade routes, the authorities were forced into action, and a trap was set.

Santia was lured into range of a vessel posing as a trader but carrying Spanish soldiers. The ruse worked. A barrage of heated shot soon turned his ship into a pillar of fire, but not before he'd delivered a devastating broadside into the Spanish vessel. Both had sunk with the loss of many lives.

Sean reflected on Pike's journal for a moment. That would explain how he had come into contact with Santia. After the *Gospall* mutiny, Santia had been sighted adrift in a small boat and rescued. It appeared the man was not only cunning but also had luck on his side.

Sean turned another page to reveal an artist's impression of Francois Santia. The pirate appeared to be mid-thirties with long dark hair. A tapering moustache ran the length of his upper lip while his beard was little more than a whisper of hair.

There was preciseness to the artist's interpretation; it was sharp yet almost too clearly defined, and this made it all the more fascinating.

Something stirred within that pencilled sketch.

He blinked and looked again.

No. It had been a long night and he hadn't slept well. *It was tiredness, that was all … just … tiredness.* Yet as he stared at the picture he felt a sudden coolness brush past him.

The image began to stir. *Or* was *it all in his head?* It was as though the depiction of Santia exuded a dark energy.

How could that be possible?

The picture was changing, becoming something more, gaining life with a momentum all of its own. Santia's pupils widened, until they were like huge dark caverns, bottomless pits, arousing dread. Sean could only stare, the hypnotic grip too powerful to resist. He heard a dreamlike voice and the sound of the ocean … gushing waves breaking against the shoreline.

The room had become bitterly cold. He swayed on his chair, his head drooping, struggling to keep control. There was a very faint but distinctive drumbeat that was joined by strange voices, a loudening chorus of laughter, cries and chants rising into some kind of discordant anthem.

Sean began to visualise something, figures *dancing … flickering firelight.* All the while he could hear the incessant drumbeat being hammered out with incredible vigour. He was drifting, becoming part of this ethereal event.

What was that? A noise, laughter, but not in his head.

Reality washed over him. His fingers tightened on the book. He listened for a moment, galvanised into alertness.

Nothing, it was nothing, just an overactive imagination, but why was it still so cold? *He was exhausted. Perhaps grief was conspiring to drain him of what little resolve he had left. Should he speak to Dr Alexander again?*

'No,' he muttered, answering the unspoken question. *It was a cliché, but time was a great …*

There it was again, the sound of laughter.

He looked around the room, and saw it was deserted. Even the librarian seemed to have vanished. *Where the hell had it come from?*

Sean was puzzled, not just by the raucous sound but by the fact that it had seemed so close, almost beside him.

His hand trembled and his attention was drawn back to the book and Francois Santia.

He blinked several times. He must have been mistaken, yet he was sure that when he had first looked at the picture Santia had not been grinning. He'd allowed the gruesome accounts to fuel his imagination; there was no other explanation for it. *That was all it was; imagination.* He looked back down into those disconcerting eyes and realised the pirate's grin had grown wider.

'Oh, God!' he muttered.

The picture was animated with a life of its own, and that laughter Sean realised was coming from the book itself.

10

Sean boarded the early train, as he did every Monday morning. He walked along the underground platform, which was surprisingly empty. In the distance he heard the familiar roar of an underground train as it rattled toward the platform, its arrival preceded by a gushing warm wind that scattered a discarded tabloid across the tracks. The newspaper fluttered along as though ghostly hands were encouraging it to move. Sean watched the pages scurrying and tumbling, and pondered on troublesome thoughts.

The grinning picture had been a product of his own imagination. There'd been no point in telling Sophie about it; she would have just worried about him. It had all been a result of grief, stress and many restless nights. Anyway, it was all over now, the funeral had been and gone, and life was supposed to be returning to normal. Once the grief receded so too would the hallucinations, as they had done in the past. But the past was an uncomfortable place for him. It was somewhere he didn't want to go. Remembering the past could result in him slipping back into madness, and that was what he feared the most. Insidious voices inside his head had suggested things, wicked things. These thoughts had risen from nowhere, malign and twisted, the urge to hurt Sophie. No! Not just hurt her … kill her. He suddenly felt nauseous.

Footsteps on the platform distracted him for a moment as a young couple passed by, whispering to each other.

How could he have thought such things? He had forced the memories to a safe place in the back of his mind, where they had taken root and festered. It was inevitable that sooner or later, without help, they would return; and when they did he would be driven to nervous collapse. A part of him couldn't help but blame himself for what had happened.

The train doors hissed open, startling him. The carriage was half empty, and what few people there were, exited through the open doors. He waited for a moment and stepped onto the train.

The doors swished shut, and the automated voice announced departure. He stared through the window at the usual array of posters advertising West End shows.

A tall man who'd entered behind him at the last station sat down facing him. He took off his jacket, folded it, placed it on a nearby seat, then opened his briefcase and removed a newspaper. He grunted, moving the case from his knees to the seat, resting it on top of his jacket. Just as Sean caught a glimpse of official-looking documents, he snapped the case shut. His gaze shifted to the man; early sixties, bald with white temple hair, his suit giving him the look of a banker. The sharp way he turned the pages of the paper suggested he was agitated about something.

Sean caught the headline of *The Times*, which read 'Middle East in Crisis'. Extremism was on the rise, while Egypt and parts of Africa were introducing Sharia law into their constitution. Another sidebar spoke of Iran's weapons of mass destruction and the threat posed to Israel and other regions. Within moments the train plunged into the tunnel. Sean stared impassively from the lightened compartment into the darkness outside before yawning aloud. He needed a long holiday, somewhere nice in the sun, perhaps Spain. He held onto that thought for a moment as the train rattled through the tunnel.

Around the litter-ridden compartment, hand straps hung from above like nooses swaying in tempo with the shaking carriage, its general condition dismally poor. Heating would have been a bonus; it felt cool. Sean turned his attention back toward the bald man. His head was bowed as if asleep and the newspaper was now discarded on the floor. He held in his hand a notepad and pen. As the lights dimmed unexpectedly, the man's head snapped backwards with a sudden jerk. He sat, features stiff, eyelids locked tightly closed, his face pale, ghost-like in the semi-darkness. Chest heaving, his lips parted.

'*Sean!*'

The voice was a woman's.

'*You're in terrible ...*' The words faded into the man's rattling gasps, then returned. More faint this time. '*Get help ... You must ...*' And once again they ebbed away. The man tried to get up, but it was as if invisible hands were pushing him down into his seat.

'What?' The word slipped out of Sean's mouth.

He shook his head, denying what was happening. Then he realised that the bald man was scribbling on the notepad. Sean heard the sound of pen against paper; the man's writing was becoming more frantic. Just as suddenly as it had started, it stopped, and the man stood up. He walked toward Sean with the sheet of paper in his hand.

'Take it ... please ...'

Sean sat in stunned silence. There was no mistaking that the voice was his mum's.

As if a spell had been broken, the man's eyes snapped open. He looked around, confused, unaware of what had just occurred.

Sean rose from his seat. 'What do you want?'

Uncertainty brought a look of fear to the man's face. He backed away, his body trembling.

'I just want to talk,' Sean said, their bodies jittering back and forth in the swaying carriage. 'Listen to me ...' he called out against the sound of rattling carriages, 'I just want to talk to you, that's all.'

The train came to a stop and the tall man put more distance between them, stumbling as he moved backwards. He grabbed his briefcase, then jacket, and clutching them to his chest he headed for the doors as they swished open. He forced his way through a crowd of people bunched around the open doors. Sean tried to follow but was pushed back onto the train by jostling commuters.

The doors closed, and as the train moved off, the lighting

flickered for a moment before returning to normal. Sean stood breathing heavily, surrounded by people, then realised he was still clutching the piece of paper in his hand. The scrawl appeared to be an address.

He stared at it in bewilderment.

11

Sean shifted gear and looked ahead. It was still pretty bright for six o'clock, although dark clouds were forming overhead. The lights of the Nissan in front glowed red and Sean slammed on his brakes. Both vehicles came to a halt. He looked out of the driver's side window and noticed a bulldog strolling across the road. It stopped for a moment, looked in his direction, then mounted the pavement and disappeared from view. A horn blared from behind and Sean glanced in his mirror. A grey-haired man mouthed something and gave another blast.

Sean considered giving him the finger but decided not to bother. He just turned and started driving again.

Sean turned off the main street, into St Mary's School. The wrought-iron gates were open but still a bit of a squeeze to get through. After finding a place to park, Sean turned off the ignition and regarded the secondary school. It was a flat brick building with white UPC windows and two large meshed glass entrance doors.

Sean's jacket lay on the back seat and his shirt sleeves were rolled up to his elbows; he'd removed his tie earlier, soon after finishing work. He'd thrown a bag into the boot with his karate gear inside, just in case Sophie texted to say she was working late. She had.

More cars arrived, and soon people were making their way into St Mary's for the session. Sean opened the car door as a tall, sandy-haired man approached smiling.

'Hello, haven't seen you for a few weeks,' he said.

'Had a few personal things going on, Pete.'

'Sorry to hear that.'

'Sophie was attacked.'

Pete's smile dropped. 'What happened?'

'Two thugs grabbed her on the street, in broad daylight. Can you believe that? The bastards dragged her down an alleyway. God only knows what would have happened if I hadn't been there.

'Is she okay?'

'Yeah.'

'What happened to the thugs?'

'I did!'

'I know I'm your sensei, but I hope you kicked the shit out of those bastards.'

Sean nodded.

'What did the police say?'

'Usual crap. It's a big city and all that.'

'So, they didn't find them?'

'I'm afraid not. They weren't in great shape when I finished with them. I left the pair of them on the ground, but they must have staggered off later.'

The tall lean man shook his head.

'It must have been pretty terrifying, but I'm glad your training kicked in. That's why I always say practise makes …'

'Mum passed away as well,' Sean cut in.

'I'm really sorry to hear that, mate.'

'We were really close.' Sean's lips trembled as he spoke, and his shoulders sagged.

'Life can be a bitch sometimes. It takes time, but you will come to terms with it.'

Sean knew he would eventually accept it, but he didn't want to.

'I lost my father five years ago,' the instructor continued. 'Not a day goes by that I don't think of him. But it does get easier. C'mon Sean, let's get some training done. It might take your mind off things for a while.'

They pushed open the double doors. A large wooden crucifix adorned one of the walls and beneath it stood a statue of the Virgin Mary with arms outstretched. Several light-coloured doors led into various classrooms, and at the far end of the room Sean saw computer monitors mounted on long wooden desks. Another door opened into the gym that doubled as the dojo. The room boasted enormous windows, wooden wall bars and a hard wooden floor with numerous coloured lines emblazoned onto it for sports purposes.

Both men bowed before entering.

Changing, as always, took a matter of minutes in the back room. Sean slipped into his Tokaido Gi, the heavy fabric of which felt comfortable, a good fit. He tugged the corners of his jacket down over his drawstring pants, wrapped his belt around his waist and knotted it.

'Line up,' the call came, prompting everyone into action.

Sean and the rest of the group moved quickly to the dojo. The line-up as always was done in position of rank, from right to left facing the instructor. The highest rank, a 2nd Dan, stood to Sean's right at the end of the line. The young man next to Sean stood fidgeting with his brown belt, while others wearing purple, green, yellow, orange and white belts prepared themselves for the start of the class.

The group stood with feet together and bowed to their sensei.

The instructor started the group off with a series of warm-up exercises, preceded by combinations of kicks, punches and elbow strikes, and other set routines. Kata followed, each one differing to the appropriate grade but with plenty of yells echoing around the room. Each Kiai was a personal vocalisation unique to each student, drawn not from the throat but from deep within the abdomen.

Sean finished Bassai-Di and stood with arms extended and fists clenched, while the 2nd Dan nearby finished off Tekki Nidan.

'Good,' the instructor said loudly. 'A little scrappy in places, but it's coming together. Partner up for some Kumite.'

This was the best part of the class for Sean; he loved the freedom of freestyle fighting, although in Shotokan Karate, it was only semi contact with the body, lightly connecting with your opponent, a touch to score a point.

Sean looked into the eyes of his muscular opponent; the 2nd Dan stared back unflinching, his eyes focused on him alone.

They bowed to one another and got into stance with hands clenched into fists.

'Remember, control,' the sensei told the group, but his attention was drawn to the man facing Sean. He'd been known to be particularly aggressive, sometimes to forget his own strength and fully connect, knocking the wind out of more than one student.

'Hajime,' the instructor shouted.

Sean reacted quickly, bouncing up and down on his feet, keeping his body loose but always moving. His focus was on the man in front of him. The burly man struck first, throwing a jab. Sean parried it, moving backwards as a roundhouse kick came toward his head in a sweeping arc. He ducked, threw a reverse punch into his opponent's stomach and moved away quickly.

Constantly moving backwards and forwards, and side to side, they continued to size each other up. Sean's attention shifted for a moment. In his mind he was back in the library in Somerset.

Sean stumbled backwards as a punch struck him hard in the gut.

He looked back to his sparring partner, who stood grinning.

Both resumed position again.

The book was there before him, its pages flipping over one at a time.

'Oh,' he grunted, receiving a kick in the ribs.

The smirk was still there on the burly man's lips.

Moving backwards, Sean quickly adjusted his Gi and straightened his belt, but the sketch was there in his thoughts, every line sharp and clear. Santia's dark eyes staring back at him.

He reacted to the man in front of him, blocking each strike from instinct even though his mind was somewhere else. He saw the pirate's face, grinning, taunting him. Sean blocked a front snap kick with a downward stroke of his arm, evaded another kick and slapped away a punch.

He was in a dark place, reacting without thought or

consideration. Sean spun, lashing out with a back fist, and it connected with a fleshy smack. He followed through with an elbow strike to the jaw, and as the man staggered backwards, Sean lifted him off his feet with a side thrust kick to the stomach.

The big man landed hard on his back and Sean leaned over him, following up with a flurry of punches.

'Yamae!' the instructor shouted, but Sean was lost to the spectre within his head.

'Stop!' his sensei cried out, running toward him from the other end of the room. 'Stop!'

'What?' Sean felt the instructor's hand on his arm, his eyes widening.

'Snap out of it.'

Sean stared at him uncomprehendingly, then to the man lying on the floor, blood spurting from his nose.

'What the fuck's wrong with you?' the man said as he was helped to his feet, his white jacket smeared red.

'Get him to the back room,' the sensei said. 'You can use some wet paper towels to stop the flow of blood.' Two young men helped him away.

'I'm sorry,' Sean said.

'I've never seen you lose control like that before. I know you've been through a lot recently but ...'

'I know Pete, it's just ...'

'Sean,' he interrupted. 'It's like you were possessed.'

The lesson had ended abruptly. Pete had drawn it to a close, having advised Sean to get some rest. Sean had returned to his car and sat there watching everyone exit St Mary's, with the thought of what he'd done fresh in his mind. He hoped he'd only bloodied his sparring partner's nose, not broken it, but losing control to such an extent was not acceptable. The whole thing had felt surreal, as though he had had no control over his actions. He couldn't even recall punching the man, because his mind had been elsewhere. He was back in the library, looking at that book, at Santia's face and those eyes. It was like being in a bad dream.

'Oh, God,' he said. 'What's happening to me?'

The last of the cars exited through the school gates and Sean leaned forward, about to press the ignition button, when his attention shifted to one of the windows.

A reflection?

Someone was in there, high up in the extension block attached to the side of the building. A face stared down from an upstairs window, blurred, too far away to be able to identify.

Sean felt increasingly uneasy.

The face was partly in shadow, but the eyes were clearly fixed on him. Was it the cleaner? If so, why was he just standing there and staring down at him? No, the cleaner usually came well after karate practice.

He leaned forward, staring harder, and could now make out dark hair framing a grinning face and eyes that were somehow familiar.

The figure remained still.

It was irrational, but he had to know who was up there. Something was wrong. Sean opened the car door and strode toward the school. He moved through the reception area and past the gym.

'Hello?' he called out.

No answer.

A door stood open on his left. He hesitated for a moment before entering, then moved quickly down a long shadowy corridor and up a flight of steps.

He paused as he heard a noise. Laughter faint, almost whispery.

Ahead of him, the door was closed, but the door to his right was ajar.

'Who's there?' he shouted, pushing it fully open.

The room was stacked with chairs, small tables and teaching supplies. Sean approached the window. There was condensation on the glass, the merest hint of a breath on its surface. He looked down into the car park and saw his car, where minutes earlier he'd been sitting, staring up at this very window.

He scanned the room. An unrolled poster lay across a table; *Toys From Our Past* the banner read in bold black print. Scattered around it were children's painted pictures. A shabby teddy bear's head peeked over the lid of one box; behind it lay a broken mechanical robot. More children's playthings were scattered around the room in groups relating to their time period. Wind-up toys like those from the Victorian era, a jack-in-the-box, a small monkey with outstretched arms ready to crash its cymbals together, and porcelain dolls with stern faces alongside ragged stuffed animals. His eyes shifted to a marionette dangling from a disused coat stand, its limbs suspended by strings, its jointed face and hands carved from wood and crudely painted.

In the far corner of the room a small figure was sitting on a child's chair. Sean's heart skipped a beat, but the child didn't move, and when he approached he realised that it was just a vintage ventriloquist's dummy. It wasn't pleasant to look at, with its wild orange hair and its plastic face twisted into a weirdly contorted grimace. He stared, strangely drawn to it. Its eyes and mouth were locked shut, its small body dressed in a white shirt, black waistcoat and tatty trousers.

Sean prodded it, felt an irrational need to.

It's a toy, for god's sake, he told himself.

'*Pop!*'

Sean turned with a startled shout and saw that the jack-in-the-box had leapt from its home. The clown's head bobbed almost as fast as the thudding in his chest.

'Jesus!' he muttered, looking back to the dummy.

Its arms were still by its sides, but its head seemed more upright and the eyes were open, staring back at him.

'No way!' the words spilled out but were little more than a whisper.

Sean stood rigid, momentarily confused. Moments earlier those eyes had been shut, but as he took in the face, the orange hair seemed wilder, the expression more manic than before.

Sean stepped backwards, sure those eyes were following him.

'Enough!' he said aloud. *It's a fucking doll*, he told himself.

Sean laughed at the stupidity of the whole thing. *Imagination could really …*

Its jaw dropped open.

'Christ almighty!'

He took another step as a nauseating odour swept over him, a sickly-sweet stench like charred skin. He'd smelled it before at the crash site in the United States when that American airlines plane had crashed into a field near where he was staying in New England. The smell of burned human flesh and bone had stuck with him for a very long time after. Here it was again, filling the air, as though a memory had been drawn from within. Sean took out a paper handkerchief from his pocket and coughed and spat into it. For a moment, he was back at the crash site, staring from a distance at the blackened debris and roaring flames. That smell again, mixed with the pungent stink of aviation fuel. At one point the whole field seemed to have been engulfed. The Boeing was little more than a twisted shell, with luggage, wheels and mechanical parts strewn everywhere. Alongside burning and blackened debris were bodies. A woman in a grey top lay on her back, blood smeared across her face, her left arm missing its hand. Another victim lay on the ground, his grey hair covered in grass, one arm badly broken and legs at a right-angle to his body. A young girl, perhaps nine or ten, lay on her side with a T-shirt that read 'Stay Cool'. But the most disturbing sight was of a passenger still strapped into his chair. Somehow it had been blown away from the aircraft and come to rest on its own in an upright position. The passenger's hands gripped the armrests, his charred body melded into the seat.

Sean remembered returning to the scene, cordoned off by the emergency services by then. He didn't know why he'd gone back. He had felt a need, out of respect for the dead, those innocents who'd perished so quickly. He couldn't help but wonder what it must have been like up there for the passengers, knowing they were about to die. Were they screaming, praying, or just accepting the inevitable as the plane hurtled to oblivion? The blackened wreck of the plane was still smouldering, even though the fire services had responded quickly. Black plastic body bags had lain in neat rows, all filled, ready to be taken away. Sean felt sweat trickling down his forehead; the past could be a terrible place to find yourself. His attention returned to the present, to the ventriloquist's dummy. It sat looking at him, its open mouth seeming to leer. Yet the smell was there, like burnt flesh without the noxious fuel mix.

There was something else there, mingling with the putrid stench, another aroma, very faint like salty air.

'Hey,' a voice called out.

Sean whirled around to see a small balding man standing with a mop in his hand.

'You shouldn't be in this part of the building,' he said, with a deep frown creasing his already lined faced.

'I was looking for the toilet,' Sean lied.

'It's downstairs,' he replied. 'You're one of that karate lot, aren't you?'

'Yeah,' he said as they moved down the stairway together.

'Tell whoever's in charge not to leave the place in that state again. There was blood all over the place.'

Sean nodded as the man prattled on, but the words washed over him as the face in the window swam into his thoughts once more, somehow clearer, the over-tanned skin, dark eyes and lank black hair framing his stern face and streaming down onto his shoulders.

Santia. The name spilled from his lips as the old man stared at him in confusion.

12

The wind struck Sean relentlessly as he ran across the clearing, a track that would eventually lead him to the shoreline of the sea. In the short time it had taken him to get this far the breeze had become a gale. He raised a forearm over his face, forcing his body forwards, pushing against the dry storm with the wind whipping at his clothes and ruffling his hair. His feet pounded the ground and he couldn't shake the feeling that this freaky weather was a portent of some kind, a warning to stay back. But he couldn't. He wanted to find out what was beyond the woodland ahead.

Grey clouds loomed in the distance, illuminated by flashes of inner lightening, and as the wind began to howl, it grew darker by the minute. Night was closing in, and with it an inner fear.

The woods opened up before him and a branch caught his outstretched arm, narrowly missing his face as he sped along the path. Young saplings bent against the onslaught, and high above tall trees shook, their leaves rustling fiercely. He slowed his pace, breathing heavily; it was becoming too dangerous to run. Lightning flashed followed by the slow rumble of thunder.

Sean stopped and looked around, patchy moonlight his only ally for now. Another flash erupted, and in that glare the woodland became a ghostly visage of bleached limbs and deep shadow.

He took to walking, resisting the urge to run, as too many broken branches littered the rutted ground. Up ahead, an enormous beech loomed, its canopy drooping as if to block his way. He didn't want to risk leaving the track and getting lost, so decided to negotiate his way around its low boughs. Ever vigilant to the falling branches, he crouched, pushing the heavy limbs away from his body, weaving his way through the tangle of branches. Some were entwined so tightly he thought they'd never move. He struggled to push them aside and eventually did so with some sense of relief.

Just as the last of that tangled mess was behind him, he tripped over something, pitched forwards and threw his arms out but hit the earth hard, smacking the side of his face. It took him a few moments to regain his senses before he realised he'd snagged his foot on a tree root. As he got to his feet he brushed a hand across his face and felt blood on his fingers. Sean pushed on, breathing heavily, as more lightning flashed.

'No,' he cried out.

The path ended in a wall of foliage. Where had it come from? He was sure it hadn't been there a few moments ago.

He gritted his teeth, determined to battle this hostile place, and ran into the surrounding undergrowth in an attempt to get around the obstacle. He pushed leaves and branches away from his face, blundering through the shrubbery, engulfed in prickly blackness, fighting through bramble and other rough foliage. Sean became disorientated and, with his vision limited, he screamed in frustration.

Another flash illuminated a jagged hole to his left, visible for just long enough for him to realise it could be a way out. He made off in that direction, his clothes torn, his arms and face bloodied, scratched and stinging. Sean fought through more brambles, pushing himself through the narrow opening. He fell to the ground, felt sand beneath him, and realised he'd escaped the woodland. Sean rolled onto his back, his eyes closed and breathing heavily. He lay, his chest heaving, the sand cool against his sweaty body. Within moments he was on his feet again and taking in his new surroundings. The wind was less turbulent and the howling had ceased. But he couldn't shake that inner feeling of dread.

Sean looked heavenward, away from the oil-black sea, as thunder boomed, echoing across the ocean. Huge clouds boiled and furled, twisting restlessly in the night sky, spreading out over the water.

He dropped his gaze to an approaching vessel. It cut a line

through the fog surrounding it, and within those yellow-tainted vapours was a peculiar luminescence. His feet felt rooted in the white sand.

His body tensed. The ship was tall and dark, a relic battered by the passage of time. It turned, moving toward him.

Nightmare. The word burst into his mind, but the notion was short-lived as fear rose on hearing a scream rip through the night. Perhaps the fog had made the sound more terrifying than it really was. Sean didn't try to understand; he didn't care. He just wanted to get away from there.

The place was unbearable; somehow corrupt, jangling every nerve in his body. More sounds came to him, the groans and cries of people in torment; heightening the feeling of fear.

Even as he watched, a bolt of lightning ripped through the air and appeared to strike the ship, but it was only an illusion. The ship remained intact, brooding against the volatile sky.

His body began to sag, and he felt his knees weaken, to the horrendous screams of people in agony. The voices were everywhere, seeping through the atmosphere, a gabble rising to a torturous crescendo. People cried for help, and he felt their anguish, their despair. Pestilence, starvation, disease and death surrounded them like a ravenous predator.

It seemed to last for eternity, but just when this nightmarish scenario was beyond tolerance, the sounds began to wane, then fell silent.

With breaths coming in short, sharp gasps, he slowly turned his head, and a dazed consciousness returned to his brain as he focused once again on the ship. She appeared grey in the swirling mist, although something dark was seeping down her frame. In the smudge of bluish-white light that remained, from a moon that had almost disappeared, he was just able to see through the drifting fog bank below. The ship was now no more than shadow.

Sean wafted a hand in front of his face, trying to disperse the vapours. The mist was gauzy and the air cold, but the sickly odour that clung to it was repulsive. It hung in the air like the small of rotting offal, a cloying stench that instantly aroused revulsion.

A terrible scream, a fearsome screech, sent Sean stumbling backwards.

'Jesus ...' He spun around but could see nothing. 'Who's there?'

The fog closed in around him, and within it he heard something else. The sounds had returned, except this time they were more intense, a bizarre mishmash of noise, a loudening chorus of chaos. The sounds were quickly followed by others: staccato gunfire, missiles launching, ear-bursting explosions and people screaming.

'No,' he mumbled. The sounds were getting inside his head, hurting him. It felt as though his brain was expanding at an alarming rate, putting pressure on every nerve in his head.

Thunder pounded the night and lightening ripped through the tumultuous sky, charging the very air itself, but the celestial display had little effect on him. He couldn't stop the barrage of noise that crowded his mind. His senses were in turmoil, the pain almost unbearable. Sean sank to his knees, clutching his ears.

'Stop ...'

He barely heard the word against the cacophony of other sounds, and as the noise increased, his mouth fell open and he joined the chorus of screams.

His eyes sprang open. He lay in bed shivering, staring through the darkness of the room, his body soaked with sweat. 'Just a nightmare,' he said in a hushed voice. Yet the spectre of the dream lingered, tormenting him. 'Just a dream,' he told himself again. He closed his eyes with the thought and eventually fell back into an uneasy sleep.

13

Sean made his way down Arkwright Street toward Brosswell College. The tall building looked dated. The blue window-frames were faded, the paint cracked. Built in the late '70s, it was now surrounded by contemporary high-rise glass-reflecting architecture. These modern commercial buildings made the technical college look like a relic.

He pushed open the double doors and walked briskly into the foyer. The receptionist behind the desk, a dark-haired woman looking mildly frustrated, was surrounded by a group of abusive teenagers.

Sean strode across the black and white chequered floor with a sense of urgency. The meeting was due to start at any moment and time was against him. Sean was always punctual for work. He hurried up two flights of stairs before pausing to catch a breath.

Why was the lift out of order so often? More than a few laboratory doors were open, revealing empty, dimly-lit rooms. Broader corridors stretched left and right but no sounds came from them, no muted conversation or the clatter of footsteps. The absence of people in this part of the building created an unsettling silence.

Sean quickened his pace until he reached the Hairdressing Department on the fourth floor. Even with all of the Department's attributes it was an area he didn't like to venture into. But he had to. Part of his duties, aside from teaching kids IT, involved staff development, assisting with the implementation of new systems in the Hairdressing Department. As a part-time lecturer, Sean felt alienated from the hairdressing team. He could always sense an atmosphere when he entered the room; conversations would stop and there was always that uneasy silence. Perhaps it was just down to the fact that they didn't like change and resented him. He'd had to endure this kind of crap for over two years and was getting sick of it. The job just wasn't worth it anymore. Sean smirked. It was good to know that his application to join the IT team at Remmington College had been accepted.

He entered room 310, where three wooden tables had been pushed together to form a kind of square horseshoe effect. A smaller table and grey plastic chair were strategically placed in the recess as the focal point for Pauline to chair the meeting.

Sean took a seat next to a thin woman with dark shoulder-length hair. She gave him a cool stare and forced smile. Almost immediately she turned her back on him and began talking to an obese lady on her right. Sean was used to this supercilious crap and paid little attention to it. They were a close-knit group and best left to it.

Twelve people sat around the table in muted conversation with their immediate neighbours. Others silently studied documents in front of them, underlining text with coloured markers in preparation for contributory comments during the meeting.

To his left another false smile graced another woman's face. Her large spectacles made her eyes look extremely small, like two tiny specks. Her smile of acknowledgement was almost believable, but lacking genuine sincerity.

He returned the gesture, sat back in his chair and took in the room. It had two glass doors, one leading out into the main corridor, the other into a small office. He saw Pauline approaching the office door. She marched forcefully toward it, pushed it open and made her grand entrance. In an instant all conversations ceased. As Head of Department, this was the respect she demanded. The group cast nervous glances at her. They were reminiscent, he thought, of a class of children. Little wonder, she was known as 'the Bitch of Brosswell'. When she spoke, you listened. She had a fierce temper, with a sharp voice and a choice of words so scathing it had reduced many members of staff to tears. There was no doubting it: she was formidable, with wild blonde hair, razor cut into a style way too severe for a woman in her late fifties.

'Let's begin.'

As she began to talk, Sean almost groaned; another boring ritual had begun, a monotonous regurgitated dialogue of curricular issues. Three things were certain in life: death, taxes … and Pauline's uninspiring speeches.

The meeting dragged on for longer than he had expected, but eventually Sean walked down the narrow corridor, his mind awash with thoughts.

He paused, feeling a sudden chill, looking down the long science corridor with its array of doors and bleak classrooms.

A frown disturbed his brow as his attention was drawn to the end of the shadowy passage that seemed darker than when he had come in. An overhead fluorescent strip flickered, providing an insubstantial light. He stared into the semi-darkness, with the strangest feeling that he was being watched.

Imagination?

As he turned to walk away, something moved. His eyes darted along the gloomy strip to the end of the corridor again.

'Who's there?' He squinted, peering into the murk, but could see nothing.

He felt it again, not just cold, but an unnatural chill at odds with the usual warmth of the building. The central heating system could be temperamental at times, but he'd never known it this cold before. He drew a breath and shuddered.

'Is anyone there?'

No answer.

He shivered again. Something had disturbed him, but he didn't know what.

Get a grip, man.

Sean closed his tired eyes and ran a hand through his hair. He couldn't allow himself to be carried away by irrational thoughts.

Yet, he felt confused, and that confusion was beginning to dredge up past emotions, past turmoil. A shadow passed before his closed eyes and he quickly opened them.

No-one there.

He looked around uneasily and became aware of the faint sound of music. A notion entered his mind: it belonged in another place, another era.

But were these sounds a product of his imagination?

Sean began to sway, and his eyelids felt heavy. He closed them again and listened intently, trying to understand what he was hearing. It sounded like a squeezebox, but the lively sound swelled and ebbed. Yet it seemed familiar.

Yes, in his dreams. He'd heard it in his dreams.

The tune continued, followed by voices; ethereal singing that came from the walls, ceiling and all around him.

> *'Slice em up, run em through,*
> *'dance with the devil our course*
> *'is hell ...'*

Sean's head fell forward and his shoulders sagged. The boisterous shanty took on a darker tone as the voices drew closer.

> *'Our souls are doomed, we repent not,*
> *'death and doom, the reaper is near ...'*

The tone steadily rose, echoing along the corridor, closely followed by a breeze. He stumbled backwards, managing to keep his balance. It was as if icy hands were pushing him from the midst of the glacial onslaught.

Through the commotion he sank deeper, becoming part of something he couldn't understand. Sean knew that it was impossible, but he could smell fresh sea air, even taste the brine in his mouth.

A peculiar sensation gripped him. He felt light-headed, as though his body were floating.

An image flickered in his mind, slowly swimming into focus, expanding into something else. He felt himself rising, then falling, as mind and body became fully integrated with the vision. Unrestricted by the constraints of time, he became part of a new reality.

> *The deck of the ship creaked below him; every sail was filling and slacking as she tore through the waves. He put an open hand across his brow, shading the glare of the sun, and felt a spray of seawater against his face. Sean glanced over the bare backs of the crew along the frigate's wide deck, toward her Captain. Their eyes met, but the man stared through Sean as though he were a ghost. The tall man stood firm, his hands clasped behind his back.*
>
> *'Steady as she goes,' the Captain said. 'We will steer a course for Haiti, and God help us.'*

As the Englishman's voice faded, so too did the vision. Aside from confusion. Sean was left with a curious feeling, that they were destined to meet again. As he pondered on this, he was dragged from the vision back to the real world.

> *'Follow our master, through the seas of time,*
> *'soon we'll return and it's the end of ...'*

The freezing air became rancid, masking the stench of decay, and vapours at the far end of the corridor, with long glowing tendrils, weaved their way toward him. The accumulation surged along the floor, spreading up the walls and across the ceiling. Shadows shifted in the rolling fog, spectral figures that had once been human but bore little semblance to that now. Their patterns were sheer, undefined, yet desperate to acquire substance. The dark wraiths hovered above and around him, their featureless faces blurred by mist.

He suddenly went weak, felt blood draining from every part of his body as if his veins had been opened up and his life force was ebbing away.

The passage shuddered to the sound of thunder, with one door after another banging open in an unstoppable wave.

A harsh jolt shook the corridor again, shuddering through the walls, ceiling and floor.

The pounding grew louder and faster, throbbing at an alarming rate.

'No.'

Still they continued.

'Stop.'

Faster and faster.

'No more!'

Louder and louder it resonated, the clamour reaching a deafening pitch.

Sean cried out again, clapping his hands against his ears.

He stood in the doorway in the dim light, but there was no music or voices, just silence. Among the thoughts tumbling chaotically through his head, one stood out from the rest.

You're losing your mind again.

14

Sean spent most of the next morning and early afternoon making duplicate records of completed assessments, projects and assignments. Regardless of his progress in the department, he always tried to add something new to the standard format, offering struggling students a lifeline wherever possible. He stared at the laptop, feeling tired, although his day hadn't been hectic. Normally Sean possessed sharp powers of concentration, which served him well in classes where some of the kids struggled getting to grips with even the basics. He'd have plenty of time to get through what he needed to, because Sophie would be working late that night, and he really wanted to get this finished.

As he worked, his thoughts shifted repeatedly to the mysterious episode at Brosswell College, and the sense of peril latched onto him again.

With the laptop turned off and working by the light of a small table lamp, he was still at his desk past four o'clock, when spatters of rain against the window drew his attention. It was as if dusk had crept in ahead of time. The clouds hung low in an ever-darkening sky, as grey as smoke from a cauldron. Sean stood, stretched his back and walked across the room to the settee where Pike's journal lay. The man's life had not been an easy one, yet as Sean continued to comb through the journal he could not help but be drawn back into the first lieutenant's life. He was undoubtedly a brave man. To take command of *Gospall* and defeat an enemy ship must have taken brass balls. But what of Captain Tanner? Sean studied the recorded entry.

> *During our last battle, Captain Tanner rested in his cabin, troubled by an ailment that confounded our surgeon.*

There seemed little doubt that the man had bottled it. Was he a coward? One thing was for sure: Tanner was a sadist. The crew had been flogged, beaten and punished for little reason. Could Tanner have been resentful, because they had seen him for what he really was? A coward trying to use power and fear to gain their respect? If so, it had been futile, ending in mutiny. Sean thumbed through more pages. Pike was a man in torment. If caught, he and his fellow mutineers would all be executed. The pressure on his shoulders must have been unbearable. The crew were looking to him for answers. Sean read on.

I have plotted a course for Tornave, a small island off the coast of Haiti. This will be our new home, God willing, for the remainder of our lives.

He moved across the room, switched on the laptop, put the journal on the table next to him and typed 'Tornave' into Google.

Tornave stood 35 -five miles off the northern coast of Haiti. It was mountainous and rocky; the rocks were especially abundant on the northern part of the island. In the early 17th Century, the population lived on the southern coast, which was divided into three parts. The first was the low country containing a port. The second was a small town called Caitan, a former tobacco plantation. The third part was known as Mòn Lan or the mountain. The French had colonised it for a short time, only to leave because the island was too small to be of any importance.

It must have been an ideal destination back then. One of those islands few had heard of in England, yet large enough for Pike and his men to make a life there.

His attention returned to the journal, to Santia. He recalled how Pike had rescued him and what had been left of his crew. It hadn't taken Santia long to start an insurrection of his own. The man was a first-class bastard, ruthless, sadistic and by all accounts insane. For a moment, Sean was drawn back to his visit to the library, to the pencilled sketch of Santia. He was sure that as he stared at it he'd heard a faint drumbeat, a tribal chant; but it was the face of the Frenchman that had disturbed him.

Lightning flashed. Its intensity cast shadows against the walls of the dimly-lit room. The sudden crash of thunder that followed didn't bring Sean to his feet, until his desk lamp blinked out. He bolted out of his chair during the next lightening flash as something dark moved across the room. He tried to dismiss it as a shadow, but that rationale was flawed. He spun around wildly looking for the source of the shadow but to no avail. He looked back to the window, thinking that maybe a structure outside was causing it. Impossible! The featureless shape was the height of a man and dark as sable. He felt a pang of fear as he turned back, realising that the black form was moving independently from the effects of the storm, its motion smooth and continuous.

It was ill-defined and could not assume full delineation. It seemed to dissolve, evaporate like driven steam from a spout.

Sean strode across the room and turned on the central light. It blazed into life, revealing that there was no-one there. He considered the possibility that he may have hallucinated the whole thing. No, he chided himself; it had to have been an optical illusion, an image created by the pyrotechnics.

Yet as he stood by the rain-lashed window once more, staring through the blurred glass, a coldness gripped him like a frigid hand against the nape of his neck.

15

Sean had a restless night. It was cool, but he felt sweaty drifting in and out of sleep. He pushed off the clinging damp bedclothes and sighed. Drinking a few beers just before going to bed hadn't helped. During the course of the night his bladder had demanded to be emptied more than once. He'd taken care not to disturb Sophie, using light from the partly-open door to make his way to the toilet. She'd had a busy day and was exhausted. She had got home late, having been caught in the storm. Drenched and thoroughly miserable, she'd had a hot bath and an early night. After a long yawn, he rolled onto his back and stared at the ceiling, wondering if sleep would ever come. Eventually his eyelids closed, and his consciousness began to drift.

Sean found himself standing on a long, desolate beach, looking out over a murky sea with the moon the only source of light, reflected off the water's surface.

The night was chilly with a cool breeze coming in off the ocean. Water gushed as it rolled onto the shore, covering his feet, its icy touch causing him to shiver. In the distance palm trees rustled, and he shuddered; staring out over the moonlit expanse with a feeling of dread slowly rising.

Far out at sea, a light flickered through the blackness. It moved toward him, gradually increasing in size as it approached. Soon he saw the source of the glow: a lantern swinging from the yardarm of an old ship. The ship was weatherworn, and although the lettering was faded, he could just make out part of her name below the stern cabin window.

Gos—

He stood silently in the moonlight and realised that his surroundings had dissolved around him. He was on the deck of the ship. High above, the trailing masthead pendant flicked out like a whip and loose gear rattled almost in protest at his arrival. The ship's wheel juddered, then slowly turned. Beneath his feet, wood creaked, the timber rotten in parts and reeking of decay. It was an odd sensation walking her boards. He could not help but imagine how it must have been a century before, with men moving along her gangways, rigging and yards and the thunderous roar of cannon fire as her frame shivered in the fury of war.

'Who's there?' he called out, distracted by a faint scratching noise within a darkened recess of the ship. He turned toward the source of the sound, listening intently but unable to see what was making it. Something was gnawing but then stopped and moved fast.

'Who's there?' his voice echoed again, before fading into oblivion. For a moment there was silence, then the scrabbling began again.

'Sean …' a voice called to him.

Rushing across his path from the shadows came a mass of black furry bodies. Rats scrambled past him, around him frantically, and leapt over the side of the ship into the water below as though preferring death to the alternative.

'Sean …' the voice returned.

The ship dipped into a steep trough, then pitched, swaying in the swelling waves. He staggered forward, the ship's hull still rising and falling as he made his way toward a grimy wooden construction. The doors swung open and closed, creaking in the growing wind. He shivered as he opened them wide and peered inside. A flight of steps led down into a black abyss, but the sour dankness of the air, so strong, so intense, made him retch before slamming the doors shut.

Unfettered by cloud, the full moon cast its light onto the deck of the ship. She groaned as she rose, then ploughed forward through the water into the fog.

All the time the ship moved beneath his feet, forcing him to walk forward, checking loose boards, several of which had sprung. Each step gave rise to concern; this ancient deck was in danger of collapsing beneath him at any moment. Torn sails flapped in the growing wind and he shuddered, feeling an abrupt drop in temperature as the tiny hairs on his neck stiffened. Accompanying the icy breeze came a distant sound that was fast approaching. Soon he recognised it. An incessant drum beat. Behind him an unsteady glow emanated from the island, an orange glow that flickered through the mist. Shadows danced around the swelling flames; ill-defined shapes, silhouetted before the dim blaze.

Wails could be heard, wretched and racked, a resonance of abject misery. Other sounds permeated the atmosphere too; chants and laughter, a gabble that steadily rose. Still the drumbeat thumped, adding to the clamour, increasing all the while, filling the space with a confusing blend of insistent chanting, wails and screams.

Like dry ice, clouds of vapour poured onto the deck. The fog flowed along her boards, and her frame trembled.

He stood, alone in the swirling mist, as a limb-freezing paralysis gripped him.

A whistle shrieked. An asson rattled.

Incantations were bellowed out in ancient dialects. He gasped, almost forgetting to breathe, and sucked in a lungful of air, but the air was pungent; an aroma of spices infused with musty odours, vaguely reminiscent of incense used in church. But this stench was not for the glorification of God. He shook his head but saw nothing, just patterns in the fog as it shifted restlessly in the breeze. The ritualistic chant lasted for some time before it ebbed into the night.

Sean felt the breeze strengthening as it brushed against his face. Through skeins of fog he realised there were gaping holes everywhere. There was a precariousness about the ship. As if to mock Sean's trepidation, her timbers creaked and part of the deck behind him collapsed. Another crash spurred him into action. **Keep moving,** he told himself, praying that the deck would not give way.

The hull pitched and buffeted as the rudder gave in to sudden pressure from beneath the sea of mist. The deck tilted, and the wheel spun as if unseen hands had gripped its spokes, trying to steady the ship.

Something thundered, an overwhelming sound from all around him. Fissures appeared on deck and rigging fell from above. The vessel shook, with a jolt like a shockwave causing the whole frame to shudder. A bell chimed from the forecastle, a warning tone buried within the sounds of crashing timber resounding from below.

He lurched from one side of the vessel to the other, losing balance as a fresh jolt threw him onto his back. Sean rose apprehensively. Could the souls of the dead crew be here? he thought. Or was all this an echo from the past?

The wheel moved again.

Peering through patches of fog he saw the ship's wheel, partly obstructed by shadow. Only two semicircles could be seen at either side of the blackness that consumed its centre, almost as if it was split into two parts. The wooden handles were long, and spokes ran from the brass rim into the darkness in front of it. Within that darkness something was changing, taking on shape.

Sean watched the amorphous configuration. It wavered, illuminated by inconstant moonlight, taking time to form, to solidify. Head bowed, the enormous cowled figure curled its spindly fingers around the wheel.

The dark host made no effort to turn and face him.

Nightmare. The thought flew through his mind, repeating itself again and again, until he heard goading laughter, coming from the unworldly thing in front of him, which appeared as real as any living person. He stared, watching the figure subtly shifting its posture, and he tried to breathe calmly.

The wheel moved slowly to the right as the ship sailed swiftly on, cutting a line through the foggy sea. The ghostly guide steered, taking him on a journey to an unknown destination.

'Where are you taking me?' Sean demanded.

'Don't you know?' it whispered. 'Time is running out.'

'What do you mean?'

'Your time is almost up.'

'Face me!'

The shape released its grip on the wheel and whirled around, its long robe flapping in the hard-driving wind. Sudden darkness swept across the giant figure and rolling black clouds smothered the moon again.

The ship rocked back and forth in a freak gale that came from nowhere and rain lashed down, pounding the vessel. She swayed on the choppy sea, rising then falling, sails booming and cracking, her fragile structure shuddering with a sonorous groaning as though the ship itself was in agony.

A heightened sense of delirium gripped him. His mind tried to grapple with what was happening as thunder boomed and lightning flashed. In that transient blaze the wind hurled stinging rain into his face, stunning him. He rolled over the handrail, almost tumbling overboard, but the ship pitched and threw him onto the deck. His body slid along the wooden surface and, although disorientated, he soon realised that he was heading straight for a gigantic hole.

Sean clawed at the deck on either side of him as the pit came closer, its jagged maw wide. He thrashed wildly but the wood beneath him was just too slippery. He couldn't stop himself. Lightning flashed as his perilous descent continued and a gut churning fear swept through him. Yet within that immense flash his hand caught hold of something, a frayed rope attached to the mainmast. He held on, his instinct for self-preservation kicking in.

Another crash of thunder hammered the night.

Heart thumping like a jackhammer he raised himself to his feet, using the rope for leverage.

Lightning blazed, so bright that the sky itself seemed to burn as Sean gripped the handrail again.

A thunderbolt ripped through the darkness, making contact with the top of a mast only a few feet from him. The huge pole burnt with incandescence, like a glowing iron rod, before the ship's yards and sails exploded into an enormous fireball. Burning embers scattered all around him and the air reeked of smoke. He felt the skin on his hands and face prickling from its heat, but the conflagration was short-lived as fiery debris fell into the cold damp mist.

With a trembling hand, Sean wiped sweat and rain from his brow. A thought remained pushed to the back of his mind. He was held by the conviction that this was a harbinger of some kind.

Once again, he was rocked from his thoughts by the bizarre storm. Jagged lightning cracked across the sky, swiftly followed by two more fearsome bolts that hurtled downward from the tar black heavens and crashed into the tumultuous sea. Sean had never known a storm like this, so intense, so unnatural.

The subsequent thunderclap was by far the loudest; it rattled the night. He stumbled backwards, his ears ringing, as another bolt ripped through the clouds. The discharge lit the whole ship long enough for Sean to glance into the face of the shrouded figure, which now loomed over him.

It stood tall and dark against the brilliant sky, an imposing ugly thing.

It looked down on him, a hideous grin on its face, baleful eyes piercing Sean's like white hot skewers causing agony beyond imagination.

The sentinel crept closer. Sean didn't want to see this grim creature or that face; gaunt, hollow-cheeked and with eyes glowing like smouldering coals.

Sean clamped his eyelids tightly shut, the pain intolerable. Like a psychic rapist its thoughts reached deep, ripping away his protective consciousness, delving into the core of his mind. Mental images flickered, horrific visions of murder, mutilation and carnage. Confused and bewildered, he staggered backwards and dropped to his knees He released an agonised yelp, an involuntary reaction to the unremitting sounds that now crowded his mind.

'Stop,' he groaned, clutching his head with his hands, and as another thunderbolt struck, the pulsating sounds became louder, expanding with the visions, and for a moment everything became clear.

Sean awoke with a start. His body felt heavy, he was exhausted and weak. Tears had gathered in the corners of his eyes. The nightmare had left him with a deep overwhelming sadness. He couldn't fathom it. Apart from the turmoil of the dream, it was the innumerable cries of people in torment that troubled him the most. He had felt their fear, their confusion, as if their minds had been crying out to him. Yet even though he had heard their death screams he was aware of something else. It had happened so quickly, and the people had been unsure of what was killing them. It was an irrational thought, but he'd felt that those people hadn't known what was happening right up until the moment of the catastrophe. What had killed them?

Sean lay in the darkness, his breathing slowing as he forced an uneasy calmness upon himself. He shuddered as he tried to make sense of the thoughts tumbling through his mind, but as he tried to focus on them the images faded to gossamer.

He lay there for what seemed like an eternity, telling himself that it was just a dream. A light sheen of perspiration had formed on his brow and he wiped it away with the back of his hand. The nightmare had really got to him. He listened to

Sophie, breathing gently, lost to a dream of her own. She lay on her side, in an almost foetal position, her head bowed; back curved with one knee drawn up. The bed sheets lay crumpled beside her, so Sean placed them carefully back over her. He desperately wanted her to wake so he could talk to her. For a moment she murmured something, but his hopes were dashed, the words were ill-formed, just remnants of her dream.

A slip of moonlight shone through a small gap in the curtains, but it was several moments before Sean noticed a shadowy form near the end of the bed that moved slowly into the light. The figure was dressed in partly scorched rags. Frozen with fear, Sean tried to dismiss the image, believing it was just an after-effect of the nightmare. No, he thought, this wasn't a trick of the light either. His flesh prickled, and he felt the tiny hairs on his exposed arms and neck stiffen. He lay motionless and cold. Something glimmered in the insubstantial light: a silver pendant hanging loosely around the intruder's neck. Sean felt vulnerable, trying to shake off the drowsiness. He needed to act quickly. Just as he made the decision to leap from the bed and confront the intruder, more light poured through the gap in the curtains. The figure stood unmoving at the foot of the bed. As Sean stared into that face, the true horror of what he saw almost froze his heart. It couldn't be possible. What was left of the skin of the face was badly decomposed and hung in rotted slivers. The scalp was bare in parts as though charred by flames, revealing the darkened surface of a skull. One of its eyelids had shrivelled, leaving an incredibly large, staring eyeball. Sean's heart was pounding yet his mind was burdened by disbelief as the figure turned to expose lipless teeth rooted in darkened gums.

Heart still hammering, Sean's thoughts were in turmoil. This was an illusion, it had to be, but the image remained. Still he watched, too stunned to act, even when it began to laugh …

A scream pierced the night. The sound was clear and sharp beside him. Sean's head swung toward Sophie, whose trembling hands covered her mouth as she screamed again. At first, he could not respond, fear kept him quiet, but not for long.

He grabbed her by the shoulders and pulled her to his chest, then looked back, but the intruder had vanished.

'What the hell was that thing?' she sobbed.

'You saw it too?'

'Yes, I woke up and it was there.'

'Christ, I thought I was still dreaming.'

'What was it?'

'I don't know,' he said, his chest heaving. 'I really don't, but it scared the hell out of me.'

16

Sean woke early but didn't want to disturb Sophie. It was a miracle either of them had gone back to sleep after the night's occurrence. He showered and slipped on a pair of joggers and a T-shirt before eating a slice of toast with black coffee.

What had they seen? How could they both have witnessed the same thing if it had been in his imagination? In his mind's eye he saw those hideous features staring back at him. There was something else too: the figure had been dressed in partly burnt garments, but those clothes looked strangely familiar. How could that be? In that insubstantial light something else had caught his eye: the silver pendent.

Sean pushed the thoughts aside for the time being and watched a news bulletin on the television. The United States had deployed the USS *Dwight D Eisenhower*, a Nimitz class carrier, eighty miles south of Iran amid fears that an oil blockade might be about to come into effect. Iran had threatened once again that it was considering closing the Strait of Hormuz, a narrow waterway through which twenty percent of the world's oil was shipped. With forty-four jets, Carrier Strike Group 8 were patrolling the skies across the Middle East, Pakistan and Afghanistan day and night in order to keep the world's oil supply moving. Sean watched attack jets from the most powerful country in the world take to the sky.

'Friggin' hell,' he breathed slowly. Was it just Iran the US were bothered about or were they worried by newly-formed alliances between Middle Eastern countries?

'Hey!'

Sean spun around to see Sophie behind him.

'Jesus, don't frighten me like that.'

They both laughed for a moment, as it masked the events of the night.

'What do you think we saw?' Sean asked.

'I don't really …'

'Do you think,' he cut in, 'it's possible that we experienced something supernatural?'

'Are we talking ghosts?'

Sean fell silent.

'Honestly, I just don't know what to think,' Sophie replied.

'So, you do believe there was something?'

'Sean?'

'I'm sorry. I thought I was the crazy one,' he said.

She fixed him with an uncompromising stare.

'It's just that I thought you didn't believe in stuff like that,' he said.

'Well, I can't deny something weird happened last night.'

Sophie leaned over the back of the chair so that her face was looking into his. He felt the warmth of her breath on his cheek but resisted the urge to reach out and kiss her. Her eyes displayed an anxiety he found troubling.

'I guess,' he began, 'there are things we don't understand, perhaps never will.'

'What are you saying?'

'Since Mum died things have not been the same.'

'Well, that's to be expected.'

'I know what you mean Sophie, but that's not it.'

'Then what?'

'Think of everything that's happened.' His body stiffened. 'The moment I was told she had died, I knew that something was wrong.'

'Sean, Christine died from heart failure.'

'Yes, but something caused that.'

'Something?' Sophie almost whispered the word.

Sean let the question hang in the air for a moment and gazed out of the window as drifting clouds began to smother the sun.

'James said he heard strange laughter coming from the cottage the night she died.' Sean's eyes locked onto Sophie's. 'He said her eyes were frozen wide.'

She shuddered unexpectedly. 'I know where you're going

with this.'

'Yes Sophie, I think she was scared to death.

'If that's true then we are missing something.'

'Like what?'

She thought for a moment. 'Do you remember the three books and newspapers we found at Bramble Cottage?'

'Of course.'

'They puzzle me. In all the time I knew her, she never expressed an interest in history or prophecies and I still can't get my head around those headlines. They were pretty gruesome.'

'Yeah,' Sean said. 'Mutilated bodies don't make for good bedtime reading.'

'I'm still confused by it all. Someone broke into Christine's cottage but didn't steal anything?'

'You're forgetting that there was no sign of forced entry either.'

'So, what then?' Sophie frowned.

'Shortly after the funeral,' he continued, 'I took a stroll into the village to clear my head. I looked in the library when I was there. I wanted to find out more about the mutiny. They had two books. Mum had previously requested them both.'

Sophie raised her eyebrows in surprise.

'Mum had wanted those books for some reason. One of them described a British frigate named *Gospall* under the command of a man named Winstanly. His first officer was William Pike. In 1809 they were engaged in battle with the French National Frigate *La Mort*, which was much bigger and considered to be the best in the fleet. *Gospall* defeated the French vessel and on return to Portsmouth both men were declared heroes. The next person to captain the ship was Edmund Tanner, a harsh, sadistic man. The frigate sailed to the Mediterranean and was never seen again. We know from Pike's journal what really happened. There was a mutiny and Tanner and two officers were cast adrift in a small boat. There was no mention of this in the book at the library, so we can assume they died at sea.'

'Why didn't you tell me any of this before?'

'Because I was worried you'd think I was mad.'

Sophie shook her head, her face a mask of confusion. 'So aside from your mum, we might be the only people who know about the mutiny. What else aren't you telling me?'

'The second book,' Sean hesitated for a second, reluctant to continue, 'spoke of Francois Santia. Remember, the journal said he was taken on board *Gospall* with his men after the mutiny. He was responsible for the deaths of hundreds of people, including women and children. There were even accounts of his cannibalism.'

Sophie winced at the thought. 'What kind of man could do such a thing?'

'One with no remorse. Even after numerous land raids, and amassing huge sums of money, it wasn't enough for him. Love of money wasn't the only thing that motivated him, that much was evident. His reputation for butchery grew, so much so that the authorities lured his ship into a trap and destroyed it. But he escaped in a small boat with some of his crew. That's how Pike came across him.'

'Oh, God,' Sophie said. 'Imagine being stuck on board a ship with a monster like that, and not even knowing it.'

'Pike figured it out soon enough, but I guess we'll never know what happened after that.'

Sean felt his shoulders sag.

'There's something else, isn't there?'

'Yes. If you don't think I'm mad now, you will when I'm finished.'

'Go on,' Sophie urged him on.

'Inside that second book was a sketch of Francois Santia. As I looked at it, something felt terribly wrong. I tried to convince myself my eyes were playing tricks with me. But they weren't.'

'No.'

Sean was becoming more anxious by the moment. 'Staring at that picture felt weird. I've tried to dismiss it, but can't. The room actually seemed to grow cold, as though the whole atmosphere had changed. The image seemed to be vibrating, shimmering as though it were leaking some kind of dark energy. I remember thinking, it was impossible, it couldn't be happening. I could hear confusing sounds, the ocean, and an incessant tribal drumbeat. Then there was laughter, a low, mocking laughter. I tried to reassure myself that it was just my imagination, but when I looked back into that face, and those eyes, without pity or remorse, Santia's grin had grown wide. That horrendous laughter was coming from the fucking book.'

Sophie suddenly took his hand.

'You must think that I've lost it again.'

'No, Sean, you haven't. Something's wrong, but it's not you. We need to try to figure out what's going on.'

She lifted his chin up with her finger and stared into his eyes.

'Okay,' he said. 'But why do I get the feeling there's worse to come?'

17

Sean moved at a sluggish pace, catching his reflection in one of the large windows as he crossed the plush carpeted concourse. He'd decided not to tell Sophie of the experience at Brosswell College – she'd been through enough – but he had shared some of the bad dreams with her. His emotions were in turmoil. It was hard enough losing a parent, but dealing with these bizarre events was definitely heightening his stress levels. She'd seemed confused, so frightened. He needed Sophie to believe in him again, and she had, even after everything he'd told her.

Sophie had persuaded him to meet with Dr Alexander, and this was something he really needed to do.

From behind the reception desk, a young girl in her early twenties looked up at him.

'Can I help you?'

'I'm here to see Dr Alexander.'

'And your name is?'

'Sean Webster.'

'Won't be a moment.' She began tapping the keyboard in front of her.

Sean hadn't been there for quite a while. The Deystrom Institute was a large building, originally built by the Ashworth family in the 15th Century. It had been rebuilt in 1900, giving the hall its square sandstone finish, although the masonry was barely visible now because of dense green foliage. Sean had always loved the look of vines covering the facade of a building; it wasn't just aesthetically pleasing but was good for the environment. Climbing plants not only provided insulation, they helped filter dust particles from the air and reduce both atmospheric greenhouse gas emissions and run-off during rainstorms. It wasn't all good, though: over time the vines would weaken the mortar and could potentially cause penetrating damp. But, he supposed, it was a trade-off. The grounds of the hall were breathtaking and very extensive, boasting ornamental lakes, a raft of ducks and a vast array of colourful shrubs. At the back of the Institute stood a private chapel, built in the 1800s and now used as a treatment centre. The grounds were encircled by a fifteen-foot-tall weather-beaten wall with access from the South and East through two ancient, yet still operational gatehouses. The Deystrom Institute was nestled in the countryside setting of Wellsborough, just an hour's drive from the hustle and bustle of city life.

Sean looked back, toward the two large doors he'd just come through, and saw an elderly couple blocking the doorway, having a hushed exchange. To his right, at the end of a narrow corridor, was a waiting room; to his immediate left, a chequer-tiled floor led to myriad corridors, all branching off in differing directions to various consultation and patient bedrooms. The Deystrom Institute specialised in helping people who were suffering from a range of mental and psychological problems. It was a fully-functioning psychiatric facility with state-of-the-art equipment and resources providing long- and short-term care, including the treatment of brain injuries and juvenile care.

'Mr Webster,' the receptionist prompted. 'He'll see you now. Room four, if you please.' She indicated the way with her hand.

Sean didn't need to be directed, he'd been often enough. It was always the same room. He approached the consultant's door and gave a timid knock.

'Come in,' came the hearty reply.

He pushed the huge door open and entered.

The consultant extended a hand across his desk without getting out of his seat.

Sean shook it. The grip was firm, but not too much.

Alexander was a silver-haired man, well over six feet and smartly dressed in a Taransay tweed jacket, light brown waistcoat, crisp white shirt and a sharp blue tie. Sean figured him to be in his early sixties, and although he seemed of a relaxed manner, his eyes were penetrating. His eyebrows were knitted together in earnest, and he stared through rimless glasses, swiftly appraising Sean.

'Please take a seat,' he said.

Sean sat down and released a long, unexpected sigh.

'Surely,' Alexander said with a broad smile, 'it can't be that bad?'

Sean returned a weak smile. 'You tell me, doc.'

'Okay, then, what's brought you here today?'

Sean told him about the bad dreams, his mum's death and the man on the train, but left out the story of the unwelcome visitor and the incident at Brosswell College. The silver-haired man listened intently, not speaking until Sean had finished recounting events.

'It sounds like you've been under a great deal of stress. The death of a loved one is one of the most traumatic things a person has to deal with. It's little wonder you feel on edge. I really wouldn't want you to read too much into the dreams. Perhaps in your case, dreaming of a dark ominous figure could symbolise death – the death of your mother.'

'I don't understand.'

'Some scientists believe that our brains are hardwired to react to situations, no matter how unbelievable they really are. The brain rehearses for things that will never happen.'

'Like,' Sean broke in, 'a black belt practising regularly for a confrontation that might never occur.'

'Exactly. Perhaps analysing dreams can help us focus on the problem and hopefully find the solution. There are lots of different theories. We do know that modern technological breakthroughs have allowed scientists to map specific areas of the brain that are active when we are in a dream state.'

'Really?'

'Oh yes.' Alexander stared into Sean's eyes, his inflection genial, and paused for a moment as if to gather his thoughts. 'Research would suggest that what we dream is entwined with our own individual behaviour. People dream of what is relevant to them. The current consensus is that dreams have very little purpose to our lives. So please don't read too much into your dreams. You could be chasing shadows, and shadows blur the mind from the truth.'

'I understand what you're saying.'

'We both know the problems faced with your condition - delusional disorder,' the psychiatrist continued, 'but in your case anger and violence have occurred only in thought, not in action. I must admit, your case fascinates me. You see, the central delusional theme usually persists after treatment if medication is withdrawn, but not with you, and that puzzles me.'

Dr Alexander performed a series of tests on Sean as the consultation progressed, and after an hour or so looked into the young man's face and smiled.

'I don't believe you've had a relapse. Nothing I've seen would indicate that at all.'

Sean breathed a huge sigh of relief. 'I was worried you were going to put me back on the antipsychotic and antidepressants again.'

'No, that's not necessary. However, you are quite an enigma. In all my years, I've never known anyone make a full recovery from this type of disorder. Neurochemical imbalances compelled me to prescribe medication, as you can appreciate, but the voices and hallucinations forced me to consider the classic symptoms of schizophrenia. I wasn't convinced. Paranoid schizophrenics can have all kinds of grandiose delusions, believe they're a servant of the Devil, or Jesus Christ incarnate, but you were different, your symptoms were atypical. You display symptoms of both delusional disorder and schizophrenia. The fact that you no longer need medication astounds me. We will schedule some more appointments just to keep an eye on you, if that's okay?'

The consultant's tone was relaxed but Sean knew that the 'appointments' were not just a request. He was still under Dr Alexander's care.

'Of course, that's fine.'

'The receptionist will sort out all the dates and you'll get a letter in the post.'

'Thanks.' Sean looked at the open magazine on the

consultant's table. He strained his eyes, trying to make outthe text.

'It's no good trying to read that,' Alexander said. 'Unless you can read Arabic.'

Sean looked back up at the silver-haired man, slightly puzzled.

'I've always had a fascination with Middle Eastern culture. Millions of pilgrims will be arriving in Mecca this year for the Hajj pilgrimage. The Masjid al-Haram mosque,' he gestured with an open hand to a photograph in the magazine, 'will be teeming with pilgrims from all over the world. Hajj must be performed, according to tradition, at least once in every Muslim's life.'

'That's quite a commitment.'

'Yes, it is. And this duty applies to both Sunni and Shia.'

'I thought those sects didn't get along with each other?' Sean said.

'That's true. Each believes the other has distorted the Quran. There has always been a tension between them, until recently. Muammar Rafika is changing all that. He is seen as both peacemaker and modern prophet. As a psychologist, I cannot help but be fascinated by their cultural differences, yet these sects are drawn together by this belief system and now this man.'

'He sounds like an enigmatic person. There's no denying that many people are being drawn to Islam from all over the world.'

'Of course, but politics plays its part.'

'In what way?'

'Saudi Arabia, mostly Sunni, has always had a rivalry with Iran, which is predominantly Shia. Politically-motivated disruption is usually a given in the area, but not now. I've been astonished at the newly-formed alliances between Riyadh, Tehran, Syria and even Turkey.'

'I've been listening to reports on the news myself. Isn't that a good thing?'

The tall man stared at him as though lost in thought, then

seemed to regain his composure. 'I've been following events very carefully. Take Afghanistan, for example. After the troops withdrew, the country gradually descended into chaos, fracturing along the same ethnic lines as it did when the Soviets retreated in the late '80s. Even they are now part of this unified alliance. A new jihadist leadership is emerging, and this one will have real teeth.'

'I understand what you're saying, but despite the terrorism of the last fifteen years, these countries couldn't really pose a nuclear threat to us. They just don't have the hardware.'

'Don't they, Mr Webster?

Sean was surprised by the exchange. He didn't know how to respond, so chose to say nothing. Dr Alexander was an affable man but also a brilliant and perceptive psychiatrist. However, what he was saying seemed implausible.

'Coming back to the man on the train,' the psychiatrist switched direction of the conversation. 'The one who seemed to fall into trance. There are all kinds of people out there with various emotional conditions …'

'You think,' Sean cut in, 'he might have had psychological issues?'

'I don't like to speculate, Mr Webster, but his actions don't seem rational.'

'What about the note he gave me?'

'Ah yes, the note. It was probably nothing more than the first address that popped into his mind. Just a gibberish scrawl of a random thought at that particular moment, nothing more than that. Sometimes we read more into something than we really should.'

What about the fact that his voice sounded just like Mum's, Sean thought. He listened as the psychiatrist rambled on, but he wasn't convinced. Not at all.

18

It was a miserable day. Bloated clouds moved sluggishly across the darkening sky, threatening rain. Sophie heard tapping against the huge salon window and it soon became an all too familiar pitter-patter. People rushed to find cover outside and umbrellas opened as the clouds shed their load. Rain bounced off the roofs of slow-moving cars as the deluge continued.

A middle-aged woman sat in front of her, jabbering on about work, family, and practically anything else she could think of. Sophie raised a well-practised smile and caught her own reflection in the mirror. She looked tired. She ran her fingers through the freshly-cut hair and began blow-drying it. Five other women worked in a line along the huge mirrored work area, which practically stretched the length of the room. A senior stylist was busy with a trainee, foil highlighting. Two others worked quickly razor cutting client's hair while another, much younger than the rest, was at one of several basins at the far end of the salon shampooing a young girl's hair. As manageress, Sophie liked to keep a close eye on her staff. Everyone was doing their jobs the way they should, yet today she was the one struggling to maintain focus.

Sophie found her gaze drifting over the reception area, where more clients waited patiently with refreshments in hand. She'd worked as a stylist since leaving school, just like her mother, but things hadn't been easy. In the summer of 1997 her father had lost his job, in a bout of shock redundancies. Things had gone from bad to worse; the salon her mother owned had to be sold because of ever-increasing financial commitments, creating immeasurable emotional distress. But in all that time she had never heard either of them complain. After a few years things had improved. Her father had secured a job as a maintenance mechanic, although the pay had been low, and her mother had got back into part-time employment. She was always of a sunny disposition and it had rubbed off on Sophie, until recently.

As rain rippled down the window glass Sophie realised she was thinking of her ex, Ricardo, a long-term mistake. He was artistic director at the prestigious Farrington's hair design studio in Kensington. At the time she had thought she loved him. Perhaps she had. Over time, she had realised that, at least in part, she'd been drawn to him because of his charismatic charm and trustworthiness.

In Ricardo's case, the charisma was genuine, though sometimes she had sensed a hidden vulnerability in those beautifully dark Italian eyes. But the trustworthy persona he projected was little more than an act. What she had thought was vulnerability was in fact deceit. The false front presented to his clients had been used in private with Sophie, masterfully disguising his fascination with all things female, regardless of age or marital status.

Over the years he'd left a trail of emotional destruction behind, been responsible for several divorces, his conquests including not only his best friend's wife, but one of his private clients, a middle-aged soap star, who'd bought into his lies and ended up in the middle of a media scrum.

He seemed to take pleasure not just from sex, but from the attention he received from other women, many of whom were vulnerable and soon had their own sense of self-worth ripped away with a callous and cavalier attitude. He had always treated Sophie affectionately, but that respect did not apply to the other unfortunates he bedded.

After the news story had broken about the minor celebrity, she had known she no longer loved him. She had needed no more time to realise she'd been a fool. The signs had been there, and she'd missed them, but she hadn't been going to let it blow her life apart. She had left the flat early one morning without a word and had never seen him again.

Two years later she had met Sean, and since then life had been not just good, but great. There had been problems, major problems with his breakdown, but he was an honest soul and gave her the love she needed.

A rumble in the storm-torn heavens distracted her, and as her eyes rested on her own reflection, she was oblivious of the babbling woman sitting before her. In her mind's eye, she saw the grotesque features of the night stalker in their bedroom and felt a juddering chill dart down her spine.

'Sophie?'

'Yes, what is it?' She turned to the young, pretty-faced receptionist behind her.

'Can you take a look at the computer? It's on the blink again.'

'Okay.'

She made her excuses to the client and made her way to the reception desk.

'See,' the receptionist said, pointing to the blank screen. 'The appointment schedule is down.'

'I'll see what I can do,' Sophie replied. 'You might as well take a quick coffee break while you have a chance.'

Sophie sat down at the desk and started tapping the keyboard. The computer screen came to life, displaying the list of scheduled clients. Everything seemed fine, no problems at all.

She felt the receptionist behind her, almost breathing down her neck. She was well and truly invading her personal space, making her feel very uncomfortable.

Sophie spun round in her chair. There was no-one behind her.

She turned back to the monitor, only to see the schedule vanish. It was replaced by a flickering message.

YOU ARE ALL GOING TO DIE!

Sophie leaped out of the chair, her heart pounding, looking around wildly. Clients and staff were glancing at her with bemused expressions.

She stared back at the screen, but the words were no longer there.

19

County Offaly, Ireland. 22 October 1974.

Father Seamus Mallom buttoned the collar of his cassock as he ascended the dimly-lit stairs. He'd been given instructions to see a 13-year old boy named Jacob Weir. His mother had found him using a Ouija board in his bedroom, and soon afterwards, the boy had begun to change. He had become aggressive, even violent at times. 'Sinister' was the word his mother had used. The priest knew most of the background: the anxious parents, a good Irish family from Tullamore, had taken the boy to various doctors and child psychologists. All had diagnosed Jacob as being perfectly healthy in body and mind. In desperation, his parents had contacted the church, convinced that he was possessed. Church officials had been reluctant to take on the case at first, but the family had continued relentlessly, bombarding them with letters, pleading for help. After long and careful deliberation, Father Mallom had been asked, because of his experience, to determine an appropriate course of action. He knew, as a trained psychologist, that most so called 'spirit possessions' could be explained in terms of multiple personality disorders or related disturbances, such as hysteria, paranoia, schizophrenia and compulsive behaviour. Most cases he had dealt with were of an emotional nature, but there was always the odd one that defied scientific reasoning. This was the grey area in which he ventured now.

Preparation for the ritual had been intense, both physically and mentally demanding, leaving him exhausted. Father Thomas, his aid, was to have assisted him in the rite of exorcism but had become violently ill and couldn't help. So, he was proceeding alone.

He continued up the flight of stairs, each step an effort.

Although he was only in his early thirties, there was no doubt that incessant prayers, fasting and careful, painstaking study of the case had taken its toll on him. The groundwork had been exhaustive; it had always been that way for him. He was conscientious in his preparation and knew that lack of faith was like a virulent cancer. He'd seen evidence of this within the church itself. Exorcists were on the verge of extinction. Many within the priesthood preferred to rationalise possession as a psychological phenomenon. Clearly in some cases it was, but not all.

He knew that every possession was different and some required unique ways of dealing with it. Situations could be fast-moving, relying on the exorcists' experience, and an inexperienced exorcist could lose control very quickly. Father Stamford, his mentor, had taught him how to approach each exorcism, adding additional prayers and reciting biblical scripture with the use of specific relics. The church turned a blind eye to this practice, because of their success in the field. Even now, many years on, the young priest knew that the greatest danger of all was to become possessed by the demon himself.

Few exorcists would work alone. Father Stamford had done so on occasion, when it had been absolutely necessary, but it could be extremely dangerous. He was faced with this dilemma tonight, and under different circumstances he might have called it off, but the child was rapidly deteriorating. Yet part of him knew carrying on was a mistake.

Mallom approached the boy's bedroom door then paused to gather his own mental energies. He stared at the Georgian wood panelling and drew a deep breath to compose himself, but as he reached for the brass door handle a voice growled from within.

'Enter.'

He eased the door open, recoiling from the foul stench that filled the room, and glanced at the figure strapped to a chair near the bed. Jacob had recently been put there for his arrival. Fear was a natural human reaction to something unnatural, but it was imperative to control it. As his eyes became accustomed to the poor light, provided only by a low-wattage bulb hanging from the ceiling, he shivered, feeling the effects of the frigid air. Almost gagging, he looked around. There was little furniture in the room, a necessary precaution; just a small rug on the wooden floor and a circular table. A few Hot Wheels cars were scattered in the corner and an Evel Knievel toy lay on its side. High above, stuck to the back of an airing cupboard door, was a tatty *Six Million Dollar Man* poster.

The exorcist stared at the wall behind Jacobs's bed. More graffiti had been scrawled across it since his last visit, daubed with vomit and excrement. The demonic ciphers were disturbing to look at, forming strange symbols. A loosely-formed pentagram with two points up inscribed within a double circle: the Sigil of Baphomet, a finger-crafted goat's head in its centre. It was a crude depiction moulded from faeces, which gave off a putridity that instantly aroused revulsion.

When the thing in the chair, for this was no child, had turned fully toward him, it was distressing. Even the soft glow from the lamp above could not soften the effect. The boy glared at him, his eyes gleaming.

'Oh, dear Lord,' the Irishman whispered to himself.

The child was dressed like any normal kid, with a long-collared shirt and tank top, and his figure was slight, with stick-like legs visible through denims, but the real horror that gripped Mallom's heart like an icy claw was the sight of his face.

Saliva drooled from his mouth onto grey skin. His blond hair was wild, matted together with bodily fluids. Jacob's parents had tried to make him presentable but had struggled because of his violent outbursts; even strapped to the chair, they said, he'd tried to bite them. Perhaps the truth was that they couldn't bear seeing their child like this. Some of his hair lay in clumps near his bed, and his face bore deep scratches raked across the flesh. The cuts and lacerations had been cleaned with antiseptic, and his arms and legs had been restrained by brown leather straps for the priest's safety.

Mallom ignored the cries and placed his briefcase on the circular table beneath the bedroom window. He opened the case slowly, walked toward the bed, stopped and looked directly into the demon's eyes. For a moment there was silence, then laughter, abrupt maniacal laughter.

Mallom forced himself to remember that this was no child, it was an entity inhabiting Jacob's body. It wasn't just the hideous grinning face and crazed features that characterised demonic possession. Jacob had begun to speak various languages, and caused mirrors to crack and objects to move around the room, even when restrained. His voice had deepened, making him sound more like a man than a child.

Jacob's body was already wasting away, and now he resembled a starving child from a third world country. Mallom understood how malign forces could generate such a wretched metamorphosis in someone like this.

Jacob sat in the chair, one hand pressed down into the armrest, the other twitching as though he had no control over it. It was rapidly moving up and down and from side to side, resisting the restraining strap. This terrifying sight forced the priest to avert contact with the boy's bulging eyes for a moment. When he looked back the boy was perfectly motionless but still staring at him, and grinning.

The priest bowed his head reverently.

'Lord have mercy.

'Christ have mercy.

'Lord have mercy.

'Christ hear us.

'God, Father in heaven have mercy on us.'

The priest raised his hand and traced the sign of the cross above the demon's head. There was an uneasy stillness about the room; it was stifling. The putrid stench of urine, dried faeces and body odour assaulted his senses. It hung in the air, choking his breath, so much so that he coughed harshly.

'Want some ass, Father?' The boy wriggled a blackened tongue suggestively, then withdrew it and began to snigger. 'You arrogant shit!' it croaked.

'Holy Mary,' the priest looked up. 'Pray for us.'

Mallom knelt by the bed in prayer while Jacob flung a barrage of abuse at him.

Silence followed.

After a few moments, the priest eased himself up, removed a small vial of holy water from his pocket and began to sprinkle it onto the demon.

'Bastard,' it rasped, struggling against the restraining straps. 'Bastard … bastard …' Fetid breath wafted from its mouth.

'Our Blessed Lady pray for us.

'Virgin of Virgins,

'St Michael,

'St Gabriel,

'St Raphael,

'All the angels and archangels.'

The exorcist continued with the recital. He spoke gently, with both reverence and respect. When the prayer had been concluded the priest walked back to the table, placed the glass vial in the briefcase and removed a black leather-bound book. He studied the text for a moment, before raising his head.

The demon watched warily.

Mallom closed his eyes and prayed:

'*Adjure te, spiritus nequissime, per Deum omnipotentem.*'

Jacob's jaw dropped open and he screamed.

'I adjure thee, most evil spirit, by almighty God,' the priest continued. 'Leave this child. It is He who commands you. He who died on the cross for our salvation, the great redeemer of sins. Leave this innocent. *Per Dominum nostrum Jesum Christum.*'

'You are off script and on your own. Come. Come closer, priest. Let me smell your fear.'

'*Per Dominum nostrum Jesum Christum, Per Dominum nostrum Jesum Christum.*' His eyes flicked open once more. '*Per Dominum nostrum Jesum Christum.*'

The exorcist walked slowly toward the raging demon and placed his hand on its head while continuing to read from the book. 'Lord God creator and defender of the human race, liberate this, your servant Jacob Weir, from this unclean spirit, I beseech you.'

The demon snapped its head away from him with a yelp of despair. Then, in complete contrast, a soft but undeniable hiss emanated from its mouth, a sound that grew in volume to a kind of guttural snarl like that of a caged predator. He glanced down to see the boy again and looked back at his text with a pounding heart.

'Deliver us, O Lord,

'From the snares of the devil,

'From anger and hatred,

'From every demonic force in hell. Lord we beg you, save your servant from the son of iniquity.'

The boy laughed, then snarled.

'Lord, hear my prayer.' Mallom's voice steadily rose amid nightmarish wails and cries. 'I liberate thee, Jacob, from the destructive power of this evil spirit, in the name of Christ.'

'Arrogant shit,' it croaked.

'Forgive us, O Lord, our offences and those of our forefathers, I beseech thee.

'Our Father who art in heaven, hallowed be thy name. Thy kingdom come, thy will be done on Earth as it is in heaven. Give us this day our daily bread and forgive us our trespasses as we forgive those who trespass against us.'

'Prick licker. Whore fucker.'

'And lead us not into temptation, but deliver us from evil,' the exorcist concluded.

'Yes ... yes ...' the demon grinned. 'Yes,' it cried out mockingly. 'Yes, oh yes!' as though reaching the peak of orgasm.

Head still bowed, Mallom continued. 'Christ our Lord, drive out this servant of darkness from this innocent child ...' As the exorcist embarked on another prayer, 'Heavenly Father, Creator of all that is seen and unseen ...' he heard a familiar voice, and his heart froze.

'Seamus, you can't beat it, it's too powerful!'

The soft Irish accent was unmistakable. He raised his eyes from the book and found himself absorbed by what he saw.

Mallom shook his head to reassure himself, but the face that stared back at him was no longer a little boy's, it was that of his mentor, Father Stamford. There was a deep weariness to the old man's countenance, and his skin appeared weather-beaten.

20

'It can't be,' Mallom muttered, the sense of loss renewed within him. Stamford's passing had been so cruel; to be mutilated in such a way while performing the Lord's work was inconceivable. But it had happened. During missionary work in Kenya, a possessed Maasai woman had attacked him so violently that she'd ripped his tongue out and blinded him.

Mallom shut his eyes, but the ghastly vision blazed in his mind. 'Illusion,' he affirmed breathing heavily.

'Illusion,' the old man's voice returned. 'See me as I was. See me as I am!'

Mallom opened his eyes, slowly. 'Oh, dear God,' he moaned.

The old man's features had changed monstrously; a slick dark liquid oozed down his cheeks, leaking from deep eyeless sockets, and a thick river of blood poured from the pit of his mouth onto his vestments.

'Help me.' His pleas were nothing more than gurgling sounds, caused by the gore pouring down the inside of his throat.

As Mallom looked down into Stamford's face, the old Irish man's silver hair sprayed out as if charged by some unseen force. He gibbered uncontrollably, his body trembling from the wretched pain.

'Lord Jesus, don't let this be so.'

The priest winced, looking away from the madness, his resolve suddenly dwindling. For a moment he could not move, his thoughts were focused on the man before him, the only family he'd ever known. Fighting back tears, he was gripped by the burden of loss, which left him exhausted and weak. He stepped backwards, gripped the bedpost and stood unsteadily on his feet.

In the cold silence of that room Mallom realised he'd been

deceived.

'No!' he shouted through gritted teeth. The demon was mocking him.

As the vision diminished, the demon grinned and threw back its head, laughing hysterically.

'Stamford was a fool!'

'No.'

'He's in here with us. All the faithless reside with us.'

'Stop!'

'Do you want to see him again?' it chuckled.

'No.'

'Sanctimonious scum, you've lost.'

Mallom shivered; the air was as cold as a tomb. This child was not only a conduit for fallen spirits but something far more sinister. Instead of becoming weaker the evil was getting stronger. *Was he losing the fight?* The priest grimaced; he'd begun to feel another presence coming through the child, much more powerful than any he'd encountered before. With the help of Father Stamford, he would once have felt able to cope, but since his mentor's death things had changed.

He closed his eyes in whispered prayer. 'Our Father, the judge of the living and the dead ...'

A thunderous blow shook the room. 'Creator and defender of the human race,' the priest continued without pause, 'have mercy on this child.' Another jolt hammered through the walls. 'In the name of your only begotten son.' He finished the prayer as the sounds intensified, a thumping that came from all around.

The exorcist clapped his hands across his ears. The sound continued, lasting for a few moments before gradually slowing to a faint throb until it ceased.

'Be gone, child of Satan!' he lashed out, his voice resonating around the room. 'It is Christ who commands you. God the son commands you. God the Holy Spirit commands you. The mystery of the cross commands you.'

'Remember the orphanage,' it cackled. 'The older boys, the hurling sticks. Ah yes, priest, I know of the punishment beatings. You still bear the scars across your back. How righteous of the virginal nuns to turn away from it. They did nothing,' the demon screamed. 'Nothing to help you, did they? Poor little orphan bastard.'

The exorcist swallowed hard. 'You know nothing.'

'I admire your faith, but it's not enough is it? Yes or no,' it prodded 'Do you really think you can drive me out?'

He looked into its face without reply, and its eyes glistened with triumph.

As Mallom traced the sign of the cross with his hand, the demon laughed. '*Adeo*,' it rasped, '*ab infernis.*' Beads of perspiration appeared on the Irishman's forehead as he made a mental translation. *I am from hell!*

The creature jerked forward, babbling a mishmash of ancient Aramaic and Hebrew, rocking the chair violently. 'Look at me, holy scum. Look at me.'

Mallom took a deep breath and averted his eyes. 'Father of Heaven and Earth, God of the angels and archangels, I call on you to drive out this unclean spirit.'

'*Eloi, Eloi, lama sabachthani*?' it cried out, ridiculing Christ's anguish on the cross.

'Shut up,' he shouted.

It laughed again.

'Your words have no meaning. Depart, you monster, enemy of the human race. Your abode is with the viper. Get down and crawl with it! It is Christ who commands you! His blood was shed for …'

'A noble façade, priest, but I can see your weakness.'

'… us and all men.'

'Does your heart flutter, holy man? Does it? As your faith abandons you.' It spat in his face. 'Look at me,' it raged, as Mallom wiped saliva from his cheek with his sleeve. 'Stamford was a stronger man than you, and look what happened to him.'

'Be gone, prince of liars,' he continued, 'to the lair of the viper, God commands you. The creator of all things, he who cast you into the realms of hell …' prayed the exorcist. He reached down into his pocket and removed a small golden crucifix.

'Stick it in your arse.'

The priest walked forward and leaned over it. 'Be gone, creature of the abyss. Our lord Jesus Christ compels you.'

'Bastard,' it seethed. 'Faithless bastard, you will lose,' it screamed, body thrashing wildly.

'What is your name?'

'I was invited here!'

Mallom knew full well what it was saying. The Ouija board had opened Jacob up to this demonic entity and allowed it to take control of his body.

'I revoke the invitation. Now give me your name.'

'Nooo,' it screamed.

'What is your name?'

'Methangalic!' the demon raged. 'Servant of the most high.'

'Get out of this child.'

'Never.'

'You will abide by the oath.'

It laughed. 'You seek to emulate the Nazarene; thorns will be driven into your body also, and there will be a gnashing of teeth. I swear the time is coming, priest. It is almost at hand.'

'Leave now. God commands it through the power of Jesus Christ.'

'No,' its voice growled back, arrogantly bold.

'Leave.'

It made odd snarling sounds like a highland wildcat, a rumble that emanated deep within its throat.

'Leave.'

The exorcist felt his body tense as though a cold finger had just slid down his spine. 'Through the power of Jesus Christ, you will leave this child.'

It screamed, a guttural yet protracted cry; an unearthly wail that inspired dread.

The exorcist made the sign of the cross. 'Father, Son, Holy Ghost,' he murmured, suddenly aware that the restraining straps had burst and part of the armrest had been worked free. Mallom's head shot sideways as splintered wood sliced his forehead. He stumbled backwards and fell to the floor.

It leapt from the chair and glared at him with malevolent, hate-filled eyes.

'The child is mine,' it grinned.

As Mallom looked into its face he saw sadistic pleasure. He fought hard against the encroaching blackness but could do little to stop it. Unconsciousness would take away the pain in his head, but what of Jacob? As he slipped away he heard laughter. Demented, low rasping laughter.

What Mallom thought was only a few moments was actually almost twenty minutes. He came to slowly, shocked to see the boy's emaciated body twisted at an impossible angle, one arm thrust into the air with clawed fingers. Its head was held rigid at a right angle to its body. In the dim light the demon's eyes appeared black and dead, staring frozenly at him, and air drifted from its lips like fine mist. He stared into that horrifically contorted face as its twisted frame began to straighten. Every dislocated joint slowly crunched back into place, each sound painfully loud against the silence, like a snapping twig.

Still the thing held him in its penetrating gaze.

Mallom rose unsteadily, clutching the wound on his forehead, trying to stem the flow of blood. He tried to move, but dizziness and disorientation kept him there. The priest could do nothing as the demon floated away from him toward the large bedroom window.

A groan escaped Mallom as the glass shattered and Jacob's body plummeted to the ground below.

'Oh, no,' he cried. 'God, no.'

The priest staggered toward the broken window and looked down. The small boy's body had been impaled on wrought iron railings. His open eyes stared up at him through the darkness. Two points protruded through his chest like arrowheads, suspending his lifeless body. Jacob's legs hung motionless, his arms extended limply, mimicking crucifixion in death. The demon's final insult to the priest.

21

'I'm glad everything worked out okay with Dr Alexander,' Sophie said as they moved along the dimly-lit street.

'It's a big relief,' Sean replied. 'He thinks everything is fine, but he still wants to keep an eye on me.'

'Makes sense.'

'You seem a little distracted, Sophie.'

I've been thinking about what we saw in our bedroom.'

'And?'

'Well, I've read an article on dream telepathy.'

'Dream what?'

'It's the idea that one person can transfer thoughts to another while asleep and influence the second person's dreams.'

'Is that even possible?'

'There's been an experiment with more than a hundred subjects that suggests so.'

'I don't know, Sophie.'

'It makes more sense than the alternative.'

'Well, what about this then?' Sean held aloft the piece of notepaper in his hand.

'I can't explain why the man on the train gave you that.'

'Mental problems?' he offered.

'I don't buy it. Why scribble down an address and nothing else?'

It had been a simple matter to find directions on the internet. Curiously enough, the address had turned out to be the home of Maria Kokoschka, a psychic. Sophie had suggested they book an appointment with her, to try to make some sense of this whole thing. Although they were both sceptical, they were prepared to give it a chance.

They studied each house they passed. Edgewood Road was quiet and rather drab. The streetlights appeared dim, the darkness between them somehow sinister. Overhead the sky was dark with rumbling clouds, heavily swollen and ready to vent their anger.

'It's got to be down here somewhere.'

'There! There it is!' Sean pointed the way ahead. 'Sixty-six, it's over there.'

They hurried up the short flight of steps leading to the medium's house and Sean rapped on the old wooden door with his knuckles as thunder rumbled above. For a moment there was silence, then lightening flashed, swiftly followed by a thunderclap. He stared up into the blazing sky as another flash seared the darkness, and was gripped by the conviction that this was straight out of his dream. *Nonsense*, he thought, yet the feeling persisted as he looked back toward the door.

'Mr Webster.' He hadn't seen the door open.

'Hi, yes. I'm Sean and this is Sophie.'

'Please come in, both of you, it's a devil of a night.' The woman stood aside to let them enter.

They stepped into the hall and shivered as a cold breeze swept through the open doorway. It was narrow, with a chequer-tiled floor and a hall stand laden with coats and umbrellas. On the wall were two large framed pictures of angels, one with outstretched arms, the other ascending into a bright light.

'I'm Maria Kokoschka,' the woman said, closing the door behind them. She was small and dark-haired, her skin pale and features haggard. 'From what you told me on the telephone, it sounds as if you may have experienced something unusual.'

'Listen,' Sean said. 'We've never been to a spiritualist before, and …'

'And you don't know what to expect?' Maria smiled. 'I do personal readings here at home, but most of my time is spent at the Circle.'

'The Circle?'

'Yes, Mr Webster.'

'Please, call me Sean.'

Maria's smile broadened. 'The Circle is a spiritualist church. There's nothing sinister or spooky about it. I, or a guest speaker, will work from the platform. A member of our inner circle, those who, how shall I put it, have "the gift", will give a brief talk, a homily regarding spirituality.' The medium's matter-of-fact tone was putting them both at ease. 'Afterwards, the important business of spirit communication takes place and we invite a spiritualist to take over. Each one has their own individual style.'

'How does that work?' Sean asked. 'Do you train them?'

'Yes, I help some people develop. Others come from outside the Circle.'

'How do you know if they have "the gift", as you put it?'

'That's an interesting question. Believe me, we root out the charlatans very quickly; those who rely on guesswork or non-verbal giveaways. Some are genuine, in which case we try to bring out their individual gift. Others are not. They usually have their own agendas, and we don't approve of this. It's harmful and damages the credibility of the spiritualist community. It's important for me to explain this to you now, so that you realise who and what we are.'

'I notice you don't charge for your services.'

'That's right. We are a non-profit group. Our function is one of guidance and spiritual support.'

'How do you make ends meet?' Sophie asked.

'With great difficulty, my dear. If it wasn't for donations we'd have been forced to close our doors many years ago. We don't expect people to offer financial assistance, but it is greatly appreciated when they do, especially in these times. The recession has hit everyone really hard.'

The medium's eyes found Sean. 'Sorry, I'm wittering on again. What you need to understand is that there is nothing to fear during our meeting tonight. It will be small and informal, and afterwards you can have some tea and biscuits and get to know us a little better.'

Sean had no desire to stay any longer than necessary and

was beginning to wonder if this had all been a big mistake. Could this woman really help? She seemed nice enough, but could she really contact the dead?

'So how did you become a medium?' he asked.

She paused for a moment as if distracted by something. 'I attended a local church for a number of years and found it incredibly helpful. Mrs Dawes was a renowned medium and very gifted. She helped me flourish.'

Sean gave Maria the note. 'What do you make of this?'

She studied it carefully. 'The man on the train gave this to you? With my address on it?'

He cleared his throat. 'Like I said on the phone, he seemed to be in some kind of trance when he wrote it.'

The psychic looked directly at him. 'Without being there myself and seeing what happened it's hard to be sure, but my best guess would be that it's a form of automatic writing.'

'What?'

'Automatic writing.' Maria turned her head toward Sophie. 'It's a form of mediumship in which the writer, in this case the gentleman on the train, is used to convey a message to you from a source other than his own conscious mind. The other side has reached out to you for some reason.'

'Are you saying the man on the train was a medium?' Sean asked.

'No, not exactly. He may have been used. Sometimes, and it is very rare, someone other than a medium can be chosen to pass on a message.'

'Are you saying that any of us can be *"used"* at any time?'

'No, Mr Webster. There are rules. We believe that divine rules govern spiritual communication.'

'Who makes these rules?'

'A medium connects with their spirit guide during a séance and asks God for protection; it's a way of vetting unwanted entities.'

'What if one of these "entities" gets through?'

'If the presence is malevolent or mischievous, the medium lets them know they're not welcome.'

'It's that simple?'

'Not always. If a hostile spirit arrives and will not leave, no matter what, we end the séance. It is rare, but in my experience, chances are it's been attracted to someone in the group.'

Sean listened intently.

'It may well be that I don't enter into trance tonight but just offer psychic messages for the gathering. I can't control the spirits. My role is to act as a conduit for them. Sometimes they will choose to express themselves through me, and when that happens I slip into trance.'

Sean stared at the paper in his hand. 'Why did I receive this note?'

'I'm not sure. I can only assume that you have been given my address because I'm a medium. Perhaps the sender thought I might be able to help you make contact with them.'

Sean could not mask the uneasy feeling that gripped him. Even Maria's relaxed demeanour did little to diffuse it.

'Please, follow me.'

Sean and Sophie followed the woman to a door at the end of a long, brightly-lit passage.

'Here we are,' she announced. She leaned toward the round brass handle and eased the door open, then stepped aside, allowing the couple to enter.

A grandfather clock chimed from a shadowy corner, cutting through the silence. Wall lights gave off an insubstantial glow, and open burgundy curtains adorned the large bay windows. Sean could see an old bureau of polished mahogany against one wall, with an antique Chesterfield chair in front of it. A tall wooden bookcase stood next to the door that Maria was in the process of closing. Aside from the people already there, the room was sparse, with very little in the way of pictures, photos and the like, which surprised Sean.

'Mr Webster.' Maria frowned, hesitating for a moment as though she'd sensed something, and then gave a brief shake of her head.

'Please take a seat, both of you.'

As they sat down at the large circular table, the medium's

attention was fixed on Sean. He wondered if the anxiety in her face was for the benefit of everyone present. Maria turned to face the rest of the group, before closing her eyes.

From the corner of his eye he saw an elderly woman. Silver-haired and frail, she would have been much taller, had it not been for a severe stoop. She wasn't part of the group but stood near the dimmer switches, assisting with the proceedings. Sean inspected the rest of the gathering. Four women sat in tense silence. Two middle-aged men, one bald and obese, the other slim with silver-grey hair, were engaged in hushed but excited conversation.

The men's excited chatter ceased, and Sean's attention returned to the figure clad in black.

'Bless you all,' she whispered. 'May God protect us and grant us an audience with those who have crossed over.'

The wall lights dimmed, apart from a small spotlight that shone down onto the medium. With the room in near darkness, the group's attention focused on her. Maria's face appeared pale, almost corpse-like under its glare, until the circle of light began to soften.

'Link hands,' she murmured.

The people around the table obeyed. The presentation was effective, but it was just theatrics – or that was the way it appeared to Sean. Still, he couldn't help but watch with interest.

'Patrick.' The medium breathed the name, then opened her eyes.

Sean heard a sharp intake of breath from his neighbour, a bald man who smelled of spicy cologne.

'I'm Patrick!' The man spoke in a soft Irish accent.

'I have a message from Muriel,' Kokoschka said. 'Get on with your life!'

The old man was tearful.

'Your wife is content but misses you. She says to tell you her passing was sudden but not painful; very quick and totally unexpected.' The medium touched her chest. 'Muriel is concerned about the state of your health. You must look after yourself.'

'I will,' he said, his voice quivering.

'Ease off the whisky, it's not good for your blood pressure.'

'I will, I will,' he almost sobbed.

Smart. Was he part of the charade? Sean had his doubts about the Irishman.

'I have a young man here with blond hair. My goodness, it is long. He's wearing a black tasselled leather jacket. He wants to speak to Aunt Edna.'

'Yes, yes, I can take that,' an obese woman announced in a loud, excited voice. 'Is it Peter? Please say it's Peter.'

The medium nodded her head in confirmation.

'It was a terrible accident, but he takes full responsibility. Do you understand?'

'Yes.'

The statement stopped the woman in her tracks. She produced a handkerchief from her plus-sized cardigan pocket and began dabbing the corners of her eyes.

'He's saying it all happened so quickly. He didn't feel a thing. One minute he was on his motorbike in the fast lane, the next he was on the other side. He didn't see the lorry.'

'Is he happy?' Edna asked, her face a mask of concern.

'Oh yes, he's very happy. He's sitting on a bench with a tall West Indian man.'

'That will be Jacob,' she interrupted. 'He died a few years ago of a brain haemorrhage. They were best friends.'

'He's stepping back now, I'm losing his energy. He says to tell Mum his ring has fallen down the back of the tallboy in his bedroom. She'll find it there.'

One by one, each sitter was chosen. The messages were often mundane, but Maria seemed to know a great deal about her guests and their deceased family and friends. Unless they were all part of an elaborate hoax, she'd have to have had prior knowledge of each individual present. Sean knew that enough of this type of information could be found by hacking into personal computer records; health, education, finance, it was all there, depending on the researcher's ability. General information wasn't that difficult to find if you knew how and where to look for it. More specific facts could be gathered by combing through the rubbish in people's bins for letters, bank statements, bills, anything that could be of use during a séance. Even a postcode could tell a story in itself. Perhaps that explained why the number of people here was restricted. But he wondered if the woman looked like someone who could be involved in such a deception. It seemed so unlikely. One thing was certain, he himself had not been served with any news from beyond, nor was he likely to be. If she was a con artist, which he doubted, it would take a couple of visits before he was offered a spiritual message. This would give Maria Kokoschka and her aides time to gain the background information they needed.

'Danger. You're in terrible danger.'

Startled from his ruminations, Sean returned his attention to the medium. A sense of urgency filled her voice when she repeated the message.

'Sean?' Sophie gripped his hand tightly. 'It's Christine.'

Maria was visibly trembling, staring frozenly through the gloom at Sean.

'He wants you.' The voice was distant, almost a whisper; seeming to come from the air itself.

Sean recognised the voice. He had no doubt that it sounded like his mum. He jerked himself free from the clammy hand of the old man next to him, breaking the circle. Something about all of this was wrong. The mood had shifted from harmony to gloomy tenseness. A draught crept into the room, a back-juddering chill that did little to settle his already jangling nerves

The medium gazed around the room, no longer in a state of trance. A smoky substance began to rise from behind the sitters. The clairvoyant watched fascinated, her mouth slowly dropping open as hazy, ill-defined shapes appeared in the vapours. They were figures, fluctuating between clarity and a blur. She watched, clutching the arms of her chair.

'This isn't right,' she said under her breath.

Her hushed words fell away as a new emotion grasped her: fear, a gut-twisting fear that froze her rigid in her chair.

She screamed, then slumped forward onto the table, unconscious.

It had all begun without warning. This was the last thing Sean had expected. He'd been looking forward to tea and biscuits and a hasty retreat, not this. What the hell was going on? It made no sense, but he could not deny what was happening. Thoughts whirled through his mind, and deep down he knew something genuinely unnatural was occurring.

Kokoschka's scream had been so hysterical that the people around him could no longer suppress their panic; he witnessed their fearful expressions as they looked at one another, eager to leave the nightmare. They seemed to be struggling to get out of their seats, but as they tried to stand, something seemed to force them down.

One old man, sitting beside Sophie, was breathing in short dry gasps. He reached into the inside pocket of his jacket and removed a spray, but as his trembling hands fumbled with the top of the red bottle, it fell from his feeble grasp to the floor.

'Please.' He writhed, sucking in sharp breaths. 'Somebody ...'

The old man's chest heaved, the effort of breathing laboured, and his trembling quickly increased to a terrible shaking.

'Help ... me ...' he groaned. 'Please, someone ... help me.' His body sagged, then toppled from the chair into a crumpled heap on the floor. He struggled to breathe, his body thrashing, his chest heaving, desperately trying to get air into his lungs, but all too quickly his face took on an unnatural bluish pallor. He may have been old and feeble, but he still struggled to hold on to life. He thumped at the floor beneath him over and over, his protests becoming weaker and weaker, until finally he rolled onto his back. His body twitched, but it was little more than a shivery spasm. Sean desperately wanted to help, but it was as though a host of wintry hands were on his shoulders pushing him into the chair. Others tried to move, to get to the old man. He could see them struggling, and knew the same thing was happening to them.

Amid screams and shouts of alarm, Maria's body was flung back into her seat. Eyes flickering open, she slowly lifted her head from her chest. She drew in a gasp as her body went rigid, each vertebra cracking loudly into place. She was unable to control herself. Seat oozed from her pores, trickling from her forehead onto tear-stained cheeks. Despite the cold, sweat tainted the dark cotton of her dress. She sat perfectly still, lost in the moment.

An unnatural silence descended on the room as all movement and noise came to a fearful stop. The medium spoke, and this time the tone was masculine and filled with hate.

'*Bastard!*' she seethed.

Sean was stunned by the outburst. Maria's face twisted into a contortion of rage, and she blazed with a terrifying fury. It was as if a shadow had passed over her. The skin of her face rippled, contorting and changing her features.

The spotlight flickered, and one of the women screamed. Sean felt Sophie's grip on his hand tighten once more.

They were plunged into darkness and the room was filled with screams. Lightning flashed, blazing from the windows, haloing Kokoschka in an unearthly glow. For a moment, in that stark transient light, Sean saw something so terrifying he almost cried out himself. Maria's features had changed into a face he recognised.

'Oh shit!' He stared at the medium, his mouth slack as he realised it was the grinning figure from the book in the library. Francois Santia.

'Your whore of a mother knew too much!'

'What do you want?' he called out amid the chaos.

'You!'

Lightning flashed, and for a brief moment he saw the pirate's haunted face.

'When the ship returns, I'll have you.'

Santia's voice swiftly faded as the spotlight burst into life, showering Maria in a pool of brightness. Her own countenance had returned, but she was a wretched sight. The pupils of her eyes were upturned so that only the whites were visible, and her head was rocking back and forth. She hissed, expelling a blast of putrid air, and as Maria's groans ceased, Sean sensed something else within the darkness of the room. He heard Sophie gasp. She was looking at the other guests with terror etched onto her face. Sean turned toward the sitters. A fine mist was drifting around them, and within those icy vapours were faint shadows that sought to acquire human form. Even as Sean watched, these immaterial conformations were acquiring substance. Although the figures were dark they were visible through the haze, and as he stared at them he felt weak and unsteady, his energy dwindling. Was the same happening to everyone else in the room? Some kind of all-pervading evil had infiltrated the séance and hijacked the medium. Maria had said there were rules governing this type of thing, so why wasn't she in control?

Sounds emerged from the shadowy figures, a low chuckling laughter, heightening the unearthliness of the situation. Within that blurry mist Sean caught sight of one of the dark forms, and a breath escaped him.

Sean hauled himself up, fighting the fatigue that clawed at him from the icy gloom. Those dark figures were moving toward him. He cried out as he leapt from the chair and raced across the room, almost tripping over the body of the elderly woman who had been operating the lighting. Still the figures crept toward him, their murmuring rising in unison to a fearsome pitch.

With no time to think, Sean stretched out a hand toward the wall and flicked the light switch. The bulbs bloomed, and a searing light flooded the room. Everyone in the room raised a hand against the glare.

It took a few moments for Sean's eyes to adjust and see that there were no ghosts. Just three old ladies, two of them sniffling, the other trembling uncontrollably. An elderly man sat whimpering and Sophie was visibly shocked. At her feet lay the body of the other man, his soft flabby face bloated, his eyes wide and glassy. The corpse seemed to be staring up at something that wasn't there.

22

London - Present Day

Seamus Mallom hobbled down the stairs and entered the hall, his knee joints reminding him just how old he'd become. Aches and pains had become constant companions. Yawning freely, he answered the ringing telephone. 'Hello …' he mumbled.

'Is that Father Mallom?'

'I'm Mallom,' he replied, rubbing a hand across his bleary eyes, still yawning because of the lateness of the hour. Then he recognised the voice. 'Maria … is something wrong?'

'Something terrible has happened.'

'Calm down, Maria. Tell me what's …'

'I'm sorry,' the medium interrupted, 'I didn't mean to disturb your sleep, I know it's late, but I just had to talk to somebody. The police have been questioning me all evening.'

'The police?'

'Yes, it was awful. A man died during one of my séances.' She began to sniffle. 'He suffered a seizure and choked to death.'

'Dear Lord! What happened?'

He listened, absorbing her words, as she related the tragic occurrence and supernatural events. There was a long pause before he spoke.

'Do you believe in what you saw, Maria?'

'Yes.' She was still sniffling.

'You're convinced the spectres were real and not mental imagery?'

'It wasn't my imagination. You've known me too long for that.'

'And I've also warned you of the dangers of communion with the dead. It was only a matter of time before something like this happened.'

'I know.'

'Maria, you cannot have God's sanction during one of these gatherings. These séances may appear like divine services, but they are not. Even though you may say a prayer or sing a hymn, it is done without divinely appointed control.'

'Seamus, I have a gift.'

'Many people are gifted with clairvoyance, clairaudience and clairsentience.'

'I understand …'

'Do you really understand? Don't you see, communication in this way is wrong? It does not contribute to the purification of the soul. It focuses on satisfying people's worldly needs, and that's …'

'I'm not a fortune teller.'

'Listen to me, Maria. You have a responsibility toward God for everything that occurs during one of these gatherings. Spiritualist meetings give the impression they are like regular church services and pleasing to God, but I'm telling you now, nothing could be further from the truth.'

He combed a hand through his silver hair in mild frustration, then flicked a glance toward a large oval mirror on the wall and saw his own haunted face. The diminutive priest looked away as if disturbed by what he saw.

'In all my years as an exorcist I encountered only a few genuine instances where supernatural forces were at work. But from what you've told me, my guess is that this young man is the key to all of this.'

'You could be right. There's a presence around him; I felt it as soon as he walked into the house.'

'Then why in God's name did you continue with the séance?'

Maria's eyes were downcast. 'I don't know. I've never experienced anything like this before.'

She paused.

'Go on, Maria.' Mallom said, sensing her reluctance to continue. 'You know you can trust me.'

'Seamus, something is very wrong.'

'Of course there is, my dear. Someone died, and you've been through a terrible ordeal.'

'No, no, it's not that.' Her voice was agitated. 'I have a feeling of dread, for him. For the young man. But there's something else.'

'Go on,' he urged.

'I can sense tremendous evil, as though something is about to be unleashed.'

'Maybe you're just frightened, and fear is affecting your judgement?'

'No! I may be frightened, but I know what I know.'

'Maria …'

'Please Father. You've got to speak to him.'

'But …'

'Promise me you'll speak to Sean.'

'All right,' he conceded, 'I will speak with him as soon as I can.'

'Thank you. Here's his number.'

Mallom fumbled in the gloom and eventually found a newspaper and pen on the cabinet beneath the mirror. He stared at the headline of *The Times*: *Muammar Rafika Calls for Global Jihad.*

Mallom shuddered at the thought as he quickly scrawled the number down across the newspaper.

'As I said, Maria, I will speak to him as soon as possible; but I don't really know …'

'He's in terrible danger,' Maria cut in.

'Okay,' he conceded. 'I'll have a word with him. Now go to bed and get some sleep. We'll talk in the morning.'

'But …'

'No buts. Stop worrying and try to get some rest. I'll be in touch soon. Good night Maria.'

Mallom replaced the receiver, then stared back into the mirror. He reached up to his face and touched the small scar on his forehead. Even after all these years he was still tortured by the memories it brought, a reminder of the guilt he felt.

Moonlight shone through a side window into the shadowy hall, its radiance reflecting in Seamus Mallom's weary blue eyes. A deep frown creased his brow, and for a moment his thoughts were with the dead. The mental self-flagellation had begun once more. Appearing like photographic images in a developer tray, the unwelcome memories returned to the guilt-ridden priest, taking him back to another time, another place. The scene unfolded before him with nightmarish clarity.

Staggering forwards, his arms outstretched, he moved toward the broken window. He remembered the child, Jacob, impaled on wrought-iron railings, his lifeless body dangling there with eyes still half open. Even in the darkness he'd seen right into them. They were accusatory, blaming him and him alone for the loss of his young life.

He'd failed Jacob.

The window had become a moonlit mirror and Mallom was no longer a young man, he was wearied and old. He shook his head to clear away the memories, knowing that another battle was about to commence.

23

Tornave 1812

The evening was bright, and the moon hung in the sky like a huge lantern, with clouds gathering around it. Its luminescence shone down behind a steep slope of rock on the Haitian island, making it appear almost colourless. Far below, the tide rushed in, bringing with it flotsam and jetsam that scattered onto the beach, a curving white crescent. Out at sea a large ship lay anchored and a small boat with a party of seamen rowed away from its side, moving toward land. The oars thrashed at the water until they eventually evened out their stroke.

The island was quiet as the small boat glided toward the shoreline, scraping along the grainy surface of the beach. It thudded into a mound of wet sand bow first and came to an abrupt halt. One by one, the crew leapt from the boat into the cool water.

'Captain,' a member of the landing party called out. The tall man turned his head, angry at the sailor for breaking the silence. His eyes, fierce and dark, narrowed, as a long finger covered his pursed lips. He whispered the order to move quietly as he beckoned the rest of the men on. In his mid-thirties, he was tall, with dark hair that hung loosely onto his shoulders. Santia's features were sharp; high cheekbones, a prominent nose and fine moustache that arched over thin lips. Close to the ridge of his bottom lip was a small goatee, little more than a flash of chin hair.

The men marched, some barefoot, in search of food or anything else they could get their hands on. A small number of the crew, the lucky ones, had dark canvas jackets or coats and wore buckled shoes, while others wore knitted caps and sported beards. Other younger sailors had their long hair tied back with twine or cloth.

They negotiated their way through foliage, the sound of scurrying night creatures around them. The moon could not be relied on as huge shifting clouds drifted across it. They hacked away at undergrowth with their blades, stumbling over moss-covered boulders.

As the men approached the top of a ridge, they came to an uneven track through the jungle. The palm leaves littering the ground had been pressed into the earth; Santia's party were not the first to pass through.

Santia led the way, looking around as he stepped over the rotting carcass of a wild boar. The animal's eyes had been eaten away and its lower tusks were missing. As each man stepped over the huge carcass they grimaced, covering their mouths to keep the stench at bay.

Santia studied the boar's stomach. 'It's been slashed,' he said, staring at the coils of pale intestine lying on the ground. 'This is no jungle kill.'

Through gaps in the foliage Santia made out a broad muddy river and heard the distant cries of birds, their sound unsettling. The men were breathing heavily, becoming restless.

'This way,' he pointed away from the river.

The crew followed Santia downhill, where they were met by a wall of dense jungle. Barely able to see more than a few yards ahead, they trampled over leaves, vines and shrubs, constantly peering into the gloom. They were all aware of the dangers that lurked there.

Santia thrust his hand into the air. He listened to the sound of the wind rustling through the leafy palms. A noise like the distant crack of a musket caught his attention. He heard it again, recognising the sound of a solitary drum, its beat resonant. Santia pointed forwards and the crew moved quietly toward the clearing ahead.

Santia's eyes widened as the whole area came alive before them. Hypnotic rhythms boomed out, orange flames leapt high into the air, dancing in the darkness.

Santia crouched, reacting to the commotion, and hid behind

the cover of thick foliage, as did the others. Brushing leaves away from his face, he looked on at a small group of Haitians. A few were seated on small wooden stools with drums wedged between their knees, while others shook wooden rattles vigorously, sounding like a nest of rattlesnakes. Men and women began to circle a raging fire, swaying drunkenly, with arms hanging limply at their sides, as the flames swelled and danced, flushing the dark sky with an orange glow.

Still concealed, Santia was totally entranced. It was more than he could have hoped for.

'*Cochon Gris*,' he breathed the words out.

'Sorry, sir?'

Santia didn't look at the crewman by his side as he spoke. 'They're practicing "the work of the left hand". This sect is a splinter of the main vodoun communities and shunned by mainstream practitioners, because of their sadistic rituals. I've heard of these people. It is said they can bring the dead back to life.'

'Sir?'

'I'll wager that any local villagers are terrified of this group and will pay a hefty price to prevent a curse falling on them.'

Santia grinned, certain that human sacrifices had already been made. At least two of the men at the ceremony wore rope-like cords around their necks. He knew that these were made from human intestines.

The fire cracked loudly, drawing his attention back to the small group of people around it. Four wooden bowls had been placed around the fire, and a deep red liquid spilled over the edge of one of them. Stout candles had been pushed into the ground around the outer circle of the gathering, and their flames flickered, rebelling against the blackness like a flurry of fireflies on a warm summer's night. Soon the smell of malodorous spices and burning wax reached Santia, as faceless bodies hidden in shadow began to chant incantations. He listened, but the words were lost in the sudden clamour of drums. The tempo seemed to make the people powerless to resist the music's pounding beat.

As Santia instructed his men to spread out around the Haitians, he became aware of something else. From the periphery of his vision, four dark shapes carried flaming torches from the woodland. The flickering light outlined crooked crosses made from twisted branches embedded in mounds of sand. Staked on several of the crosses were human skulls. The drumbeat ceased, and the Haitians began shouting *'Diabolim … Diabolim … Diabolim.'* The cries, the babble, a cacophony of roaring voices, almost forced Santia to shield his ears. As this devil's symphony continued it confirmed his belief that they were dabbling in the blackest arts.

Amid the clamour, three tall men began beating their drums with human bones. Others joined in, quickening the tempo, slapping the skin of the drums with their hands. Working harder and faster, their skin soon became moist, glistening against the firelight. All the while the beat increased, becoming more aggressive, more frenzied, as hypnotic rhythms boomed out, driving the people to dance faster. Their arms rose, flailing wildly in the air, and their bodies spun, whirling like dervishes.

The drumming reached a feverish crescendo then stopped, halting the frenetic dance. All fell quiet apart from the crackle of the fire, burning fiercely, an almost mesmerising sight against the dark forest. Within those flames rose wispy streaks, like mist. They shifted, weaving and bobbing through the fiery torrent of smoke that came from the flames. Hideous faces stared from within them, demonic eyes and gaping mouths, yawning wide, screaming angrily.

A young woman broke away from the crowd. She staggered forwards, twitching and shouting, *'Hounsis … Hounsis.'* One by one the gathering began to chant, *'Hounsis … Hounsis … Hounsis,'* in a vigorous cadence of solidarity.

Two men approached her; each carried a cockerel and took up a position on either side of her. A third man untied her tribal robe as she stood unmoving. It slid from her shoulders and fell to the ground, leaving her naked.

As swiftly as it had started, the chant changed. *'Houngan … Houngan … Houngan.'*

'What are they saying, sir?'

'*Houngan* means priest,' Santia hissed to the man by his side.

A chilling silence replaced the clamour, leaving no chants, shouts or beating drums. Santia scanned the area as a tall, thin-framed Haitian priest emerged from the pitch-black woodland into the firelight wearing nothing more than a flimsy loincloth. He paused, still partly sheathed in shadow, his eyes incredibly large. Raising an arm, he pointed a long bony finger at the two men and smiled as they raised the cockerels into the air.

'*Petro Ioa,*' they chanted. '*Petro Ioa … Petro Ioa …*'

As shadows grew deep around Santia he suddenly felt edgy. He watched the men place the cockerels' heads in their open mouths, and bite down hard. The sound of screeches and flapping wings ended with a sharp resounding crack, as the animals' heads were ripped from their bodies.

They hoisted the mutilated cockerels over the naked woman, blood dripping from where the heads had once been.

'*Hounsis … Hounsis … Hounsis …*'

The woman's eyes remained open, as she tilted her head back.

'*Hounsis … Hounsis … Hounsis.*'

They poured, and she drank the blood that spilled over her lips, trickling down her face and body, dripping onto the white sand.

'*Ioa.*' The gathering chanted again, as they circled the woman. '*Ioa … Ioa …*' The pace quickened, working into a feverish crescendo once more.

It had become much cooler, a steady, creeping cold. Santia heard whispers of sorcery and witchcraft amongst the men. He saw fear in the eyes of Dunwoody and assumed it was the same for the rest of his crew. Santia jammed an elbow into the ribs of the former coxswain, annoyed at the burly man.

'If there's killing to be done,' Santia hissed, 'rest assured I'll do it.'

The bald man flinched, clutching his side.

Santia grasped the dagger in his belt. Signs of weakness usually resulted in a slit throat to serve as an example to the others.

'Do I have your loyalty?'

'Aye, sir.'

'I'm the only one you need to be afraid of, and don't ever forget it. The same goes for all of you.'

Santia turned in the direction of the blood-drenched female. With the firelight flickering and the atmosphere charged, he focused on the Haitian woman. His temples throbbed as he tried to understand what was happening. Was he picking up on the dark undertones of the ceremony? The Houngan could encourage an Ioa, a fearsome spirit, to possess another person.

Tilting his head back, he stared at the canopy of branches above, so entwined that no moonlight could penetrate. He turned his attention to the Houngan stalking silently toward the woman.

An imperious grin swept across her face as though her very look could invade the minds of the shadowy congregation.

Their murmuring ceased entirely when they heard her deep-moaned cry, *'Asmodeus.'* She clutched her ears with clawed hands, as though in terrible pain. *'Astarte,'* she continued. *'Baphomet.'*

She's calling on demons, Santia thought, but this was not part of a voodoo ritual. It didn't make sense. Demonology played no part in their belief system. So why was she doing it? How did she even know the names?

The woman cried out, a weird agonised yelp.

Santia watched, fascinated.

She shrieked, her legs kicking out, her arms flailing as if in spasm.

'Yes,' he murmured.

Her body was flung back and forth, bent double by an unseen force. It happened again and again with bone-jarring speed. Her cries were unremitting, tearing through the night, but he continued to watch, enjoying every nuance of her suffering. Her body snapped upright with a sickening crack and she screamed again, a short, agonised sound.

She hissed, *'Methangalic.'* Her eyes rolled back slowly in their sockets, blazing white, while another voice escaped her lips, *'Methangalic.'*

Her chest heaved, and she jerked, but no consciousness returned to those eyes. Other voices came though her mouth, flowing uncontrollably, intermingling with one another. *'Exorthumin ... Bethanzine ...'* Strange, diabolic words. *'Tethragrem.'*

Santia knew that this woman was acting as a vessel for demons; her body being used as a gateway to announce their presence.

The woman's body jerked, and in the flickering firelight her face began contorting; another countenance existed beneath the surface of her rippling skin.

The change was rapid.

Her bones stretched, the jawbone dislocating with a crack, developing into a vicious fanged mouth. Hair fell away from her scalp in great clumps and her eyes turned crimson, burning fiercely against the pale flesh of her face, lengthening into blood-red almond orbs. She screamed as her fingers grew, stretching into razor-sharp claws.

Santia had witnessed nothing like this. She continued to evolve, her lean body now emaciated, the skin stretched tautly over bones, as if her muscles had wasted away. Her stomach was drawn and ribs protruded. But to think this made her weak would have been a terrible mistake. The pirate knew this thing was no woman, not anymore. Its high domed head was bald, with a visible network of small overlapping scales giving it almost reptilian features. The face, no longer alluring, was long and thin, gaunt and sallow against those sunken eyes. Despite its appearance, this thing had once been human, but had now become the physical manifestation of the Ioa.

The Ioa shook its head, then again. It looked around, staggered sideways and dropped to its knees. It stayed there, looking at its hands, turning them over and back again. The Ioa reached up, running claws lightly across the contours of its face. It snarled, a raw guttural sound. For a moment there was silence, then its lips peeled back, and its jaws snapped at the air.

It got to its feet, swayed a little, but took a step forwards. It moved unsteadily, stumbled and almost fell, but eventually the Ioa's movements became more controlled. It turned, snapping its head in the direction of the woodland where Santia was hiding.

The Ioa moved toward him, its footsteps padding on the ground. Santia hissed under his breath, one hand reaching for the pistol in his belt. Eyes narrowing, he stepped backwards, using shadow for camouflage.

Could it see him?

It seemed to be staring through the foliage straight at him.

The Ioa moved within a few feet, sniffing at the air, its body silhouetted against the firelight.

Could it smell him?

He was sure it knew he was there. Its crimson eyes bored right into his. Santia tried to look away but couldn't. A notion entered his head that this creature was trying to draw him in.

It was close, very close; only a few flimsy pieces of foliage lay between them. He tried not to breathe, not wanting to give away his presence, but the twigs beneath his boots defied him with an audible crack.

It inched closer.

Fascinated, perhaps spellbound, he stood. A lesser man would have screamed or at least tried to escape. Not Santia.

It stood erect, with arms longer than any human, and raised a hand into the air. Santia saw its long, tapered fingers, which had an extra joint with incredibly sharp, discoloured nails. One of those bony fingers pointed at him in an accusatory way.

An unnatural chill wrapped itself around him. Those eyes, the colour of fiery coals and seething with hatred, held him fast.

The men around him murmured to one another, and Santia knew by their tone they were afraid, but he was calm. With incredible will, he tore his eyes away from it, slid the pistol from his belt and drew back the hammer.

The Ioa padded lightly across the ground, coming closer, its mouth opening, baring sharp teeth. He watched in awe, avoiding eye contact, for those eyes had an unusual ability.

Moonlight broke through the furled clouds, casting an eerie sheen across the Ioa. The creature turned and moved slowly toward the billowing flames of the fire, its back hunched and arms hanging limply at its sides, walking like some deformed ape. It stopped in front of the Houngan, its eyes locking onto his.

The Haitian seemed to mutter something. A prayer was being said, an invocation repeated again and again, and Santia knew the man was begging his God for protection. Clearly, he was just as afraid of this creature as everyone else.

The Houngan placed a serpent-shaped amulet around its neck as the pirate raised his pistol into the air and jerked the trigger. It cracked above his head, and his eyes blinked against the sudden glare of the fire-burst. This was the sign his men had been waiting for.

Santia lunged toward the Ioa, but instantly a Haitian stepped in front of it. The pirate took a step back, then sprang into action, jabbing the heel of his hand beneath the man's nose, snapping his head backwards. Santia's other hand wielded a dagger, which slid across the man's throat.

Santia looked up from the blood-soaked figure at his feet, his head darting from left to right with perverse excitement.

'Kill the bastards,' he screamed.

It was an ordered yet disciplined assault, and for a moment little could be heard amid roaring men and their battle cries ripping through the night. They hacked with swords and axes so that steel thumped on flesh, cutting, ripping and shredding it.

'Kill them all,' Santia cried again.

A disembowelled drummer trailed his guts toward Santia and sank to his knees with a look of horror, before pitching forward onto the leafy ground.

A crewmember smashed his fist into the face of a small man, shattering his cheekbone. The pirate, a huge hulk of a figure, jabbed another blow into the man's gut, and as he doubled up, slammed the short but keen-edged blade of his cutlass down hard onto his neck, shearing his head off in one blow.

Another man swiftly unravelled a length of thin wire with two stout handles. He crept up behind one of the Haitians and casually crossed his hands, forming the wire into a loop. The loop was flung over the man's head with breathtaking speed and an expertise born from years of practice. He pulled back and pushed his knee into the man's back. The man struggled, his body convulsing, before the wire sliced through his neck.

Santia turned in time to see a young crewman bring a wooden cosh down hard onto the head of a Haitian woman, her arms raised in a futile attempt to ward off the attack. It smashed against her skull with a bone-crunching crack before a scream had left her lips. The crewman brought the heavy weapon down again and again in a frenetic attack, sending fragments of bloodied matter onto the sand around him. With the sheer force of each blow, the recumbent body of the woman shook and sprayed fresh blood upwards, speckling his face.

Some of the Haitians ran, dazed and bleeding, others lay where they had been cut down. Three seamen kicked and stamped the broken body of a young boy, their breeches splashed with his blood. A few feet away lay the crumpled body of an elderly woman, her skull cleaved open to the bridge of her nose. A trembling man raised his arms in a gesture of surrender and received a Spanish sword through his chest.

Despite the fear and pitiful cries of the islanders, Santia observed with satisfaction that his men were working well. Killing wasn't as important as how you killed; this was what struck fear into the minds of men. It was a rule he had lived by, but also derived great pleasure from. His propensity for violence knew no bounds.

A startled screech distracted him from his thoughts. He spun around to see someone slammed against a huge tree. A heavy-set pirate squeezed a man's throat. A smile crept across his face as his fist hammered into the Haitian's ribs, then another blow cracked them. The pirate slid a knife from his sheath and jabbed it into the man's belly. The Haitian released a horrendous wail as his steaming innards spilled from his trembling body.

Santia squinted, wishing the dim light were better so that he could see every nuance of the man's suffering.

Where was the Ioa?

Santia reloaded his pistol, quickly marching toward where he had seen an enormous black drummer sitting astride one of his men, his huge hands grasping the crewman's throat. Intimidated and overpowered by the Haitian, the crewman struggled, desperately trying to fight back, with little effect. Santia took aim at the black man's back in an almost cavalier manner. The drummer screamed an agonised roar as the ball ripped through his body. Tattered flesh spattered the sailor. Instantly the grip around his throat relaxed and the drummer fell away from him.

Santia laughed at the twitching body on the ground, and with a quick downward stroke smashed the butt of his flintlock against the Haitian's head, finishing the job.

He reloaded, staring coldly into the drummer's vacant eyes. Muzzle loading a single shot gun was not only time-consuming but dangerous during a land raid. He would have discarded the gun in favour of a blade, but on this occasion, he needed it by his side.

Santia heard women screaming, the cries mingled with perverse laughter. Two pirates held a young girl down. Her frightened eyes pleaded for them to stop, but their rough hands had already begun to tear at her clothes.

Santia's cohorts treated other women in a similar fashion. Screaming in agony, a young girl was forced face down onto the sand as two men abused her, then casually slit her throat.

They were rabid wolves attacking with a savagery Santia enjoyed, but he'd noticed that a faint, sickly yellow mist had started to materialise. Slowly rising, it moved sluggishly toward the young girl's naked body.

Was the darkness playing tricks with his eyes?

It poured over the lifeless figure, growing all the while, spreading along the ground, toward Santia. It soon reached his feet and began to rise, until streaky drifts swirled around him.

Within moments it had all but smothered everything.

Santia moved through the haze, baffled by its sudden

appearance, but apprehension began to override his confusion as part of the fog thinned. Figures were forming through the blurry mist, figures he now recognised. One of them was the priest and the other was the creature, which stood with its arms dangling, claws almost reaching the ground.

Santia holstered his pistol and ran toward the Ioa. As he approached, the Houngan stepped in front of him and leaned forward.

'*Keaman chanaka,*' the Houngan shouted. '*Ashrubanipal, satiu azuzu.*' His bulbous eyes burned into Santia's. '*Ashrubanipal, satiu azuzu,*' he repeated.

'A curse!' Santia squeezed the words out through gritted teeth as the muscular man lunged at him. The pirate was fast; he thrust a dagger into the soft flesh beneath the Haitian's chin. The attack was so sudden that the Houngan's jaw snapped shut with a bone-crunching crack, stifling his scream. Santia stepped back as his attacker fell away. The man was writhing in agony, the blade lodged inside his head. He gripped the sticky hilt, pulling at the dagger with both hands, as Santia grinned. The man sank to the ground, his hands smothered with blood, and fell forwards onto his face. Santia watched the life ebb away until eventually the Houngan's eyes glazed over, frozen open in death.

Santia withdrew the dagger from the man's jaw. He peered into the mist, almost unable to make out anything. The Ioa had disappeared again. His foot snagged on something and he stumbled over the body of a partly-naked girl. Her face, grotesquely twisted, stared back at him with vacant eyes bulging from their sockets. The rope around her neck told its own story. Strangulation was an ultimate form of power. There was nothing on earth like having complete control over a victim, staring them in the eye as they struggled, gasping their final breath. Santia's sick mind relished the thought. He stepped over the corpse, quickening his pace.

He felt a deep coldness that chilled his innards, and a rancid smell seemed to come from the mist itself.

An unexpected breeze passed through the vapours around

him, ruffling his dark hair, freezing his scalp as if it was touched by wintry hands. He heard agonising groans, a weird sonorous moaning. This wasn't his crew's work. He knew the sound of dying – he'd heard it more times than he could recall – and this was different.

He tried to follow what he thought were moving shadows, but as he blinked, he realised it was just an illusion created by the shifting mist. The only thing he could make out were the dark outlines of surrounding trees. Yet the voices were becoming louder, more distinct, a dreadful outpouring of anguish. The piteous lamentation hung in the vapours around him as though it were part of the fog. His grip on the dagger tightened as the voices wailed. He whirled around, trying to locate the source of the sounds, but they wafted, mingling with the drifting mists.

Were the sounds from his own imagination? For an uneasy moment, it seemed as though something deep within the fog was staring back at him. He shrugged off the feeling.

Yet, what about the Ioa?

His steps were tentative, and his breathing slowed. There was very little light penetrating the fog, just glimmers of moonlight finding its way through the glowing mass. He was trapped with a creature out there, stalking him, biding its time.

'What!'

Santia staggered backward, startled at the speed with which it moved.

'You bastard,' he seethed through clenched teeth, struggling with his inner emotions, unwilling to give in to fear. The creature could see him through the mist, perhaps even sense his pounding heart.

'Where are you?'

He tried to fight the chill that swept through him, but a blast of cold air struck him, a glacial blast so strong it threatened to knock him over.

The Ioa growled, a deep rasping sound.

Santia's grip on both dagger and pistol tightened. Another shadow appeared, giggling within the cloaking vapours, then another. From the periphery of his vision he could make out more dark shadows with featureless faces. They wheeled about him, spinning continuously, a ghoulish carousel that iced the blood in his veins.

Santia backed away, his weapons at the ready and his attention fully on them. His heel caught a man's body beneath him. The man's face was little more than a bloated mass of purple flesh.

There were many more corpses, strewn around the sandy ground, but it was the shadows that made Santia retreat, calling out to his crew.

With an increasing sense of foreboding, he ran from their taunting laughter. Santia moved quickly, his instinct for self-survival his only driving force.

Like a drowning man, he became lost in the depths of the fog that seemed to whisper his name.

Santia looked back over his shoulder but could see just the fog. His breaths came in short gasps and his lungs ached. He felt isolated. This substance had a way of sapping a man's spirit and reaching into his very being to chill his innards.

From within the fog icy streamers skimmed his face, cold against his flesh.

Madness. He'd allowed the voodoo ritual to distort his thoughts.

Something was moving through the yellow haze, but as hard as he tried to focus upon it, it dissolved back into the writhing vapours. The crack of pistol fire echoed around him, followed by shouts and frantic running as the frightened voices of his crew called out to one another. The commotion grew louder, and he had no doubt that his men were being slaughtered.

Amid the wails and cries, there were flashes of gunfire, sharp and clear in the icy air; but soon the cacophony of sounds faded into the distance.

Santia understood. They were the ones being hunted, but by what? The Ioa? Surely it couldn't kill that many men that quickly. Something else was at work here, just as deadly as the creature. Whatever it was, his crew were being torn to pieces. This vaporous yellow mist harboured something evil, something beyond his understanding, and that frightened him.

The shroud of mist opened up before Santia, and the Ioa strode through with arms wide, its mouth fixed in a wicked grin.

'Keep back!'

Its eyes focused on him.

'Get away from me.'

It drew closer, its crimson orbs glaring and its breath visible in the frosty air.

'Keep back,' Santia repeated, moving backwards as it snarled.

The Ioa hissed, sniffing the air, capturing his scent, then growled, with a steady stream of saliva drooling from its mouth.

Driven by panic, he lunged forward, thrusting his dagger deep into the creature's chest, ripping flesh and slicing through organs. Blood slapped his face, and the sound of its startled screech sent him stumbling backwards.

As he shrank away, the Ioa howled, clutching its chest with blood spurting through its fingers. It staggered toward him, clutching the handle of the dagger, desperately trying to force itself forwards.

Santia's body stiffened. He wanted to scream his outrage at the Ioa, but the sound froze in his throat. He tried to turn away, but its fiery eyes held him captive.

Mist swirled about him, and with it came the murmurs, the babble, the rising ululation of ethereal voices, like the cries of the dammed.

Santia thought he could hear words of warning, but he paid little attention; he just stared at the Ioa. It muttered something, but the guttural sound made little sense. Unable to move, Santia was locked within the Ioa's influence. Its hand reached out and long fingers wrapped around his throat. Although the grip was weak he was dizzy with fear.

Santia grabbed its wrist, and the creature hissed, its blood-speckled spit dampening his face. The pirate struggled. 'Let me go!'

Its grip tightened as he looked into its narrowing eyes. The Ioa was powerfully built, and Santia knew it could have lifted him off his feet if it had not been in such a weakened state.

His head was reeling, but still the pressure on his windpipe increased. Santia knew that if he didn't break the Ioa's grip, he would soon be dead.

In desperation, he thrust his other hand into its snarling face, pushing its jaw upwards so that its head went backwards. The Ioa's claws dug into his neck, puncturing the flesh. Wincing in pain, he released his grip on its wrist and chopped its exposed throat with as much strength as he could muster. An agonising screech came from the creature, giving him the opportunity to break free. Santia drew in several deep breaths, sucking air back into his body. He desperately needed to get away from there, but just as he was about to run, the Ioa swiped a blood-soaked claw at him. Santia ducked and jumped away from it. The creature whirled around and its other clawed hand caught his shoulder, shredding his jacket. But the pirate was quick; he drove his elbow into its jaw as hard as he could. The creature howled in anguish. Santia recoiled, trying to put distance between them, but the Ioa reached out its arms toward him. As he backed away, its movements became slower. It grabbed the dagger with both hands, wrenching it free from its torso. Dark liquid spattered Santia and he wiped his cheek with his coat sleeve, fighting the urge to look into the creature's face yet concerned by something else. This had all been too easy. He shouldn't have been able to catch it unawares like that. This thing could have torn him to pieces before he had a chance to stab it. It made no sense, but he was glad to be alive.

The Ioa sank to its knees, spitting out more words in a weirdly distorted growl. *Was it trying to communicate with him?*

Its breathing came in short rattling gasps, becoming quieter until it could scarcely be heard. The weight of its body as it hit the ground forced a final gasp of air from its lungs and a spurt of blood from its lips.

Santia should have been elated but wasn't. A thought in the back of his head nagged him again: *this had been too easy.* He tilted his head back to the canopy above.

A sudden flash lit the whole area, the transient blaze so intense that he raised an arm to shield his face. For a moment, the forest swirled around him. More lightening followed, and peals of thunder, but it was short lived; soon the weird celestial display faded, as though it were a support act for the main event.

Santia lowered his arm, staring through the haze, surprised by the sudden cessation. The moon, unhindered by cloud, found its way through ragged holes in the canopy, its luminescence falling upon the misty ground and trees. He'd experienced many thunderstorms before, but they'd lasted much longer than this. Everything was wrong about this place; the island, the people, and the thing on the ground before him. The Ioa lay like a fallen marble statue, its domed head twisted to the side, with crimson eyes fixed in a death stare. He regarded it for a moment, thankful that the mist had receded a little. He stiffened when he heard the voices again. They fluctuated between weeping and whispers, a horrible lamentation that inspired dread.

His mind tried to make sense of the chaotic rambling. It didn't help, but what gave him hope were the gushing waves of the sea breaking against the shoreline in the distance.

Santia was aware that something else could be lurking out there. He didn't want to venture further into the darkness. But he had to. It flowed around him as though it were a tangible thing, almost choking off his breath. If it had not been for the glowing mist, he would have been relegated to a dark oblivion. The mist offered some form of light for the time being. He stepped forward, still listening, trying to determine the source of the sounds, but the insidious whispers receded and Santia's attention shifted back to the body of the Ioa at his feet.

He remembered the Houngan had placed an amulet around its neck, and even though he wanted to get out of there, he suspected the trinket would be worth something.

Placing his foot under the Ioa's midriff, he rolled it onto its back then stepped away, still wary. He pushed the creature with the tip of his boot, but it remained still. The pirate waited for a few moments, for he was a cautious man. He had seen men faking death, and lost crew to this type of deception. Santia raised his pistol and without hesitation fired. The creature's pale body twitched as though life still loitered there, but it was little more than residual nerves as the ball ripped through brain tissue. Reassured, he knelt and swiftly removed the amulet from around its neck.

Santia raised himself with a grunt and briefly looked down at the mutilated corpse as he reloaded his pistol. He backed away, luminous mist brushing against him, prickling his flesh. More air wafted into his face, its taste as foul as the vapour that had woven its way over the Ioa's body like glowing tendrils.

Deep and sinister laughter came from the glowing mass, very different from the voices he had heard moments earlier.

'Show yourself!' he shouted.

Something moved.

He looked toward the source of the movement, swiping the pistol in his hand in front of his face, trying to dispel the mist. Eventually, a shadowy figure appeared, unmoving and silent. Within the heart of the fog a small light flickered, a spectral flame that ignited the brightening mass with a thunderous whoosh. He raised an arm just in time to protect his face from the searing heat, as the ground beneath him trembled.

An explosion? As the conflagration expanded it swept him off his feet, sending him sprawling backwards, crashing to the ground. With the huge ball of fire came a roar that seemed to go on forever. Santia felt the blast of heat sweeping over him. He rolled over again and again, his arms and legs sending sand into the air, covering him in a fine white layer. It brushed against his scalded face and blistered hands. His body came to rest and he landed on his back, chest heaving. His instinct for survival kicked in and he curled up in a foetal position, fearing another blast that did not materialise.

The whole area had been engulfed in flames, but he'd been

lucky. He could have been burnt to death by the blast. It was some time before he summoned up the courage to uncover his head from his stinging hands. He raised himself to his knees cautiously, wincing as he rose to his feet. Santia raised a hand to his brow and roared as his probing fingers touched raw pink flesh. He blinked, clearing grit from his eyes, and realised that he was a good distance from the source of the blaze. Despite that, he could still feel its tremendous heat.

A figure stood in the rolling flames at the fire's core, unmoving and unconsumed by the ferocious heat. The array of bright coloured flames swirled around it, increasing into a fiery whirlwind.

'What are you?'

It stepped out of the flames, a dark silhouette against the conflagration, an oppressive shroud of blackness surrounding its tall thin body like a cankerous aura. Its pallid face visible from in the darkness seemed to hover in the turbulent air like a floating death mask.

Santia, realising he was still clutching the pistol, took aim at the tall figure and fired. The ball whistled through the air and passed through its face as though it were a ghost.

'You bastard,' he seethed.

Santia turned away from it and threw himself forward. Perhaps it was fear that spurred him on, his feet pounding against the ground. Some of the trees were still burning, flushing the fog with an orange and yellow glow and helping him see the way ahead. Santia ran faster as the sudden surge of adrenaline kicked in, giving his legs the extra strength he needed. Something thundered from behind, and the ground seemed to shake. His heart hammering, another jolt hit home, its sound like the crash of a felled tree. He ran on, hoping to find the track that would eventually lead to the coast. It had to be close; he'd heard the rush of waves earlier. A branch struck him on the forehead as he pushed through the woods, and he tripped, sprawling headlong, hitting the ground with a resounding smack.

Santia got back to his feet. He was about to call out to his crew again when something curled around his leg.

'Get off,' he shouted.

A young woman was looking up at him, her eyes widening, pleading for help. Santia wrenched his foot away and was about to strike the woman with the butt of his pistol, when she was drawn into the mist by unseen hands. He was stunned by the sheer speed at which she was taken. Then he turned and ran as her screams faded into the distance.

He slapped branches out of his way, feeling disorientated. There had to be a landmark somewhere, something he could recognise to give him his bearings.

It was with considerable relief that he caught sight of the rotting carcass of the wild boar he had passed earlier. Santia looked down at the dead animal, saw the way its innards lay in front of its slit gut. He gave an abrupt laugh, remembering stepping over them from the opposite direction. He now knew he was approaching the shore and going the right way. Sweat trickled down his face, his mouth as dry and parched as his throat.

'Make for the beach!' Santia called out, wondering if any of his men were still alive. Santia moved through the mist, continuing to call out, but there was no reply.

There was a cold silence that seemed heightened by the unearthliness of this strange, all-obscuring miasma, but it was the feeling of isolation that gripped him most. He wanted to escape this accursed place. In his mind's eye he saw the grinning spectre, floating in the swirling flames. He could still see its eyes, watching, staring at him so balefully.

The only sound now was that of his own footsteps thudding against the leafy ground below. He stopped, sensing a presence.

'Who's there?'

'Here. Over here. This way.'

Santia ran toward the source of the anxious voice. As he burst through the icy skin of the fog, he heard a deep, ominous groan from behind that became a roar driving him onwards.

He laboured for every breath, staggering in the direction of the voice before collapsing into a heap on the ground.

It took a few seconds for his brain to recognise the welcoming sound of gushing waves breaking against the shoreline.

'We thought you were dead, sir.' The unmistakeable voice of Samson Ramsay. The powerfully-built Jamaican helped Santia to his feet.

'Are you all right?' came the voice of another anxious crewman. He was old, with sagging jowls and half-moons of wrinkled flesh hanging loosely under his eyes. Santia focused on the man's weathered face as his white hair blew wildly in the wind. 'They … they …' the old man stammered, 'didn't get you?'

It took Santia a moment to focus.

'I'm all right,' he grunted, wincing in pain from the stinging blisters on his hands and face as he rose to his feet with the help of arms outstretched to help him up.

'Let's get the hell out of here,' he said, motioning toward the boat, where more of his men had gathered. 'Where are the others?' he called out.

'Dead, sir,' replied a young, thin-framed man with a mop of unruly red hair. 'Something in the fog took them. I heard them screaming, but I couldn't … couldn't …'

'All right lad,' Santia said, his voice lowered to a whisper. 'We can't fight this. It's voodoo.' He smiled nervously, fingering the amulet around his neck.

'You should have warned us,' a burly pirate said harshly, his face filled with both anger and fear. 'You didn't say anything about voodoo or those things in the fog.'

Santia looked toward him with a surge of anger.

'Are you challenging me?'

The big man didn't reply.

Santia ground his teeth and looked at the rest of his crew. 'A lot of us have died, yes,' he admitted. 'But we've lost men before.'

'Not like this,' someone said.

'No not like this, but …'

'What's going on? Those things weren't human, they

wouldn't die.' A tall sailor stared at Santia wide-eyed. 'I shot one in the face and it just became part of the fog again, then came right back at me. It took my fingers,' he held up a bloodied, rag-bandaged hand. 'There were too many of them. They were everywhere.'

'How many did you see?' another crewman asked.

'At least fifteen. Maybe more. I couldn't be sure.'

'Listen,' Santia spoke harshly. 'Has it even occurred to you that the things that did that,' he pointed at the bloody stump of the man's hand, 'might still be here, waiting to finish the job?'

His remarks silenced the crew.

'Enough talk. Let's get back to the ship. We've more work to do.'

24

The pirates had gathered on the deck of *Gospall*, and they were armed. Santia, now on board, stood boots astride, clenching his fists.

'Who the hell do you think you are, you English bastard?'

He yelled insults at the tall, well-tanned man with thick blond hair.

Pike leaned forward, the lapels of his sea-worn blue coat flapping in the cool night breeze. His eyes narrowed, watching the men peering down from the shrouds with pistols trained on him. His small crew were well aware of what was happening. Outnumbered, they stood their ground in front of him, protecting their Captain.

'A man's actions define who he is, and you have proved what you are.' Pike stared at the pirate with seething contempt. 'You have murdered defenceless men, butchered women.' He slammed his hand against the quarterdeck rail. 'You have even slaughtered children.'

His remarks provoked an angry response from the other pirates. He heard their jeers as they reached for their weapons. One of them yelled from the back of the crowd, 'Pitch him overboard!'

Santia raised a hand into the air. 'I'll deal with him.'

Pike knew the situation was hopeless. Santia had seized the opportunity to deceive many of the crew, encouraging them to join his band of felons. Seduced by lies and false promises, they had willingly became gullible collaborators in his bid to take over the ship. Only a few men had remained loyal; the others were too ill to fight.

'Remember, men, this is what we want.' Santia reached into his pocket and removed a ducat. He held the gold coin aloft for all to see. 'Follow me,' he shouted. 'There's more where that came from. Or you can rot on that island.' The pirate dropped the coin back into his pocket, grinning coldly.

'Be damned, sir.' Pike's voice rang out from the quarterdeck.

The exchange of glances between the two men was as cold as steel.

'Disarm this scum,' Pike instructed, looking toward his men.

His threat was hollow, and Santia knew it.

'You can expect no mercy from me, if you will not relinquish your weapons. Hand them over.'

Santia laughed.

'Aye aye, sir!' he mocked.

'Damn you. You will leave my ship.'

'Your ship!' Santia barked. 'You bloody fool, she's mine now.'

He drew his cutlass and thrust it firmly into the deck, the blade quivering. This was the sign his crew had waited for.

An enormous man with long hair tied into a pigtail ran across the main deck screaming, waving a sword in the air. The rest of the pirates followed, their response, swift and savage. The resounding clash of steel against steel rang out as men fell and died. Despite the screams, Pike heard the shrill cry of a young man with red hair, blinded by a single musket shot. The man clapped hands to his shattered face, staggered, then fell overboard. Two more gunshots cracked and tore through the sails in front of Pike, thudding into the deck, only narrowly missing his head.

From nowhere a huge bald pirate lunged at him. Pike had little time to react; the scarcely clothed figure was almost on him, muscular arms stretching forward. Pike was caught in a vicious headlock and both men tumbled across the quarter deck so fast and with such force that they landed on the hard wooden floor with a sickening thud.

The fall was brutal, and Pike seized the moment, rolling away from the other man, whose massive hand flailed wildly, trying to catch hold of him again. But Pike was quick, rising to his feet while the pirate struggled to his knees, screaming insults at him.

He swayed as the ship rocked, suddenly unsteady on his feet. The big man's cumbersome body was still bent over, presenting a formidable target, and Pike thrust a booted foot directly into his gut with as much strength as he could muster. The bald man roared, and Pike kicked again, trying to wind him enough to incapacitate him, but the pain seemed to spur the brute on. He stood upright, breathing heavily, and swung his arm. The back of his hand swiped Pike across the face, knocking him backwards toward the quarter deck rail. He remained on his feet and met the pirate's charge head on, but as the bald man was much heavier and stronger, Pike took the worst of the collision. For a moment, everything was hazy, but he turned in time to dodge a punch, driving his own fist into his assailant's jaw, almost breaking his own knuckles. The pirate staggered backwards, his features twisting into a sneer. Pike heard screams and yells coming from the main deck, aware that his men were losing. Pike feinted left then right as his opponent closed in. His movements were quick, but the ruse had little effect. This time he ran at the enormous pirate and jammed an elbow into his stomach just below the sternum. It worked, knocking the brute back a few feet, giving Pike just enough time to land another punch. It shattered the pirate's nose and sent him reeling down the steps and onto the main deck

A musket shot caught the side of Pike's leg, ripping his nankeen breeches across the thigh. He winced as his fingers touched the wound, then looked up, as someone yelled, 'Get Pike!'

It was Santia.

Pike saw him plunge a sword right up to the hilt into a crewman's chest. One by one his men were being cut down, their corpses littering the bloodied deck.

Even the men who had dragged themselves up from sick bay onto the main deck had been hacked down without mercy. The deck was soaked red, and for a moment it appeared as though *Gospall* was slowly bleeding to death.

Pike's face was etched with pain as memories flooded through his mind. He'd hoped to return to England one day, to his wife and his dear friend Winstanly. Having suffered terribly, he could not forget his decision to take control of the ship. He'd sacrificed everything for his men, and they had paid the ultimate price for their loyalty. He would never see home again.

The ship rolled and the swaying lantern behind Pike cast an unsteady light across his face, distracting him. His jaw tightened with the realisation that the battle was almost lost. But he'd prepared for such an outcome. He felt strangely calm as he lit the torch in his hand.

His eyes shone like glass in the firelight, clear and grey. He glanced around *Gospall*, along her gangways and the main deck where Santia stood surrounded by his cohorts. She would be a formidable weapon in the wrong hands, and that was something he would not permit.

Alone on the quarterdeck, Pike looked down and met the pirates' stabbing eyes.

'This ship has achieved great things, and you shall not have her.' There was no anxiety in his voice, only determination and an acceptance of the inevitable.

They watched him warily.

Pike moved toward three wooden barrels and prised the lid off one of them, exposing its dark powdery contents. He looked over the quarterdeck rail, staring into the hardened faces of the pirates again. They stood bemused, not knowing he'd had the barrels of gunpowder brought up from below while they were on the island. As he raised the torch high into the air, he saw fear flush through them.

With a trembling hand, he touched the locket inside his shirt and whispered, 'Forgive me, Rebecca.'

Santia reached for his pistol, but it was too late. Pike dropped the flaming torch into the powder keg and stared up into the black void above. The night was filled with a thousand shimmering stars, some so colossal it was as if they were just beyond the spiralling mastheads.

A searing flash followed by a thunderous explosion rocked the ship. The stridency of the screams rang out, terrible ear-piercing screeches heralding an end to the pirates' murderous reign.

Many of the crew were instantly burnt to death by the scorching blast. Some were not so lucky; a sailor lay dazed, and suddenly his hair ignited, before his whole body burst into yellow flames amid piteous screams. He thrashed wildly for pain-filled moments, still screaming, his body writhing, the flesh roasting and spitting onto the deck.

Another barrel exploded, and other men were swept toward the stern of the vessel by the force of the blast. Billowing fire rose high into the air, spreading out with thick smoke surging at its head, expanding at an astonishing speed.

Gospall blazed brightly, the flames spurred on by the rising wind whipping up from the sea. Those that had survived stood before the conflagration. They hadn't anticipated Pike's resolve. Burning wreckage tumbled from the ship into the water all around them as the ship started to sink. More explosions followed as the ship's stores of munitions ignited, setting off a chain reaction along the remaining deck. Spars and rigging collapsed, smashing down onto lifeless bodies below. The frigate exploded into a great column of fire. Driven by rising winds, the tattered sails were consumed, and billowing flames surged along the hull and spat through open ports. The crackling of the timber increased into a rending of wood and iron, a shrieking that overwhelmed everything else. What was left of *Gospall* sank into the murky depths, taking with her the last few survivors.

25

Father Mallom was woken by the sound of his bedroom door creaking loudly. A glance at his clock revealed that it was barely 3.30. He stared at the heavy wooden door, which stood slightly open, allowing a sliver of light from the landing to slip in. There was no-one there, but there was movement downstairs. He heard footsteps, sluggish footsteps, moving up the stairs, getting louder and closer. A small bead of sweat trickled down his forehead as he grappled with his own sense of isolation. Mallom's heart was hammering in his chest as he waited for the prowler to enter the room, but was this just the remnant of a bad dream? His mind had been drawn back to his younger days, a time he'd tried hard to forget. A child had died because of him, but he had been too weak to deal with it at the time.

Had he let pride stand in the way of duty? Surely he should have known better than to perform an exorcism on his own? Sweet Jesus, look what had happened to Father Stamford. Why hadn't he learned from that?

The presence he'd felt was worse than anything he'd encountered before. Even with the help of his mentor, could he have really driven it out? He had believed that this entity could be vanquished, but things had gone bad and he had felt the full fury of the demon. That night, he had lost faith, not in God but in himself, and he'd fled from the priesthood. He would not become involved or participate in the field again. How could he? He'd been broken, spiritually wrecked.

When he'd moved to London he'd encountered Maria Kokoschka at a social club, and they'd become firm friends. Even though he hadn't approved of her spiritual gift, as she put it, he had identified with her instincts. He had grown to understand through his own dealings with the supernatural that spirits of the dead could be incredibly dangerous.

Sometimes that fury was vented against the living.

But why was he sensing something unusual now? It had been a long time since he had felt such trepidation.

'Who's there?' Mallom managed to utter softly.

The old door's hinges creaked, the sound scratching his brain.

'Is somebody there?'

He desperately wanted to believe that it was just a case of over-imagination pushed to extremes because of Maria's story.

With a long drawn-out high-pitched creak, the door fully opened, allowing more light into the room. He watched, trying to gather his senses, expecting to see someone enter.

A mist began drifting through the open doorway into the bedroom. It quickly spread along the length and breadth of the floor. Mallom's old bones seemed to be soaking up the chilly atmosphere, and his flesh was damp and incredibly cold.

What was happening?

The mist rose until it began billowing up from below him, becoming denser, around his bed. Misty tendrils, like elongated fingers, searched the priest's body. He coughed and spluttered as they reached his nose and mouth, their stench like stagnant pond water. He gasped for breath as freezing vapours constricted his chest, making it difficult to breathe.

He couldn't move.

Mallom cried out, aware that there was no-one there to hear him.

All he could do was pray: 'Father, deliver thy servant from evil …' He spoke slowly, repeating the same prayer over and over, imploring God for help.

He had once been a man of unshakeable faith, but events had changed that. The menace of this presence made him question his own lack of belief, which had been eroded through years of self-pity and spiritual doubt.

'Father, deliver thy servant from evil …' Mallom's tone strengthened and the prayer quickened like a feverish incantation. 'Father, deliver thy servant from evil …'

Mist poured into his mouth and he almost gagged. Its taste

was putrid. He felt it burning his mouth, and although his throat ached, he continued relentlessly, unceasing in his defensive prayer. 'Father, deliver thy servant from evil ...'

The fog gained a yellowish hue, becoming thicker and seeming to throb. Something was moving in those vapours!

He prayed silently for strength, pushing aside the thought that he might not actually receive divine help. Inside the swirling mist spherical lights flickered, gradually changing. Mallom was sure he knew what was happening. He knew that energy existed in many different forms. It was his belief that spirit energy could attract moisture, gaseous vapours and loose atmospheric particles in order to materialise enough for human eyes to see. He was almost certain that he was experiencing a stage four manifestation.

Mallom blinked, almost doubting his own sanity, as the orbs became dim, then incredibly dark, while still retaining a strange mesmerising quality to them. As they hovered, every fibre in his being screamed out that these tar-black objects were malevolent. He'd seen orbs when assisting Father Stamford, but not like these. They didn't resemble anything he'd seen before. They hung several feet from the ground, the mist almost touching the ceiling.

Mallom blinked again as his prayer continued.

The orbs slowly stretched, becoming shapeless silhouettes with little clarity, but even as the thought entered his head they were altering, becoming more manlike.

'Father, deliver thy servant from evil.' The priest's words were no more than a whisper against the oppressive silence.

The ambiguous forms slowly acquired more substance. Still blurred, the dark shapes lumbered, dragging their feet as they moved through the mist, shuffling toward him. He could do nothing but raise his hand in an act of faith, make the sign of the cross and close his eyes. It was his only escape from the approaching shadows, seeking refuge in the babbling prayer within his mind.

All around him the sound of movement grew louder, causing his eyes to spring open. He gazed at the dim shapes, listened to their hushed voices. Mallom's resolve faltered and he struggled to fight the fear within him.

Within the swirling vapours the spectral shapes stood, unmoving, a few feet apart.

They watched!

Close to panic Mallom looked from one dark form to another, and through that haze he began to make out malformed ancient mariners, indistinct cutlasses raised in withered fists, a hint of scorched clothes over blackened bodies.

One of them drew closer.

Mallom lay transfixed, his eyes locked onto the dagger gripped firmly in its hand. He focused on the vicious-looking blade as it was raised to head height ready to strike.

The priest struggled as icy fingers squeezed his throat, slowly choking the life from him. The figure's eyes were dark and remorseless, projecting both hatred and insanity. The incredibly strong grip was pinning him down against the mattress. Mallom's heels dug into the bed, his hands fighting against the vice-like grip without success. He gasped for air, his senses reeling. He could feel the misty room beginning to spin around him as his arms fell to his sides, utterly useless. His only consolation was that he didn't expect the pain to last much longer.

As Mallom's consciousness began to slip he was aware of the knife-wielding grotesque standing over him, and those dark and feral eyes. He felt numb to the pain. In a heartbeat he was hovering above his own body and rising steadily toward the ceiling. Mallom glanced back, realising that he was leaving his earthly remains behind.

Was he dead?

He'd been left with a tremendous sense of freedom. Worldly ties meant nothing anymore. This revelation gave rise to an incredible sense of wellbeing. Casting off the shackles that had chained him to the physical world was liberating in a way he'd never thought possible. There were no physical torments anymore, no depression, guilt, or pain. Even the persistent ache in his arthritic joints had disappeared.

Something flickered in front of him; a tunnel with spiralling light. He moved through it, and when he awoke he was in another place.

The priest's body floated. His essence shimmered as he rose higher and higher above a dark sea. He saw rigging and tattered sailcloth spinning in a huge whirlpool. Something else was down there, sloshing around with the debris: blackened corpses being sucked into watery oblivion.

Fog was being drawn in, coming from a nearby island. Its streaky yellow vapour joined with swirling water, moving with the descending maelstrom, reaching down into the heart of the vortex. It began to amass, dense and luminous, localising itself to where a ship must have been. He sensed a malevolence emanating from the writhing mass yet felt a compulsion to go toward it. His descent was fast as thought itself. Mallom closed his mind to the fear as he plunged into the vaporous growth. Its sudden touch was like iced energy, a dispiriting cold that enveloped his whole body.

He fought the chill that crept through him, unable to shake the feeling that unseen eyes were upon him. Mallom could see nothing, only volute patterns made by swirling mists. Gradually his vision adjusted, and the gloom began to dissipate.

His mind reached out to whatever lay hidden within the shadows, unsure of the scope of his new abilities. The priest's thoughts began to meld with the fog, and as he explored its essence, dark sensations intermingled with his own, touching his very consciousness. Mallom was confused by the strange invader probing his own mind. He in turn hoped to discover the identity of the presence. It was as though he were being swept along in the swirling waters of a river, its undercurrents dragging him down deeper and deeper into the murky depths. Images flashed through his mind; the island, the Ioa, Pike and Santia and the destruction of *Gospall*. Within a moment he understood everything that had happened and realised that the debris on the sea was all that was left of the ship and her crew.

It searched for weakness.

Malign forces probed him like poisonous tendrils, relishing

the contact, gaining access to his consciousness.

No. He wouldn't allow fear to deter him.

Within the shimmering vapours were legions of hushed voices.

Were these sounds inside his head?

The sounds grew louder, and strange shapes drifted through the fog. *They were like wisps of twisting vapour, nebulous in appearance, with little form or definite substance. Could it be that these wraiths drew form from the fog itself?*

The shadows circled the priest, revealing faces with gaping mouths, wailing in terrible distress. Mallom felt weakened. These wretched spirits were draining him of strength, using his energy in an attempt to materialise into something more tangible. The spectral faces dissolved back into the fog, only to be replaced by sinister phantoms, their faces blurred with shadowed eyes. He heard their laughter, a mocking sound that breathed flesh onto the bones of this nightmare.

More spectres encircled him, their form transparent. These apparitions were unlike the others, which displayed such misery with their pitiful cries. Mallom knew by their soul-shattering lamentation that the latter were tormented souls, while these new, ambiguous conformations were tormentors.

He couldn't help but feel pity for the poor wretches held captive by this demon horde that hovered like curious spectators, staring through eyeless sockets.

In moments he was at the centre of a howling whirlwind. From within that encircling storm, hideous wraiths struck at the disorientated priest. Mallom raised a hand to protect his face, but the phantom claws passed through him.

Mallom prayed for the strength to continue. His journey had taken him deep into the heart of this lair, but if he proceeded, could he return?

A peculiar vibration thrummed through him as his consciousness detached from his spirit form and passed through the screeching maelstrom around him.

In a final attempt to discover the identity of this evil, he perceived a vague shape. Whatever this thing was, it wasn't the

Ioa. He read its thoughts and knew that it wanted revenge for the death of the Ioa and its disciples. It had witnessed the massacre on the island and was driven by uncontrollable rage. A smothering heaviness began to overwhelm him. He knew from the connection that it was out there, watching him from the darkness. Like liquid shadow it moved within the fog, expanding and contracting, stretching then shrinking as though it were trying to break free from a bubble. He caught a glimpse of a long-curved claw, a face broad and flat, pushing against the darkness that surrounded it. He felt a pang of fear as two nickel eyes blinked into existence.

Memories gushed through his head, drawing him back to his youth. He'd suffered for his failure and now this presence was picking at the scab of remorse, opening up a healing wound for its own amusement.

Every part of his being was telling him to look away, but he could not. The intangible link became stronger; soon he would be lost to its influence. He touched its mind and sensed evil, a pure and unrefined malevolence. Mallom's resolve faltered, and he saw a monstrous form so terrifying that his mind froze.

For an instant the priest was lost, then he felt an incredible force. It was bright, pumping out an intense light, yet it didn't hurt his eyes. The flash seared through the darkness as his consciousness was pulled back as though attached by an unseen flexible cord.

With a jolt he realised he was once more within the confines of the screaming whirlwind. He was too wearied to react, too drained of energy. Higher and higher he rose, passing through icy vapours, gaining height, climbing into a clear night sky.

Looking down, he saw the accumulation of spectres dissolve back into the fog, wailing in protest.

'Soon, warrior of Yahweh,' a voice whispered. 'Soon we will meet, and your God will not save you …'

He drifted over the wreckage of the *Gospall* and watched the incipient glimmer of dawn; warm light shimmered off the water's surface with a purity that dispersed the final dregs of fog.

The sun had doused not just the fog but the spectres within it. Perhaps this nightmare was at an end.

Something drew his attention to the water below: a leather-bound journal resting on top of a large fragment of wood. It bobbed easily on the rippling sea, rising on the ridge of each new wave, then falling, but all the time moving toward the shoreline.

Wakefulness brought uncertainty. Mallom sat upright in bed as morning sunlight shone through his window, brightening up the whole room. He steadied his breathing, relieved the nightmare was over. But when he glanced down at the bed sheets that had twisted around his body he almost gasped. The sheets were covered in grime and a coin lay beside his bare leg.

26

Seamus Mallom stepped from his car. Sometimes he yearned to be back in the old country, where the air was fresh, untarnished by car fumes and the stench of city life; but after all these years perhaps even the little villages in Ireland were in danger of becoming overpopulated. This was progress. He shook his head at the thought. Perhaps he'd become old and stuck in his ways. The gravel crunched beneath his feet as he walked across the car park toward the Houghton Museum. It was a large contemporary structure with a glass and steel exterior, and he took a moment to take in the building before entering.

It was busy inside. A group of children were being ushered toward the main maritime museum by three frustrated teachers. The children seemed oblivious to instruction and were excited to the point of giddiness. Their babble was deafening, disturbing not only other visitors but members of staff too.

Mallom made his way up two flights of stairs and approached a tall glass door. He tapped it lightly with his knuckles, unable to see through the dark-tinted glass.

The door swung open after the briefest of moments, and a young blond-haired man greeted him.

'Can I help you?' he asked.

'My name is Mallom.' He peered over the man's shoulder into the high-tech lab. 'I have an appointment with …'

His words were cut short.

'Peter, bring him through,' a voice called out from behind the young man.

The young man stepped aside and Mallom entered the room.

'How the hell are you, Seamus? It's been way too long.'

'That it has, Simon. That it has.'

'What is it? Four years?'

The old man smiled. 'More like five.'

He took a moment to take in his surroundings. The combination of artificial light and gleaming chrome made it feel more like a medical unit than a research facility.

Simon Massey rose to his feet, made his way across to Mallom and placed a hand on his shoulder.

'It's good to see you again, my old friend.'

'Hey, less of the old.'

Massey laughed. 'How are you?'

'Not too bad,' he said, but Mallom knew his tired eyes betrayed how he really felt.

'You're looking well, Seamus.'

'Am I?'

'Well, at least you've still got your hair,' the bald man said, running a hand over his smooth scalp.

'Stress will do that to you,' he replied, grinning.

'Tell me about it.'

'You know, Simon, I miss Phelan.'

'Yes, Father would have turned eighty this year.'

'I know,' Mallom replied, saddened.

'Cancer's a bitch,' Massey said. 'It robs you of everything you have and everything you could have had.'

'He had problems with his pancreas?'

'Yes, and by the time he was diagnosed it was too late.'

Mallom averted his eyes. He'd been content to wallow in his own self-pity for decades without conversing with friends, yet the truth of it was he'd felt ashamed. Phelan Massey had never judged him, even though he had known about the botched exorcism. He'd kept it a secret even from his son. Even so, Phelan hadn't had it easy. The clergy had turned on him too, but for different reasons, forcing him from the church. They hadn't allowed him to confess his so-called crime to the Garda, but his bishop had made it quite clear that the Catholic Church could in no way be associated with his actions and had to distance itself from him. He had left quietly, disillusioned by the politics, not even bothering to tell them about the peace deal he had been working on with the IRA to help prevent more sectarian murders. After resigning, Phelan had worked as a community leader and had even married. A short time later he had been blessed with a son, Simon. Mallom envied that. He would have liked a family of his own.

'I'm sorry I missed the funeral.'

'Dad would have understood.'

'It's just that ...' He looked into Massey's eyes, the sadness evident.

'Seamus, it's fine, really.'

'He was such a happy-go-lucky man, Simon. I'm sure he thought I was a bad influence.'

'Nonsense.'

'No, I'm quite sure he didn't like the idea of us working together on paranormal investigations.'

'Ghost baiting, he called it. It wasn't that he didn't like the idea of it. I think he was scared that it could in some way damage my career. Back then, parapsychology was ridiculed. I believe the possibility has now been acknowledged by several academic bodies. Some even have departments that delve into anomalous experiences such as extrasensory perception, psychokinesis and transpersonal psychology.'

'I've read a little about that,' Mallom cut in. 'Transpersonal psychologists draw on insights from specific areas of cognition, consciousness and the paranormal.'

'That's right. The focus is on evidence for survival after bodily death, taking into account apparitions, reincarnation and cases of possession. It's approached in a much more academic way now, with a dissertation based on empirical research at the end of the course.' Massey grinned. 'I bet they don't tell you how boring it can be in the field, though.'

'Those all-night vigils could drag on a bit.' There was banter in the Irishman's voice, but Massey realised there was also a degree of anxiety. 'Part of me wishes that we had seen or heard something credible, but there were no spirit manifestations, ghostly footsteps or mysterious knocking. It could all be reasoned out in scientific terms. I've always said that a paranormal investigator should scrutinise the evidence and find out where it leads. It's usually to creaky floorboards, clanking pipes and a vivid imagination.'

Massey smiled. 'Being ex-clergy, father never really accepted what we were trying to do, but gathering research on the subject and alleviating anxiety for people caught up in so-called "paranormal situations" helped reinforce my own beliefs. It was a great experience for me.'

'You're still a sceptic.'

'Absolutely. The only spirits I believe in come in a bottle.'

'Is that right?' Mallom reached into his coat pocket and removed a small plastic bag. 'This may change your mind.'

'What is it?'

'You tell me,' he said, unravelling the bag.

Massey's eyes locked onto the object.

'My God, where did you find it?'

'You wouldn't believe me if I told you.'

'It's an interesting piece.'

Massey put on some latex gloves, removed the small object from Mallom's hand and held it in front of his face.

'This is rare. It's a 10-ducat coin.'

'What's that?'

'The ducat was a trade coin, of a separate weight and denomination from the standard coinage. There were two separate issues of trade ducat from Zurich in the first quarter of the 18th Century; one from the Canton and one from the city.' Massey smiled broadly. 'Canton coinage was issued in values of between four and ten ducats. Look Seamus, you can just make out the arms of Zurich on one side.' He flipped the coin over. 'And a view of the city and river on the other.'

'What makes it special?'

'Mintage was extremely low, and they had more of a ceremonial use than a practical function as currency. City of Zurich trade ducats were usually issued in values of between one quarter and two ducats, but production was much higher than the Canton issue.'

'How can you tell the difference?'

'Because one side of the city coin features the oval arms of

Zurich supported by a rampant lion and the inscription *REIPUBLICAE TIGURINAE DUCATUS* and the reverse features the inscription *DUCATUS/NOVUS/REIPUBLICAE/TIGURINAE* and the date.'

'How old are they?'

'They were minted in 1702, 1707, 1709, 1712 and 1714-1727.'

'You're like a kid in a sweet shop, Simon.'

'Absolutely. It gives us a pretty good idea of the financial state of the Republic of Zurich in the 18th Century. It's probably from the town of Limmat; no other Swiss confederate state was circulating as many gold coins as them at that time.

'I'm sure there was an American trader in the 18th Century that lost its cargo to pirates and was supposed to have been carrying a small chest of these ducats.'

'Is it valuable?' Mallom asked.

'These coins were more than just money, Seamus. They were offered as prestigious gifts by the very wealthy. Only the best engravers were employed to create them. How did you come across it?'

'I was wondering,' Mallom said, evading the question, 'if you could take a closer look at it and tell me if you find anything unusual about it.'

'Unusual?' The scientist frowned.

'Yes, just check it out for me and I'll tell you the whole story.'

'How can I refuse? You've got me curious now.'

'Thanks, Simon. Just give me a call as soon as you can.'

Mallom removed a small piece of paper from his pocket. 'My number's on there,' he said, handing it to him.

Massey took the paper, and for the briefest moment Mallom felt uneasy. He almost told his friend not to bother with the investigation, but then chalked it down to tiredness. Yet as he turned and walked away, a niggling thought told him this was a mistake.

27

Massey sat on the swivel chair and glanced down at his laptop. Several paragraphs were highlighted, and some sentences underlined. He reached up to the back of his head. A dull ache had settled there and was threatening to develop into a full-blown headache. He stood up, massaging the nape of his neck, but it had little effect. He paced the floor, wanting to leave. It was late and everyone else had already left, but curiosity had got the better of him. His attention shifted to the electron microscope. The tests were complete. In the hours since returning to the lab that morning he'd been working on minute bone and cloth fragments that had been pressed into a small fracture in Mallom's coin. Dating the ducat had been easy enough. Even though most of the date had worn away from the metal surface, he'd cross-referenced it on the database and established it was minted in 1720. But there had been barely enough human material to date, and this was coupled with the fact that it had been exposed to the elements for a very long time. He'd given Mallom as much information as he could but wanted to pursue the investigation further to satisfy his own curiosity. The Carbon 14 and Nitrogen tests had been completed and he was now sure the bone samples were over 200 years old, probably early 18th Century.

What had happened? It had to have been something pretty catastrophic to split the coin and press human tissue into it. It all seemed so incredibly coincidental, almost as if this were a hoax. He'd known Mallom long enough to trust him completely, but nagging thoughts persisted. Surely the intense heat would have incinerated everything, bone and cloth, so how had these fragments survived? Even the ducat had ruptured due to extreme temperature. This whole thing felt wrong. As a scientist he went by facts, but his gut instinct was telling him something else.

He went to the worktop where the coin rested in a small glass dish and prodded it with his tweezers. He stared at it for a moment then carefully turned it over. The glass had blackened as though burnt by some kind of chemical reaction.

Massey shivered, noticing how cold the room had become. He strode toward the window and checked the radiator below it.

'Still hot,' he said to no-one, puzzled.

The scientist removed his glasses and used his lab coat to rub the lenses. Night had descended rapidly outside, and through the blinds he could see that the moon cast a weak, insufficient light over the deserted car park.

'Seven forty-five.'

Where had the time gone?

He returned to his seat and tapped the laptop keyboard. With all the other staff gone, he suddenly and quite unexpectedly felt isolated in the department. He'd worked late before, and it had never bothered him. But he couldn't get Mallom's face out of his mind; he'd looked so grim. Clearly there was something about this coin that had made him uneasy.

The ducat itself remained an enigma. What was the dark residue on the glass dish? Tired or not, he was determined to identify its source.

He returned to the work surface and carefully removed the coin. The base of the dish wasn't just discoloured; something had partly melted the glass.

'What?'

At first, he wondered if his eyes were playing tricks on him, but then he realised that this wasn't just a case of fatigue affecting his senses. Something had generated an enormous amount of energy. What could have isolated such a small area and caused it to react like that? It didn't make sense.

As he tried to consider possibilities he heard a knock at the door.

'Hello.'

Knock ... knock ... knock ... the noise grew louder, an

impatient rap.

Massey strode to the door, opened it and peered down the dimly-lit corridor.

'Anyone there?'

The noise came again, echoing along the deserted walkway.

'Peter, is that you?'

The scientist removed his lab coat. He called out again, flicking off the lights in the lab and retrieving a key from his trouser pocket. As he locked the door, he heard the sound again.

'Is anybody there?'

No answer.

It had to be an employee from another part of the building who had got lost; or perhaps Simmons, the security guard, doing his rounds.

'Excuse me,' he said loudly, rushing down the two flights of stairs. 'Can I help?'

Silence.

Surely whoever was there must have heard him. So why weren't they answering?

The bottom of the stairs was dimly illuminated, with only night lighting in operation.

Ahead, in the double glass entrance doors, Simon's own ghostly reflection stared back at him.

Another noise.

He heard a rasping of breath and swung around, his heart hammering against his ribs.

No-one there.

A bronze statue towered over Simon, its sightless eyes staring down at him. He looked up into the cold, hard face, a representation of Michal Nugent, founder of the Houghton Museum and Research Institute.

He moved along the walkway toward the museum, treading slowly on plush carpet as he passed the main reception desk.

It took him only a moment to realise that the strange sound was nothing more than a breeze rushing through the air-conditioning unit.

That might explain why it had suddenly become so cold; perhaps it was on the blink again. The bloody thing could be temperamental. But he'd never heard it make that kind of noise before.

Perhaps there was no intruder in the building after all. He'd been disturbed by the mystery of the coin. How in God's name had it melted the base of the glass dish? There was no rational explanation for this weird occurrence. It had given him a headache, and he hated headaches. Could the glass have been damaged? It was possible, but he'd need to do further investigations to test for a chemical reaction if that was what this was. Try as he might to make sense of it, he couldn't, and he was starting to feel more than a little unsettled.

The scientist gave a swift anxious look over his shoulder, feeling that someone was there.

Ahead of him, a tall black figure stood perfectly still.

'Simmons, is that you?'

He moved toward it, clenching his fist, feeling the moisture on the palm of his hand. Vapours seemed to be swirling around it.

Massey stopped. This person was much taller than the security guard and he had no desire to find out who it was.

A rasp of air accompanied a cruel, mocking laughter.

'I've called security,' he said, fear chiming in his mind.

Time seemed to have frozen, and in that moment the mist surged towards him.

Massey screamed.

28

Mallom sat in his living-room with his head in his hands. How could such a terrible thing have happened? Page three of the crumpled newspaper on the floor told the story: *'Man found dead in Houghton Museum named as Simon Massey.'*

The Irishman wiped tears from his cheeks. Simon had been found dead on Thursday morning, having suffered a major heart attack. It hadn't taken long for Mallom to realise that something was wrong; it was too much of a coincidence. He couldn't go to the police and ask them to investigate. What would he say? That otherworldly forces were in play?

The guilt was returning, compounded by the fact that he'd inadvertently caused the death of a dear friend.

He rose to his feet at the sound of the telephone ringing, the effort almost too much to bear. Mallom moved slowly along the hallway and lifted the receiver.

'Father Mallom?'

'I'm not a priest anymore, Maria,' he replied with a flicker of irritation.

'I'm sorry.'

'It's okay.'

'I think we should meet as soon as possible. We have a lot to discuss and …'

'Yes,' he interrupted.

'Your house, say Saturday at ten?'

'Yes,' he replied, unable to control the tremor in his voice.

'What's wrong, Seamus?'

There was a long pause.

'Seamus, are you all right?'

'I'm fine,' he lied.

'Please tell me what's wrong?'

'A very dear friend has … has …'

For a moment she heard a sound like muffled sobbing.

'Seamus?'

'I'm all right, just an old fool.'

'You're anything but that.'

'Have you heard about the Houghton Museum?'

'Hasn't one of the staff died from a heart attack and …'

'Yes, Maria. He was called Simon Massey. He was a friend, as was his father.'

'I'm so sorry, Seamus.'

'I know why you've called,' he said with an affected firmness forcing his emotions into check.

'Perhaps now is a good time to discuss this.'

'It is. Simon's death could be linked to the young couple you spoke to me about.'

'I don't understand.'

'The séance.'

'What about it?' she said.

'You spoke of a malevolence within the room.'

'It was the worst experience of my entire life. I have encountered aggressive spirits in the past but nothing like this. I could feel the evil emanating from them. It was as if they were trying to possess the sitters.'

'It must have been quite an ordeal for you, my dear.'

'The worst part of it was that I was trapped. My body was paralysed but I knew full well what was going on. Even though I knew that these apparitions were twisted in mind and spirit, it was nothing compared with the entity that took control of me.'

'Tell me, Maria: this entity, can you describe it for me?'

'Old, very old. He walked the earth centuries ago. He had a lust for destruction; he'd murdered men, women and children and enjoyed it. All I could sense was rage, terrible rage; yet he himself was trapped by something.'

'I see.'

'Seamus, what has your friend's death got to do with any of this?'

Mallom fell silent.

'Please tell me what you are thinking.'

'I didn't think it would get this far.'

'You're not making sense.'

'I had an unusual experience myself. It was terrifying but allowed me to see past events.'

'How?'

'It's hard to explain, Maria. I think that everything that has happened so far, is all connected. Your meeting with the couple, the séance and my experience. What you said about that entity is right. It's my belief that through our connection with each other we have encountered the same vengeful spirit. In life, his name was Francois Santia, and he's one of the vilest men that I've ever come across. I witnessed atrocious acts of violence, and he derived pleasure from them.'

'You speak as though you know him.'

'I do, in a way.'

'Seamus, what do you mean?'

'It was more than just visions, Maria. I was outside of my body when all of this occurred.'

'You had an out-of-body experience?'

'Yes.' His voice was almost a whisper.

'And …?'

'At the end of it was physical proof. A charred coin had been placed on my bed. I think it belonged to Santia.'

'But …'

'Simon was analysing it for me at the Houghton Institute, and now he's dead.'

'Oh, God …'

'Yes, quite. This whole experience has made me realise one thing. I need to see that couple as soon as possible. Their lives are in danger.'

29

Sean sat on the sofa, gazing at the darkness pressing against the window. It was late, and he'd had a bitch of a day at work; too many meetings, too much stress and a pile of paperwork he needed to get through.

He picked up the coffee cup from the table, took a sip. Caffeine at ten o'clock wasn't a good idea, but he needed something to keep him going if he was to stand any chance of finishing marking the rest of the test papers.

'You still working, Sean?' Sophie called out from the kitchen.

'These bloody papers will be the end of me.'

'You need some sleep.'

'Tell me about it.'

He stared at the small stack of papers and sighed. It would probably take at least another twenty minutes to finish off. He took another mouthful of coffee as Sophie walked into the room. She'd shared with him earlier her disturbing experience with the on-screen message at the salon, and neither of them could easily explain it away. It would have been easy to say that it was all down to imagination, but there was more to it than that. It had got to her. She looked tired; the dark blemishes beneath her eyes stood out against the paleness of her skin. She'd been having trouble sleeping, but Sean knew that wasn't all. Although she tired to hide it, she was deeply worried. Christ almighty, so was he; but he supposed they were both playing the same game, not wanting to show it to the other.

'Get some sleep, Sophie,' he prompted.

'You sure?'

He nodded.

'I don't mind staying up a while longer if you …'

'Just go to bed.'

'Okay, but don't stay up too late.' She yawned theatrically

and wandered off toward the bedroom.

The slight patter of rain outside distracted Sean. Small raindrops trickled down the window pane. The world had become something he couldn't fathom anymore. Everything had been so much simpler before his mum had died; he had seen things in black and white. But not anymore. The lines had been blurred, rationality had been tossed out of the window, and now he found himself in a world cloaked in shades of grey. A place where the unbelievable happened.

The sting of grief was suddenly renewed, and what made it worse was guilt, the thought of his mum having been alone, gasping her last breath. His bottom lip trembled. Had she cried out for him? His eyes glistened with unshed tears and his shoulders sagged. Would this emptiness ever disappear? It seemed to hit him when he least expected it.

Sean walked across the room to a small over-stacked bookshelf. He picked up the small diary and flicked through the pages. He read it again, a welcome distraction; the account of the ominous dark figure struggling with someone in a naval uniform and of how they had both vanished.

Still he couldn't understand why his mother would have had this diary. He turned the pages with the question burning in his mind. He reached the last page and noticed something he hadn't seen before. In the bottom right-hand corner were small faded initials.

'E W,' he read, his voice just a whisper.

The handwriting was the same as that in the rest of the diary.

'Of course,' he said. 'Eleanor Webster.' It was his grandmother.

He'd never had a relationship with her; she had died many years before he was born. He knew very little about Eleanor, because his mum had rarely spoken about her. He understood that she had given birth to his mum at a young age and that the family had pretty much ostracised her. Back then it had been considered a huge disgrace for a teenager to have a child. Sean flipped through the pages again, but found nothing else, so he put the diary back on the shelf. Pike's journal rested on top of Abbott Saul's book of prophecies.

Sean massaged the nape of his neck, trying to ease away the tension. He returned to the sofa. Tiredness wasn't forthcoming now that the caffeine was kicking in with a vengeance.

He picked up the TV remote and began switching from channel to channel. A geology documentary caught his eye. Barely hearing the presenter, he stared at the pictures of the rugged exterior of an American cave, its ridges of rock spiralling into blackness. Sean almost leapt from his seat as an explosion of bats erupted from the mouth of the cave, their tiny forms fluttering in a steady stream.

His heart pounded. Bats scared the shit out of him. He could put up with spiders, snakes, or any kind of insects for that matter, but not those things. Crazy as it might be, those little bastards had always frightened him, even when he was a kid. Everyone had something in their closet. Sophie was no exception: she was afraid of the dark. She'd confided to him that she'd felt that way since childhood but didn't know why. Even now, as an adult, she would become agitated in a dark place. The sweating, shaking and increased heart-rate had become less marked over the years, partly because he'd encouraged her to spend more and more time in the bedroom with the lights off. It had been the only way he could think of to get her to confront her fears. But at night, if he wasn't in the bedroom with her, he would often find the door ajar, allowing light to slip into the room.

Sean eventually settled on the Discovery Channel; it was showing a documentary about developments in weapons technology, and this drew him in immediately. It was an intriguing piece focusing on defence research projects. The presenter explained that BAE Systems had developed a device that had the ability to mask a vehicle's infrared signature, making it appear almost invisible to thermal imaging. This camouflage system used modules that looked like cells in a honeycomb; once a vehicle was covered in them, they could be heated or cooled very quickly to allow different patterns to be created.

Sean looked on with interest as the presenter interviewed a man named Powell, a powerfully-built senior naval commander, who talked about *The LCS*, one of the Navy's newest and most technologically-advanced ships. Capable of operation both in near-shore environments and in the open ocean, it fulfilled, Powell said, 'an essential role in the six core areas of maritime defence strategy; deterrence, sea control, forward presence ...'

'But,' the presenter interrupted, 'we've heard of another, much more advanced ship than *The LCS*, called the *DS1* or *Dark Star.*'

The commander shifted uncomfortably in his chair but said nothing.

'It's reputed to be operating at the naval base in San Diego.'

The commander smiled. 'I think I would have heard about it if it was in operation.'

'Well, Commander Powell, we understand that this ship is a crossover, capable of submersion.'

The black commander shook his head dismissively. 'You're talking about *The Ghost*. It can glide on water using a layer of gas generated around its submerged areas at incredibly high speeds. The technology is called supercavitation. It's something we are looking at.'

'No, Captain Powell. The *DS1* is far superior to *The Ghost*. Take a look at this,' the presenter said. He handed across a photograph, and Powell's smile wilted.

The grainy image on screen caught Sean's eye. The ship was midnight black, with chiselled angles like a stealth aircraft but very state of the art.

'From what we can gather,' the presenter continued, 'it is highly classified and rumoured to have an adaptive invisibility cloak much more advanced than *The LCS*.'

The commander sat in silence.

'Our source states that it has advanced weaponry. Can you explain to us what that means?'

Powell refused to confirm the existence of the ship, and the documentary ended with speculation and hearsay, with very little in the way of facts to corroborate the story.

Sean shook his head dismissively and turned off the television.

30

Sean lay in bed, staring up into the darkness. Sophie lay beside him, fast asleep. He listened to her breathing; it seemed uneven, as though her dreams were disturbing her. She'd mumbled something earlier that had been enough to confirm her restlessness.

Eventually, his mind occupied by thoughts of the documentary he'd watched earlier, he himself drifted into a restless sleep, which was filled with dreams.

'It's heading straight for us, Captain Powell!' the young man gasped, looking at the luminescent tracking screen.

Powell wheeled around in his chair.

'Goddam it, evasive manoeuvres,' his voice flushed between the crew's shouts and screeching alarms. 'For Christ's sake get me Communications.'

'Yes, sir.' The control panel sparked, and the young officer was thrown backwards, his fingers badly burned by the blast.

Another man rushed across the dimly-lit operational deck and took control.

'Communications are out, sir,' he called out over the sound of crackling circuitry.

Powell leapt from his chair and joined a thin-framed man hunched over an elongated computer screen. Diagnostic images flashed before him.

The Captain's eyes narrowed. 'What is it?'

'One moment, sir.' The crew member tapped the glass panel in front of him, playing it like a keyboard. 'It's impossible!' His voice carried around the small circular room. He stared at the screen, his eyes narrowing. '"Configuration Unknown." It's not possible. All military and commercial vessels are stored in our system, but this isn't registering.'

'What are you saying?'

'Nothing can track us. The Dark Star's cutting edge, but whatever this is, it's following us move for move.'

'Move for move?'

'Yes, Captain.'

'But this technology is years ahead of anyone else's. Why would someone let us see them if they have superior technology? And why confront us here in the Persian Gulf? Are they here to stop us?'

The Captain walked to his station and slammed down into his chair.

'Submerge. Let's get the hell out of here before we start an international incident.'

'Impossible, sir.'

'What!'

'She won't budge,' a voice called out. 'Systems are non-responsive.'

Powell watched from the middle of the circular bridge, scanning the crew as they worked frantically at their stations, the acrid smoke attacking his nostrils.

'It's stopped moving sir.'

'Weapons.'

'Inoperative.'

The Captain leaned back in his chair, gazing through the night-vision screen at the mist, a deep greyness pressing against the smart glass. He closed his eyes and concentrated, his brow furrowing.

It seeped in, unnoticed at first, steadily invading the bridge, surging through the gloom across the circular floor, flowing over it, smothering it. The mist began to swirl around the feet of the crew, moving upwards.

'Fire!'

Powell's eyes opened. 'Emergency procedures.'

It billowed, rising steadily.

The men shouted to one another as the floor began to vibrate, a strange oscillation like seismic trembling. Tumbling mist rolled across the ceiling, covering everything, and the light faded to nothing.

The rapping increased, becoming louder and faster like a distressed heart. Crew stumbled around blindly, their voices lost in the nightmarish resonance.

Powell leaned forward as hazy shapes moved toward his crew. The *men's screams were wild, bodies staggered and fell lifelessly to the floor. Others lay, roaring in agony as unseen figures loomed over them.*

Something wet spattered Powell. He reeled backwards, wiping crimson liquid from his face.

Soon the sound of strangulated cries was lost in the incessant pounding that emanated from the floor, walls and ceiling.

Sean groaned, drenched in sweat, but could not haul himself free from the nightmare.

The mist, with its shadows, still hid the ambiguous forms from view. They assembled around Powell, a great gathering of unseen phantoms. They shuffled toward him, breaking through skeins of fog.

'Get away from me!' he cried out. 'Get the fuck back!'

He placed a shaking hand on the small glass panel on his arm-rest and spread his fingers. Within moments his prints were scanned; luminous numerals appeared, and he tapped in a five-digit code.

The flash was blinding.

Sean woke up, confused, unsure of where he was. He lay fighting for some clarity, his brow sheathed in sweat. It took a moment to realise the dream was over. He wiped perspiration from his face with a trembling hand, but the image still lingered so vivid, so fresh.

31

Maria was doing her best not to be preoccupied, but it wasn't working. The conversation with Mallom the evening before had disturbed her and led to a restless night. Earlier in the day, she'd assumed she was in control, that much of the worry had been cried out of her system. It hadn't worked. Since the séance, things had been slipping out of her control. Recent events had left her feeling vulnerable.

A small black shadow darted in front of her.

'Oh …'

She froze.

'It's a cat,' she muttered. 'Just a cat.'

She stared into its eyes, yellow and glaring. Its black fur bristled and its tail stiffened. It hissed, leapt onto a low wall bordering a garden and was gone.

Maria felt herself drifting. Mental flashes had been coming and going through the day, and try as she might to stop them, some of these images had remained.

An island. A ship, its silhouette shimmering like a mirage. Fog, steadily surging through the gloom, swirling around the feet of the crew. The sound of men shouting.

She saw a man, yet he was a ghost in another place. A man used to controlling situations now at the mercy of something he could not possibly understand. His eyes fixed on the rolling mist.

It was happening again!

The island smothered by fog. Sailors stumbling around blindly, calling out to one another, their voices lost in a nightmare. The man, his eyes peering through the writhing layers at shadows moving through the fog.

Maria groaned, and the part of her that was remote from this nightmare pitied them, because these shadows were not the man's crew. She heard their whispers, watched their hazy shapes moving through the fog, a great gathering of unseen phantoms.

Screams.

'Stop!' Maria said aloud.

She wouldn't allow this to take control of her, but the image still haunted her thoughts, and with it came a stark realisation. The man on the island was the same entity that had possessed her at the séance. *Santia.*

'Enough,' she said.

She looked down the street, her focus shifting. Belford wasn't the place it used to be; the area had been in decline for some years, flotsam from surrounding districts were closing in, drug-addled youths and gang culture becoming more prevalent. She couldn't lose herself here, it wasn't safe. She rarely ventured out at night but couldn't stay in the house any longer.

Ahead, yellow lamps glowed, offering some comfort from the darkness. The street was wide and the houses running down either side of it were tall, semi-detached properties.

Maria shivered; she'd have to get home before it got much later. She rarely hurried these days, but she walked as quickly as she could, her black coat flapping around her ankles. The air was chilly, and the breeze wafted her dark hair around her face. She adjusted the scarf around her neck, but it did little to stop the shiver that ran down her spine.

Maria had been through a lot. She had experienced some pretty weird things in her life, but nothing like this. The séance had shaken her to the core, and with the news of Simon Massey's death, she felt rattled. Mallom's friend had died from a heart attack, but she wondered what might have induced it. She'd been told he'd started a scientific investigation into a coin found on Mallom's bed after he'd experienced what he described as some kind of a spiritual assault. The idea that spirits could leave things behind after a visitation wasn't new to her. In her experience spirits liked to place objects in the path of loved ones as a sign that they were still around. Many people from the spiritualist church had said they'd found their deceased husband's shirt, tie or keys in an odd place, somewhere they had not put them before. Others spoke of finding feathers. These were good signs from the other side, but Mallom's experience had been bad. She could sympathise with him after the malevolent attack at the séance. She had been the victim of a form of spiritual violation that had terrified her. The hatred, the anger had been so strong it had resulted in the death of one of the gathering. But how? Dark spirits fed off negative emotions, but she'd taken great care when greeting everyone at the séance, appraising them with her gift. It was a kind of failsafe, to prevent unwanted guests from the other side gate-crashing the gathering. Sean, the young man, had caught her attention. He'd suffered bereavement, the loss of someone close, but didn't harbour anything bad. He could have come into contact with some object that had drawn negative energies to the séance.

'Spare some change?'

She gasped in surprise, then looked down and saw a hand thrust out from an odiously stained quilted blanket. The huddled shape beneath it remained hidden from view.

She considered walking past the homeless man, but she reached into her coat pocket, found some loose coins and gathered them together.

'Here,' she said, extending a hand. There was no reply to her offer. The poor soul didn't even try to look up.

'Hello,' Maria said. 'Are you all right?'

There was no response.

'There's a shelter in Buchannan Street. They'll give you hot soup and a bed to sleep in. I'll call for a taxi and pay for it if you want me to.'

Whoever was under there didn't react.

'Please let me do something for you.'

The grimy arm slid backwards.

'You can have a shower and they'll give you clean clothes.' She reached forwards and peeled the tatty blanket away.

The old man stared back, shrivelled and toothless, with deep wrinkles carved into every part of his face.

'I can help.'

His eyes, framed by thick white eyebrows, seemed unresponsive.

'Can you hear me?' She asked, noticing a faint smile beneath those dense white whiskers. 'What can I do for you?'

'You can …'

'What?' she said, encouraged.

'Die!'

Maria stepped backwards, staring into that face; except it wasn't the old man's anymore, it belonged to another.

'Die, bitch!'

She turned and ran as fast as a woman of her age could.

The figure followed.

Sweat prickled her brow and her heart pounded. She reached into her pocket and grabbed her mobile, but the Nokia fell from her grasp and shattered on the floor.

Maria tried to scream but the sound locked in her throat. She thought about hurrying to one of the houses, but the stalker would reach her before she had time.

It's insane, she told herself. She was convinced that the old man had been possessed. An image flared inside her head. *A ship, people mangled, burnt beyond recognition*. She ran blindly, throwing herself forward, aware of the figure closing in behind.

Nearly home, Maria told herself. It was irrational – she could have got to one of the other houses faster – but she just needed to be home, in her own house and away from this madness.

It took everything she had to push herself those last few yards. She blundered forward, key in hand, and opened the front door of her house, slamming it shut behind her. Maria stood with tears of terror glistening in her eyes.

Chest heaving, she stepped forward in the darkness, knocking over the coat stand, before bright light flooded the hall as her fumbling fingers found the light switch.

Thank God. She hoped she'd be safe now.

She reached the telephone and put the receiver to her ear but almost cried out in despair. There was no dialling tone.

She spun around at the sound of something outside but couldn't see clearly through the window. A blurred figure moved fast, heading toward the house.

Maria stood, not daring to move.

Smack! The massive blow shook the front door.

'No!' she cried out.

Another blow followed, and another.

She fell to her knees, holding her head in her hands. Each new blow rekindled psychic flashes.

'Stop!'

Images tore through her mind, causing pain beyond belief.

'Please, make it stop.'

But the final image to reveal itself as the door burst from its hinges made her scream in horror.

'Oh, no,' she muttered. 'Not that. Please, God, not that.'

She crawled along the floor, tears streaming down her face.

'Must get to Mallom,' she whimpered. 'Tell him the truth.'

'Not today, bitch,' the possessed man seethed.

She felt his warm breath against her cheek, and an arm hooked around her throat. A moment later the world turned black.

Mallom heard a scream. He twisted in bed and muttered Maria's name. A voice called out again; it was distant, the sound muffled, but he could sense fear in the tone.

Mallom sighed contentedly as he rose gently from the bed. A moment later he was hovering above his own body and rising steadily. A small azure light sliced through the darkness, its beam broadening as it drew closer.

He moved toward the light and found himself inside a tunnel. Time and space had no hold here, and for the first time in his life he felt truly at peace. The light was soothing, like the warmth of a summer sun.

The tunnel had become a gateway, and even though he knew everything he'd believed in and sought after all his life was at the end, something slowed him down, preventing him from reaching his goal. He felt an urge to push on, but his attention was drawn elsewhere.

A figure floated through the mist toward him, a female form, and as she moved closer, the Irishman could see her shimmering.

As Mallom gazed into her essence, the spirit became sharper, taking on the form of an elderly lady. Her silver hair was swept back, and although physical age had not affected the smooth skin of her face, there was a small scar above her right eyebrow.

'The past events you witnessed must be heeded.'

She drew nearer, and her eyes softened.

'This path, if you choose it, demands sacrifice.'

Mallom nodded.

She lifted her hand and touched his forehead. He fell backwards, tumbling through a black void, and in the moment before he lost consciousness, he heard her voice once more.

'Help him.'

Her words petered out as Mallom's eyes opened.

32

'You look worn out,' Sophie said as she poured herself a cup of tea.

Sean smiled wearily. He slumped into a chair and fumbled with the remote, looking for the latest news headlines. 'I've got a stack of reports to get through by Monday, but I just don't seem to be able to concentrate on anything at the moment.'

'I'm not surprised; its past 9.00. Have a break.'

'Yeah.'

'You need a good night's sleep,' Sophie said, walking into the living-room. 'The reports will wait.'

'I suppose you're right,' he said, staring at the TV, scanning live news streaming along the bottom of the screen.

Muammar Rafika calls for global Jihad after wreckage from suspected US naval vessel washes up on shoreline.

'Sean?'

'Yeah?'

'Are you okay?'

'Sorry, just a bit distracted, that's all,' he replied.

'What is it?'

'You'll think I'm crazy if I tell you.'

'What do you mean?'

He pointed to the Sky news story. 'I had another nightmare last night, except this one involved some kind of state-of-the-art US naval vessel.'

'And?'

Sean rubbed the back of his neck, trying to relieve stiff muscles. 'I don't know. Something invaded the operations centre, some kind of mist. Whatever it was killed the crew.'

'Surely it's nothing more than a bad dream? You probably

saw something on TV and it resurfaced while you were asleep.'

'Maybe. But it was very vivid, almost as if I was watching a movie.'

'Don't read too much into it, Sean.'

'You're probably right. The whole thing is probably just coincidence. Besides, we've enough shit going on without worrying about something else.'

'Exactly,' she smiled reassuringly.

Sean scanned another story.

Two senior CIA officials killed in car bomb explosion in Washington. Islamic militants claim responsibility.

He sat back in his chair, listening to the main news, a live report with Professor Hans Dietrich, who was meticulously examining documents in front of him.

'You say you have unequivocal proof?' asked the grey-haired TV presenter.

The Professor looked toward her. 'Yes, of course. Here it is.'

He handed a file to the presenter, who looked at it and for a moment was lost for words.

'I have approached you directly,' Dietrich continued, 'because I believe it to be in the public interest, and because I now fear for my life. This knowledge has already cost the lives of two CIA operatives. During a two-year investigation into the whereabouts of Dr Raymond Kemp, head of the US biological weapons defence program, I discovered something quite alarming. Dr Kemp, a genius in the field of biological warfare, disappeared four years ago. I can now confirm that Muammar Rafika has had secret meetings with Kemp. Together, they have been working on the development of a genetic weapon.'

'How does it work?' the presenter asked.

'In theory, once all genetic markers have been identified for a specific ethnic group, a virus could be designed to look for them upon entering the body. It would scan the DNA of cells, seeking these genetic markers, and once they were found, the process of infection would begin. This virus would target only people who had the target genetic make-up. This now brings genetic targeting onto our own doorstep. A sustained biological attack with such a weapon would overwhelm medical and civil defence services. What we're dealing with here is a genetically-engineered virus that could wipe out a whole population. There is no vaccine or antibiotic capable of dealing with this kind of threat. This is a doomsday weapon for specific races of people.'

Another man, announced as Tom Marsh, the foreign affairs editor, joined both men at the table.

'Am I correct in saying,' Marsh asked, 'that this biological weapon could also be put into the water supply?'

'It's possible.'

'And you are telling us there's no cure?' he asked.

'We will find one,' Professor Dietrich assured them. 'When we know what we're dealing with we will work to develop a serum, through research and analysis. But this will take time, and we may not have much left.'

'A virus,' Marsh continued, 'can be spread in many ways, by warhead or by simply releasing it into the atmosphere. But is it all rhetoric? There are many who believe, and this may be playing into Professor Dietrich's theory, that Rafika is using Khaled Abdel Taha, a wealthy Saudi dissident, to wage a war against the US and the West.'

'This is obviously a cause for concern,' the grey-haired newsman remarked.

'Absolutely. In this country we have lived by the concept of Mutually Assured Destruction. If they launch at us, we launch at them. But it doesn't work anymore. It might have worked in the 1980s when there were only two real superpowers, but we don't have that today. Plenty of countries possess nuclear capabilities; China, India, Pakistan to name but a few. We have a world community that has the capability to wipe each other out with a single strike. We need to assure the more moderate Islamic Nations that America and its allies are concerned only with terrorist groups that pose a real and definite threat to the West.'

'Why use missiles when, as we have already discussed, they

could simply put this virus in our water supply?'

'Yes,' Marsh replied, 'I believe they could; but these fanatics will want to make a statement first, by taking out a major city to incite as much terror as possible.'

'Where do we stand on missile detection?' the presenter continued.

The young man forced a smile again. 'The US have large computer systems that analyse information from space. They constantly scan the world for signs of launches. Detecting an Inter-Continental Ballistic Missile is relatively straightforward. Stopping it is something else. Defending against an ICBM is tremendously difficult. In layman's terms, if it's launched from one side of the world, it proceeds into space and then re-enters the Earth's atmosphere almost straight down, moving faster than a mile per second.' As he paused for a moment, the presenter interrupted.

'Are you telling us we don't have a system in place that could effectively take out the deliberate launch of an ICBM?'

'If a missile strike,' Marsh continued, 'is launched from anywhere in the world, NORAD will be first to know; but we cannot make any contingency for other types of weapons of mass destruction such as "nuclear backpacks."'

'Correct.' Dietrich spoke as a lecturer might. 'The "nuclear backpack", as you call it, is an extremely lethal and effective weapon. It is basically a cylindrical fusion bomb containing five kilograms of plutonium.' He removed his thick-framed glasses and pinched the bridge of his nose with thumb and forefinger. 'Primarily it is a warhead that is transportable in backpacks by two soldiers, or in a worst-case scenario, two terrorists.' He placed his spectacles back on again. 'It's crude but devastating, with a capability of one kiloton of destruction; and if that massive capability were to be unleashed on London, for instance, it would bring about severe destruction. There would be an enormous loss of life, massive radioactive contamination and chaos unlike anything we've dealt with before.' He leaned forward, placing a hand on the table in front of him. 'There may be as many as a couple of hundred nuclear backpacks in existence today, out there for sale on the black market. We realise that there are those who would use them to dominate and control other people and affect world policy. We are under threat not only of a biological attack but of a nuclear one as well. It is imperative that we act decisively. A full accounting of these weapons must be the government's number one priority, otherwise we could find ourselves at the mercy of …'

A loud rap at the door startled Sean. He glanced at his watch and saw that it was 9.30. He opened the front door slowly, peering into the semi-darkness.

'Forgive the intrusion. My name is Mallom. I need to speak with both of you.'

Sean took in the small man dressed mostly in black. His head was downcast and his eyes in shadow.

'About what?'

'It really is quite urgent.' The man's eyes were still in shadow. 'I'm here on behalf of Maria Kokoschka.'

Sean felt uneasy but beckoned the old man in.

'She thought that I might be able to help you.' He ran a hand through his silver hair, sweeping loose strands back from his forehead.

'Maria told you about the séance?' Sophie said.

The man flicked a glance at her with a look of concern that was all too apparent.

'Dabbling with the occult can be dangerous.'

'What's your interest in this?'

'Many years ago, I worked as an exorcist.'

'Oh,' she said.

'My task in part was to validate incidents of the paranormal. To root out genuine cases that could not be explained away rationally.'

'Which parish do you represent, Mr …?'

'Call me Seamus. I'm not in service anymore.'

'Where are my manners,' Sophie said. 'Please take a seat.'

The young couple sat together on the sofa and watched Mallom sink into the armchair opposite.

'Would you like a tea or coffee?' Sophie asked.

'Not at the moment.' He gave them a warm, tired smile, clasping his hands together as he leaned forward.

'You asked me why I've shown an interest. Well, initially it was to help an old friend; Maria persuaded me to offer my services to you. But since she and I last spoke, I've had something of a disturbing experience myself.'

'Really?' Sean cut in.

The old man looked at him with a weary expectation of ridicule.

'I think what I experienced could be connected to what happened to you.' His penetrating gaze never left Sean. 'Tell me, is your mother still with us?'

'No, she passed away recently.'

'Ah, I see.'

'Why do you ask?'

'Because I believe she contacted me last night.'

'How?'

'During a dream.'

'I don't understand.'

'Tell me, Sean, did your mother wear her hair back off her face?'

'Lots of women do.'

'Did she also have a small scar above her right eye?'

'How could you possibly know that?'

'She asked me to help you, and that's part of the reason I'm here now.'

Sean paused for a moment, unsure of the man, then saw the comforting smile had risen to his eyes.

Mallom broke the silence. 'I think you both need to tell me what's been going on.'

'Where do you want me to start?' Sean asked.

'The beginning's always a good place.'

'Well, I guess, it all started about the time of Mum's death.' Sean averted his eyes for a moment. 'She died from a heart attack, but I'm convinced there was more to it than that.'

'How can you be so sure?'

'Because I think she was quite literally scared to death.'

'Go on,' Mallom urged.

'We spoke to James,' Sophie said, 'a friend of Sean's mum. He discovered her body. He thought he heard laughter coming from the house just before he forced his way in. But there was no-one else there. He checked every room.'

'And?'

'She was sitting rigid in a chair, her eyes wide, staring into the corner of the room.'

Sophie fell silent.

Sean stood up and walked to a small table. 'We found three books at my mum's home.' He picked them up and returned to his seat again. 'This,' he held up the scuffed leather diary, 'is from 1939. A child's record of daily events, you might think; but you'd be wrong. It describes an attack. From what we can gather, the little girl, my grandma, believed she was attacked by a dark figure, then saved by a man in naval uniform. These figures, she says, fought with each other, then evaporated.'

'Do you mind?' Mallom pointed to another book on Sean's lap.

'No, not at all.' He passed the frayed volume to the priest.

'*A libri of oraculum,*' the old priest said, his voice but a whisper. He opened it to the first page and ran a hand across a large, intricately designed black cross. '*In nomine Jesu Christi, hoc est verbum et haec veritas.*' Mallom stared long and hard at the book before speaking again.

'This was at your mother's house?'

'Yes.'

'This volume is not only incredibly valuable but contains a collection of apocalyptic prophecies by Abbot Saul. He was burnt at the stake for witchcraft, in the 16th Century. I see someone has already translated the Latin predictions.'

He scrutinised a passage underlined twice, in red ink.

Before the fall of man, through the mists of time, thrice it shall come, a leprous vessel, the bringer of great evil and destruction to mankind. Heed the warning, before my prophecy is fulfilled.

'If you think that's curious, look at this.'

'*The Journal of William Pike.*' Deep lines creased Mallom's brow. He scrutinised each entry in the book, right up to the last one.

'The journal ends abruptly,' Sophie tore him from his thoughts.

'That it does.'

'They managed to reach Tornave and Pike gave the order for his men to be armed, ready to make their stand against Santia.'

'Yes, that's how it happened,' Mallom said.

'How can you know that?'

'Because I saw what was left of the ship sink.'

'That's not possible.'

'I didn't think so either, until a couple of nights ago. I was spiritually attacked, and during that assault experienced supernatural visions.'

From what he'd read of the Captain's journal, Mallom was able to fill in historical gaps and describe the atrocities on the Haitian island, the mutiny by Santia and the eventual destruction of *Gospall* at the hands of Pike.

The young couple listened intently, until Mallom had finished.

'I think you might want to look at this as well,' Sean said as the retired priest put Pike's journal down on the floor near his feet. 'It's a copy of *The Times* dated 1939.' He tapped the musty newspaper with his finger, drawing Mallom's attention to a highlighted headline.

Slaughter on the Streets of London. Three Mutilated Bodies Discovered.

Mallom noticed another piece of underlined text.

Child attacked by spectre.

And another,

Ghostly ship sighted in Grime Street.

'Interesting,' he said.
'Here's something else.' Sophie gave the old Irishman a copy of the *Globe.* He studied the headline.

Two bodies found in Grime Street.

Other reports caught his eye, pertaining to a strange mist and spectral vessel, all in the same vicinity.
'This occurred in 1914,' he said. 'We need to find some kind of connection. It's here, I'm sure it must be.'
Most of the evening was spent going through Sean's story in fine detail again and meticulously examining the evidence at hand.
Sophie eventually broke the silence. 'The *Globe* and *The Times* talk of murders, although the time period between them is 25 years. But those killings took place in the same area.'
'Clever girl,' the exorcist said. 'So, we now know where this paranormal activity will occur.'
Sean was puzzled as he stared into Mallom's tired eyes.
'Where?'
'Grime Street,' he replied. 'Both murders occurred in the same location.'
'Forgive my ignorance, but why of all places would a street in London be the focal point of supernatural activity?'
The Irishman was staring at Sean, and in his expression, there was little in the way of surprise.
'Evil knows evil.'
'What do you mean?' Sophie asked.
Mallom flicked a glance at the young woman.
'Grime Street has a dark history. I gained an understanding of spiritual hotspots when I was an investigator. This is one of them. There are records from the 1560s concerning the village that used to stand there. All the inhabitants were executed for practising witchcraft and the whole place burned to the ground.'
Mallom continued. 'A hundred years later, more villagers

were put to death, for taking part in rituals involving human sacrifice, orgies and the like. A place that is inherently bad can draw evil to it.'

Sean felt the old man's eyes boring into his.

'I sense a malevolence around you, and it's been there for some time. The visions you spoke about earlier might have been intended to drive you insane.'

'I don't understand.'

'Because of your grandmother.' He paused for a moment. 'Did she not survive an attempt on her life when she was a little girl?

'Yes. Mum didn't talk much about her, but from what little I do know about grandma, she died in mysterious circumstances.'

'What do you mean?'

'Mum never went into detail.'

'And,' Mallom continued, 'your mother died from an unexpected heart attack.'

'What are you trying to say?'

'Don't you think it's a little strange that both your mother and your grandmother died mysteriously? I think whoever, or whatever, attacked and eventually killed them wants you now.'

'Why?'

Mallom's eyebrows knitted together. 'Maybe because, like your mother, you have uncovered some secrets of *Gospall.* Or maybe the driving force is purely revenge.'

'Yes, it's beginning to make some kind of sense. Grandma's diary spoke of an attack by a dark figure. It doesn't take a genius to work out that was Francois Santia. And I'm pretty sure that the man in a naval uniform who came to her defence was William Pike.'

'That would explain part of what's going on, Sean, but there are other forces at work here. You are just a small part of it.'

'If the visions were intended to push me over the edge, then what about the nightmares?'

'My feeling is that these nightmares could be some kind of warning.'

'A warning?'

Mallom saw Sean's eyes flick to the TV and back again.

'What is it, Sean?'

'Nothing.'

'Are you sure?'

'Yeah, it's just my imagination.'

'I think it's going to be a long night,' Sophie said. 'Would you like a coffee now, Father?'

'Thank you,' he replied. 'Black, no sugar.'

'Sean?'

'Please.'

She stood and made her way into the kitchen.

'She's on edge,' said Sean. 'Christ, we both are!'

Mallom was silent.

'Sorry, Father, I didn't mean to offend.'

'No offence taken.'

'It's just that it's all so confusing, so frightening. We're both struggling to deal with it.'

'You've been through a terrible ordeal, but you need to be strong, both of you. I'm not going to lie to you. This thing is going to get worse, much worse.'

Sean nodded.

'We must meet whatever is behind it head on.' Mallom leaned forward. 'We will get through this, Sean.'

There was still much to learn from the old documents. The search continued as Mallom busied himself trying to bring some kind of order to the records, painstakingly combing through and scrutinising every scrap of information. Eventually he slumped back into his chair, exhausted.

'We're missing something.' Mallom looked down and began rifling through the old newspapers. He stared at the headlines again.

Slaughter on the Streets of London. Three Mutilated Bodies Discovered.

He focused on the date, 1939, then shook his head. 'The key

question is, when will this supernatural activity occur?' He studied the *Globe* dated 1914, and yet another grisly story:

Two bodies found in Grime Street.

'What's that?' he muttered, looking from the papers to Abbot Saul's book of prophecies. Mallom lifted the volume so that the table lamp shone through one of the pages. Running across one of the predictions were numerals, almost invisible to the eye, yet the light allowed them to be read. He squinted, realising that they formed a date.
'Good Lord,' the Irishman said, raising his head sharply.
'What is it?'
'It's going to happen on 22 October.'
Sean stared at him, his face a mask of incredulity. 'That's tomorrow night.'

33

Seamus Mallom stood by the window in his living-room. It was a quiet morning, just a couple of people in the street: an elderly man with a newspaper folded under his arm, and a short squat woman walking a shih tzu.

Where on earth was Maria?, he wondered. She should have arrived more than an hour ago. Surely she couldn't have forgotten. They'd agreed on it only a couple of days before. He needed to talk to her and get some insight into what might lie in store for them that night. He was hoping she might accompany them to Grime Street. He could certainly use her abilities, for God only knew what they would be up against.

The television caught his attention. It was showing a news bulletin dominated by a report about three explosions. Manchester, Birmingham and Central London had been hit, and the loss of life was staggering: 320 victims so far.

'Good Lord,' he said aloud.

Another report spoke of a detonation in Paris and another in Luxembourg. He picked up the remote and turned off the TV, sickened by what he had seen.

Mallom finished his tea but couldn't help feeling pity for the families of the poor souls who had lost their lives in the senseless terrorist attacks. More bombings had been threatened, and that thought made him shudder. He made his way into the hall and picked up the telephone, slowly tapping Maria's number into the key pad. He waited for a few moments.

No answer.

Mallom replaced the receiver, a frown adding more creases to his brow. He caught his reflection in the wall-mirror, and something else. A word was beginning to form on the glass as though finger written in condensation on a bathroom cabinet.

YOU

Then another.

ARE

He blinked, but wasn't afraid; there was no hostility here. He didn't sense or feel that he was threatened in any way.

Another word appeared.

BEING

He focused, straining his eyes, waiting for more.

Slowly, it materialised.

DECEIVED

'Deceived by whom?' he found himself saying. 'Who is trying to communicate with me?'

MAR …

The name faded before it was completed.

'Please, tell me. Who are you?'

Nothing.

Mallom picked up the receiver and redialled.

This time, someone answered. Even before the voice spoke, Mallom knew what he was going to be told.

34

The night was closing in ominously fast. Father Mallom, Sophie and Sean eventually found Grime Street, although it had been a hell of a drive across London. All thoroughfares in every direction were congested, and this had made the journey extremely frustrating. Recent terror attacks across the country had people worried, especially in the capital. Two tube stations had been targets of suicide bombers. Police had killed one of the terrorists but the other had detonated his vest, packed with explosives. Holbrook station hadn't stood a chance; fifty people were feared dead and the toll was rising. More attacks had been threatened by a group of British-born Islamic extremists who had in recent months been involved in a spate of car bombings, kidnappings and random acts of violence. Terror had come to the streets of London, and people were responding to the threat. Muammar Rafika's calls for a global Jihad were being repeated at an alarming rate, and security forces were now faced with not just well-planned attacks but indiscriminate attacks by individuals and groups. People were leaving the capital, if they could.

They had all been shocked to learn of Maria Kokoschka's murder, coming so quickly after Simon Massey's death. It was an alarming twist of events that made them all realise just how dangerous the situation was. Mallom was wearing his vestments, saying that it was time to remember his vows, to be a priest again, even if not sanctioned by the church.

Grime Street was some way out of the city. The whole area had been earmarked for a development of apartments and three- and four-bedroom homes. Wire mesh fencing stood tall, grey and ugly, erected around its perimeter. There was a dampness in the air and a distinct smell of dust. Most of the remaining houses were derelict and in various stages of decay, as if residents had abandoned the entire street and left it to die a slow death. Sean's eyes darted around the surrounding wasteland. A large 'No Trespassing' sign hung from the double gates.

Sophie pointed to the padlock.

'I hope you don't expect me to climb that fence,' she said. There was no humour in her voice.

Sean tried the gate. 'Shit.' It wouldn't budge. He forced it forwards then pulled it backwards, but still no joy.

'Well that's just great,' Sophie muttered. 'How are we going to get in?'

Sean stepped back, surveying the fence.

'I suppose I could climb, but …'

'Wait. Over there,' Mallom said, pointing to some heavy twists of wire a few feet away from them.

'Well spotted,' Sean said, and rushed to the car. As the boot light came on, he rifled through his belongings and removed a pair of winter gloves.

'Be careful, Sean,' warned Sophie, 'that wire is sharp.'

'I will,' he grunted as he peeled it back. 'Someone's had a good go at it already. It's pretty weak,' he said, ripping it open.

Each of them in turn used the hole to enter Grime Street.

They looked down the darkened street, its emptiness an oppressive thing. A stale heaviness hung in the atmosphere like floating decay. Mallom's purple stole flapped against his dark cassock, like a winged creature desperate to escape.

'Can you sense it?' he asked with a tiredness in his voice.

'What do you mean?' Sean asked.

'There's something here.'

'Are you sure?'

'You must prepare yourself. Do not accept anything that you see or hear without question.' He leaned in toward them. 'Take great care,' he said. 'What we discover tonight might well destroy us.'

He made the sign of the cross, blessed himself. 'At times it will be terrifying, but we must stay together and have faith.'

Sean and Sophie listened, hanging on to his every word. The

implication of the old man's words hit home.

'Listen to me.' He placed a placating hand on Sophie's shoulder. 'I know that you're afraid, but I must be truthful with you. There are malign forces here now, I'm sure of it.'

As Sophie looked into the old man's face she was suddenly frightened and felt like running, getting the hell away from this place.

The Irishman's eyes returned to Sean. 'You think that over the past few weeks you have had the most frightening experiences of your lives. I can assure you that they were nothing compared to what awaits us tonight. So be afraid, but don't let it control you. Have faith, it is your armour. Evil is insidious, devious and ultimately deceptive. We must take great care.'

He removed his hand from Sophie's shoulder.

'Something has been unleashed, something terrible,' Mallom continued. 'Tell me, do you both have faith?'

'I believe in God,' Sean said. 'But not religion.'

Sophie nodded in agreement.

'Faith and each other are all we have, but that may not be enough.'

Sean had started to feel a little too sure of himself, and that could be every bit as dangerous as fear, perhaps even more so. He peered into the darkness that was Grime Street and once again felt anxious. He really didn't want to go down there but knew he must.

35

The moon glowed faintly, casting a sickly glow over Grime Street. Mallom walked ahead of them, along the dim road, his shoulders slightly rounded, his footsteps loud against the ground. Sophie followed, almost dwarfing the priest.

They avoided the debris that littered the road, which separated tall grey-bricked houses standing like crumbling monuments to the dead. To their right stood an old Victorian building, its shattered shell no longer a home.

'You feel it as well?' Sophie whispered.

Sean nodded. Something within the silence, a tension, like pulsing energies, was slowly building.

His phone pinged, and he slipped it from his pocket.

'Who is it?' Sophie asked.

Sean didn't reply, he just looked down, puzzled by the text. Odd looking symbols flashed intermittently.

'What?' Sophie caught the disturbed look on his face.

'Have you ever seen anything like this before?' He turned the screen so she could see for herself.

'That's weird!'

Sean tapped the handset with his finger, but the power ebbed away. 'Maybe the battery's dead?' he said, trying to mask his unease. He slid his iPhone back into his pocket as Sophie voiced her own concern.

'My phone's the same.'

He saw the blank screen and her worried expression as she fiddled with it, almost willing the thing to work.

'Those symbols, Sean, I saw them for a moment too.'

He looked back to her phone. No power.

'What's going on?' Sean asked.

'That won't work here,' Mallom said.

'I don't understand.'

'It takes a lot of energy for a manifestation to occur. A fluctuation in the electromagnetic fields usually follows. What is happening around us will drain any electrical devices.'

They continued their journey down the deserted street, unwilling to be distracted. Sean looked across at the jagged-eyed windows of the surrounding buildings. He stopped for a moment, slid a torch from the pocket of his jeans and shone its powerful beam in the direction of one of the houses.

A gaping hole revealed a dilapidated room. The air was musty and dank, the walls were little more than bare brick and matted with cobwebs, but in the corner of the room was a shadow that seemed deeper than the darkness around it. Sean's attention was quickly drawn to the anomaly, and his heart began thudding. *Was it starting to move?*

'What is it?'

'Christ Almighty.' He whirled around toward Sophie, who had crept up behind him. 'You scared the shit out of me.'

'Sorry,' she tugged at his arm. 'Let's get back to the road. I don't like it here.'

'Okay,' he said, as she pulled at him again. He resisted the urge to share what he thought he'd seen, not wanting to alarm her, but he had the weirdest feeling that he was being watched. The notion made him stop.

'Sean?'

He blinked.

'What's wrong?'

He gave a brief shake of his head. 'I thought … Never mind. It's nothing.'

'It's started,' stated Mallom. He pointed toward the end of the street. 'Shine your torch down there.'

Sean complied, but as the circle of light swept along the road, the beam started to diminish as though its luminosity was being devoured. The crawling darkness approached as if it were a tangible thing.

'It's a trick of the light,' Sophie said, moving backwards. 'Check the batteries.'

Sean didn't have the time. The darkness edged closer,

growing all the while, until it was like a huge black bank of cloud, obscuring everything.

Mallom was lost to prayer, seemingly oblivious to it. Only when it was almost on top of him did the old man react. He raised a hand and traced the sign of the cross, staring commandingly at the awesome black mass, then repeated the gesture, reciting some words in Latin. It retreated slowly along Grime Street before disappearing from view.

'What the hell was that thing?'

The Irishman eyed Sophie serenely.

'Illusion, my dear,' he said, matter-of-factly. 'Evil will attack in many ways. It will force you to face things you fear most and use them against you. Be ready to …' He stopped mid-sentence, his eyes searching the wasteland around him.

'There's a distinct coldness here,' he said. 'It's not the first time I've felt it, but it is always present in places that need spiritual cleansing.'

Sean watched Mallom walk forward, a breeze ruffling his hair. The moon was brighter now and bathed the ruins about them with a harsher glow. As irrational as it was to Sean, it seemed the land was frozen beneath the moon's glare.

Something flew across his line of sight, disappearing through a glassless window into the shadows of a derelict house, its fluttering movement erratic.

'Listen,' Sean whispered.

The sound was distant at first but was approaching fast; a frantic beating of wings, growing louder.

He caught a quick glimpse of the moon before it became lost in a dark, writhing mass. A great gathering of bats descended from the sky at an alarming speed. They swooped down, their screeches drowning out all other sounds. Sean's heartbeat raced almost in time with the flutter of approaching wings, and the torch fell from his hand onto his foot before rolling onto the ground. He stood unsteadily, his legs useless, as if his muscles had somehow wasted. His fear of bats was overwhelming him.

They circled Sean and began swarming over him. He tried to fight them off amid the turmoil of flapping wings, lashing out wildly at first but soon growing weaker as more creatures joined the terrible onslaught. Sean fell to his knees, beating at himself, but it was useless, his body was smothered by the creatures. They plucked at his clothes, their teeth digging into his back, neck and throat, tearing and raking flesh. More bats settled on him. They struck from the shrieking mass, ripping slivers of skin from his face like paper tissue.

The black-winged creatures snatched at his eyelids and raked at his arms and legs. Everything was a blur, but though the pain was excruciating, Sean could hear Sophie screaming and Mallom calling out to him.

'It's a phantasm, an illusion. Reject it.'

Sean closed his eyes against the madness. He soon realised that this whole experience was just a ghastly nightmare with no substance. He heaved a sigh of relief and tried to stand but staggered backwards, then felt himself falling, his senses numbed. Sean's eyes closed as he slumped to the ground, and when he opened them again the street spun dizzily about him.

A face swam into focus.

'Sean. Are you all right?' Sophie asked, fighting back tears.

He gave a brief shake of his head. 'The bats …' he murmured, as he was helped to his feet by the former priest.

'There were no bats,' Mallom replied.

'But you saw them, didn't you?'

'Yes, but they were a product of your own mind.'

'So how come both of you could see them?'

'Because they were a visual projection from your own mind. Your fear of bats was used against you to exploit your own inner weakness, and we were forced to watch you suffer.'

'But …'

'Just as the dark was Sophie's fear,' the Irishman continued.

Sophie turned to Mallom.

'There's no time for explanations,' the exorcist said quietly.

They both heard him, and something else; a child's laughter. The Irishman glanced around as the mocking voice drifted toward him.

'Who's there?' Mallom's voice was no more than a whisper.

More laughter floated through the night, weird and chilling. It lasted for only a few moments before fading away to nothing, but the silence that followed was not comforting.

'Who's there?' he repeated, his face pale in the silvery light. *No answer.*

The stillness of the night had become a smothering silence, almost choking off the air itself.

Mallom moved away from the young couple. He stood with his head tipped to one side, listening to another sound.

'What is it?' Sean called out.

'Listen,' he replied, his face set in grim lines.

They all heard it this time, a solitary child's voice, clear and distinct like a choirboy's.

'Oh, dear Lord,' Mallom said. He lowered his head as it continued.

A little boy stood before them, illuminated only by moonlight, his hands pressed together as if in prayer, and out of his yawning wide mouth came a softly sung hymn.

'Numberless toils and suffering,
'bloody sweat, mockery, threat,
'anguish till thy sinking breath,
'pray to God before thy death.'

The old man crossed himself, repeatedly, and muttered something.

Sean thought he heard him say the name Jacob but couldn't be sure. He was too mesmerised by the small figure. It stared back at them through dead eyes, upturned in their sockets.

With nightmarish slowness the boy's head turned toward the exorcist, and the singing stopped.

The image had been drawn from deep within the old man's mind, and even though he clearly grappled with the ugly memories, they pushed all other thoughts aside. An old nightmare had returned, rushing toward him with horrifying clarity.

'No,' the Irishman protested. He opened his eyes and the

boy grinned.

'You're not Jacob!'

He lowered his gaze.

'*Abnego te,*' his voice was firm. '*Discede in nomine Christi.*'

Mallom moved toward the apparition in murmured prayer. Sean and Sophie followed close behind.

'*Abnego te in nomine Christi,*' the priest continued. '*In nomine Christi.*'

Yet the figure lingered, almost as real as any of them.

'Be gone in the name of Christ.'

He moved toward it.

'*Abnego te … abnego te … abnego te.*'

The vision shimmered like a painting doused in turpentine, becoming distorted and blurred before fading to nothing. All that remained was chilling laughter, and that faded slowly until there was silence once more.

Mallom faltered. The illusion had been transient, but its effect lingered. He took a step backwards and stumbled.
Sean grabbed him by the arm preventing him from falling. 'Are you okay?'

'Thank you,' Mallom said with tears glistening in his eyes.

'Seamus, are you strong enough to …'

'Don't worry about me,' he cut in. 'I'll be just fine.' He smiled at the young couple. 'It's playing on our fears and weaknesses, even your concern for me. Nothing can be allowed to stop us. Do you understand, both of you?'

They agreed.

'Something other than the creature I saw on the Haitian island, is controlling this series of events.'

'What do you mean, creature?' Sean asked.

'From what I've discovered, it's a dark spirit known as an Ioa and is associated with voodoo folklore. But there is another force here that has not revealed itself.'

What was it about this place that inspired such dread? Sean thought. There was a canker here. It was as if the ground were sour, the surface a façade for something dark, something that lurked deep within the earth. Something was certainly wrong about this place.

He moved ahead with the exorcist, who walked with an awkward hobbling motion, his arthritic legs struggling to keep pace. Sean slowed down a little, noticing just how slight Mallom was when he came alongside him, although his presence was commanding. His gait might have been withered by age but not his spirit.

Sean heard a noise and glanced around warily. It was a low rumble, growing louder by the moment.

The shadow of a shattered house stretched in front of them like a ghostly marker, directing them somewhere he didn't want to go.

Why hadn't Mallom heard anything?

He felt his heart beating faster.

Or had he?

It became louder, more disquieting, like a seismic throb.

Both men stopped dead.

It returned again, as though the ground had been jabbed from below.

A coldness gripped Sean when he looked over his shoulder and realised just how far behind Sophie was.

She was standing, almost frozen in place.

'Stay there,' he called out, moving toward her, with Mallom close behind.

A deep, ominous rumbling rose up through the bowels of Grime Street until the surface started to vibrate. Its intensity increased violently, an uncontrollable seismic wave. They staggered, then fell.

Sean felt it deep down in the ground, something moving. The pounding was getting stronger, and for a moment they remained still. Sean placed a hand on the ground, hoping that it would stop, but instead it just got stronger. Buildings shook, and he felt a gush of panic.

'What's going on?' he called out, but his words were lost in the chaos.

Sean got to his feet, as did Mallom with a grunt. Both men called out to Sophie, moving toward her while trying to protect their heads from falling debris.

Sophie screamed as she was brought to the ground by the sheer force of the tremors. All around them buildings shook fiercely, and fissures appeared in the walls of derelict houses before masonry began to fall.

They helped Sophie to her feet, but another jolt sent the old man staggering sideways, while the young couple clung onto each other.

'We need to get away from here, Sophie!' Sean called through a cloud of dust.

He coughed, swiping a hand in front of his face. Soon they were enveloped in a fine grey powder that stung their eyes. He looked through the tainted clouds swirling about him, his hair and clothes covered, and felt the earth shake crazily.

Sean tried to blink away dust as the whole street shook once more.

'What the hell's happening?' he called out to the priest.

'It's testing us.'

There were more sounds, more jolts, as bricks continued to fall around them, and from nowhere something smashed into Sean's back. Luckily the small piece of rotting timber shattered on impact, but it still hurt like hell.

'Where did that come from?' He looked around confused and frightened but couldn't locate the source. 'We've got to go,' he called out, wincing against the pain.

'Wait!' Mallom shouted.

A tall Victorian villa shuddered, the moonlit sky visible through the windows of the roofless house.

'Careful now,' Mallom told them as they watched the fabric of the building falter. It leaned toward them with a horrendous groan.

'It's going to collapse!' Sophie gasped.

'No, it's not!' the priest replied.

'Yes,' Sean raised his voice. 'It is.'

'It's not!' the priest reiterated.

The old man sank to his knees and closed his eyes. He made the sign of the cross and placed his hands together in prayer.

'Seamus!' Sean shouted, but the Irishman didn't respond.

'What's he doing?' Sophie cried out with a look of incredulity.

'We've got to get out of here,' Sean replied. 'It's too dangerous.'

'What about …?' As she spoke, the ground shook so violently that they were pitched forward.

'Seamus,' Sean screamed, but the Irishman was lost in prayer.

'Why won't he answer?'

Sean gave a brief shake of his head, then grabbed Sophie by the wrist.

'We're getting the hell away from here.'

'What about Mallom?' she protested.

'He'll have to take his chances.'

'But …'

'We have to hurry before this place rips itself apart.'

Sophie gave a small cry, and as Sean turned he froze. The shaking culminated into one great juddering motion and the building toppled onto all three of them. Instinctively the couple threw their arms across their faces, and for a moment amid the chaos all Sean heard were Sophie's screams.

36

Silence replaced the turmoil and they lowered their arms cautiously. There was no dust, debris or rubble. The street was as it had been before the quake.

Thank God,' Sean said breathlessly.

Sophie opened her mouth.

'Imagination,' he said, answering her unspoken question.

'But …'

'Don't try to make sense of it; this is a fucked-up place.'

Head bowed and shoulders hunched, the exorcist seemed unaware of what had occurred. He was still locked in prayer, as though trying to protect them from something else.

Sean felt it first. It was as if all the mud, clay and murkiness that lay beneath them wanted to reach up and pull them down. It was a crazy notion. How could he possibly be sensing or feeling that?

'Impossible,' he muttered, but Sophie had felt it too, he was sure of it; he could tell by her anxious expression. A wave flowed along the street, then another, as if a stone had been dropped into a calm body of water and the ripple was spreading outwards. The skin of the earth was changing. Sean watched the undulating earth move with the fluidity of the ocean, rising and falling with a regularity that was mesmerising.

'Over there!' Sophie screamed. She was pointing beyond the priest, where odd shapes were moving.

Sean blinked, but the illusion didn't fade. Whatever these things were, they appeared to belong deep underground, their abode darkness, not light.

They moved beneath the street, lifting their belly scales, hauling themselves forward. Sean saw the scales of their backs as they just broke the surface, deep brown and rough as pumice.

One of them stopped, and for a moment seemed oblivious to their presence.

Sean froze when it moved suddenly and with great speed. It sent a shuddering wave down its frame, rolling its body from head to tail. Portions of it lifted, pushing against the now thin skin of earth as it moved snake-like toward all three of them.

Sean didn't wait any longer. He dragged Sophie away from the advancing monstrosity.

'Seamus!'

It was moving toward Mallom at an incredible speed.

'Seamus,' he cried again.

The old man didn't acknowledge him but remained kneeling in prayer.

They called out again, watching as the creature broke through the earth, its enormous body uncoiling, its mouth gaping with needle-sharp teeth. It rose above Mallom, ready to strike.

Sickened by the inevitable outcome, they took another step backwards.

The exorcist fell silent, his hands clenched tightly together in defensive prayer.

More serpents reared high into the air, their avaricious jaws wide. They descended on the old man, and for the briefest instant his whole body flared, an aura pulsating outwards, expanding until the street was illuminated by an almost blinding incandescence.

It was over within a heartbeat.

'Sophie? Sophie, are you okay?'

Sean gently pulled Sophie's hands from her face but could see that she was still lost to the effect of the light.

The peculiar waves had disappeared, and the ground was still. The only sound was Mallom's voice, low and whispery. These phantasms had malevolent intentions but not enough power to harm them physically. Sean had felt their insidious will weaving through his mind, like an icy mist mutating reality. What it had conveyed was their contempt and sheer hatred. The longer he, Sophie and Mallom remained in that place, the more certain Sean became that they would die there. But a physical attack had not happened. Not yet, anyway.

Sophie was breathing hard. Her body was trembling, and Sean wondered if it was because of the cold or just plain fear. Mallom had said it would be difficult, but he hadn't expected this. Sophie had coped well, but there was only so much either of them could take.

The emanations from the structures that surrounded Sean induced an inner fear, like a stalking predator waiting to take hold of him, assault his mind with a wickedness he was sure was inherent within every single stone of every miserable house. Was strength of will enough to oppose this insanity?

The buildings seemed to leer back at him. As the priest prayed, Sean summoned enough courage to approach one of the rows of derelict terraced houses. Shadows moved inside; shapeless things without substance.

'Sean.' Sophie's voice wafted across the street. 'Come back over here. It's not safe there.'

'All right,' he replied.

'Sean!'

This time he turned away and hurried back to Sophie.

'Stay with me.' Sophie was staring beyond him at the cluster of houses. 'I really don't want to be on my own, not here.'

'Okay,' he conceded, looking toward Mallom, still lost in prayer.

'What's that?' Sophie asked. She gave him a gentle nudge with her elbow. 'Listen.'

He heard it this time, a scratching of claws against earth.

'Oh, God. Rats.'

'No, it's not,' Sean replied. 'It's coming from over there, underground.'

Sophie shrieked when she caught sight of something prodding at the earth from below. 'There!' She pointed toward the source of the noise.

The rubble moved, as dark soil was pushed to the surface, spilling onto the grey powdery surface, staining it with fresh earth.

'What the hell's down there?' She gave another cry when small, skeletal fingers burst through the cracked earth. The rest of the hand reached up, pushing until the whole arm was exposed. The limb could have belonged to a malnourished child, although the skin was pale and encrusted in grime.

Another hand appeared through the muck, then another; more and more of them began to appear. Sophie shrieked as something clammy grasped her ankle. Small fingers curled around her leg, yanking it violently. She crashed to the ground, screaming as more bony hands reached out, clawing at her face. Sophie wrenched her foot away from the thing still clinging to it.

Sean kicked several grime-smeared limbs away, grabbed Sophie by the shoulders and hoisted her to her feet and away from the sea of writhing hands.

'Mallom,' he cried out, unable to control his rising panic.

Claws raked their legs, tugging, pulling them down, their grip unrelenting, too strong to break. Sean tried to lash out with his feet, but the things held him fast.

'For God's sake,' he screamed again. 'Do something!'

The exorcist rose from his knees and made the sign of the cross. He faced them and raised his arms into the air. '*Dominus salvatio mea? Non timebo malum quod tu es cum me, deus meus, potestas mea, domine omnipotens, domine pacis, pater saeculorum.* God our Father,' he continued, 'creator and defender of humanity, I humbly beg for your protection. Be gone, demon, in the name of Christ.'

The atmosphere of this place was becoming more dangerous by the moment. It was possible to believe that the bodies of those iniquitous inhabitants of Grime Street might lie beneath its surface. Its history was dark and blood-drenched, and these fleshy stalks rising out of the ground were another manifestation of that evil.

Mallom stood holding a small round pendant out in front of him. '*Ut piisima et Immaculata caelorum Domina vos protegat atique defendat.*' The recitation was hushed, but the words seemed to exude an unseen power. The undulating mass of erratic movement ceased, and the grubby limbs began to sink, retreating as swiftly as they had emerged.

'Seamus,' Sophie asked as they approached the exorcist. 'What were they?'

'The question is,' he said, placing the pendant into his pocket, 'who were they?'

She looked on, confused.

'This is where the dead are,' Mallom continued. 'I warned you about Grime Street's history. You can feel that hatred and thirst for violence yourself. It's becoming more and more oppressive. It's tapping into an existing malevolence and amplifying it. All the manifestations generated so far have been evoking your innermost fears. But I suspect that all of this has been just a prelude to the main event.'

37

'Look!' Sean called out, staring at the far end of the street. An unusual yellow mist had begun to form, and it was moving toward them incredibly quickly. A coldness crawled up his spine.

'This is weird,' Sophie said.

'It's just fog,' Sean muttered. It was a lame attempt to rationalise the phenomenon, but he knew that reality was out of control. The mist swiftly spread along the breadth of the street, its murky vapour enveloping everything in its path.

Sean spotted Mallom slipping a small silver crucifix from his pocket. The priest used it to mark a six-pointed star in the dust around them, then drew a curved line that intersected each point. Sean watched with growing curiosity as the exorcist began scrawling names around the perimeter of the circle: *Tetragrammaton, Jehovah, Jeiah* and *Emmanuel.* Mallom drew another circle around the previous one.

'What are you doing?' Sean asked.

'This area is being prepared as a refuge.' The exorcist began sprinkling something between the two circles. 'Vervain, a holy herb that is extremely powerful against demonic attacks. On no account must either of you step out of this circle.'

Sean turned to Sophie. He saw the pallor of her skin and the fear in her face; a raw visceral terror.

Sophie raised a trembling arm and pointed at the mist. Dark spectral shapes were moving in the accumulation, surging toward them. Disembodied voices, deep and whispery, swelled to a ghostly chorus of wails and cries. Sean wanted to clasp his hands over his ears to shut out the horrendous sound.

'Souls of the damned,' Mallom shouted above the uproar.

The fog swirled around them as though it were somehow alive, testing the circle's strength, constantly probing but unable to break through its protective boundary. The circle was keeping the mist out, retaining within its confines some kind of invisible force that guarded those inside.

How could this be possible? It was like staring through a window on a foggy night; everything on the outside was hazy but inside remained clear and unpolluted. Sean could not escape the notion that this holy circle exuded a hidden power. But it was just a circle drawn in dust.

He peered into the murk, to the sound of the wailing increasing. Amid the yellow-tainted mist inchoate faces floated, their gaping-wide maws screaming furiously.

Sean turned to find both Sophie and Mallom watching the horrifying vision. As they looked on, the ghostly faces dissolved, only to be swiftly replaced by more spectres, their faces blurred, with shadowed eyes.

The phantoms acquired more definition, their hands evolving with clawed fingers that raked the unseen barrier but were unable to penetrate it.

'Is this in our mind too?' Sean called out.

'No.' The exorcist shook his head fiercely. 'These spirits can kill us.'

'What?'

'They are extremely dangerous. Their power is drawn from this substance.' Mallom pointed to the mist. 'It isn't fog, it's a realm of trapped souls.'

'Trapped souls?'

'Tormentors and the tormented,' the priest replied. 'The tormentors are vicious, cruel and unrelenting in their attacks on other wretched souls, deriving pleasure from their perpetual suffering.'

Sean heard an inhuman cry, a piteous squeal like a frightened animal caught in a snare, but the sound was short-lived. It was swiftly followed by another, a brutal expression of rage so intense, so chilling, that he wanted to believe it was only the skirling wind of his imagination.

'The tormentors are not spirits, they are a dark breed almost demonic in nature.' Mallom pointed to the fog again. 'This is where our fight will be.'

The ghostly assembly had begun to swell, wheeling about them, slowly at first but gradually picking up speed. The storm demons' hideous laughter rang through the turbulent air. They were unending in their attack on the holy circle; they scratched, shrieked and raked at the invisible barrier.

'Let me go,' Sophie cried out, struggling against Sean's grip. 'I've got to get out of here.'

'Stop it,' he pleaded. 'They'll tear you to pieces.'

Still she struggled.

'I can't take any more. I've got to get out … I've got to …'

'No!' Mallom shouted. 'We can't leave. It would mean certain death.'

Sean held Sophie tighter. 'We've got to stay within the circle.'

'We're safe,' the Irishman said. 'As long as we remain on consecrated ground. Are you listening, Sophie?' His eyes shone with benevolence and kindly understanding. A serenity seemed to pour from him and flow right through the young woman.

'Trust me, please.' Mallom's tone softened.

'I'm sorry,' she found herself saying. 'I don't know what got into me. I just …'

Sean hugged her close, kissed her hair, and she buried her head against his chest, shutting out the sight of the raging spirits.

'I'm scared, Sean.'

'Me too,' he whispered.

They stayed within the safety of each other's arms for a few brief moments, before she drew away and looked out from within the eye of the storm. The alliance of howling wraiths whirled about them, their claws lashing out wildly against the unseen barrier, scratching at it with icy-sharp talons.

A prayer was being said, a fevered mantra repeated again and again. Sean knew it was Mallom imploring God for help, although he could not make out his words. They were lost within the cacophony of other sounds.

The exorcist paused for a moment, raised his hand unhurriedly and traced the sign of the cross into the air four times. Then slowly, deliberately, he lowered his head in murmured prayer again.

Suddenly the exorcist jolted the air with his voice.

'Be still!' he commanded. 'Our Lord compels you. He who once stilled the wind and the sea and the storm.' The words of his prayer were loud. 'Let this enemy have no power over us …'

The legion of dark spirits spun faster, moving at a speed beyond imagination, a swarm of black death. Sean pressed his hands against his ears, desperately trying to shut out the noise amid the mad hammering of his heart. The reverberations continued, rumblings that shook the very earth, while the howling persisted.

Mallom drew out a small black pouch, loosened its ties and poured a white powder into his hand. He closed his eyes, blessing it, then threw the fine dust high into the air. It scattered above the three of them, floating as though suspended by some unseen force before being sucked into the dark vortex.

It was difficult to make out anything clearly beyond the circle. The world beyond was a dense black and shrieking rage. The hideous manifestations were now little more than blurred suggestions of what they had once been.

Sean dropped his hands from his head. 'It's slowing down,' he said.

The darkness started to thin, become less intense. Like oxygen being consumed by a hungry firestorm, the cruel spirits were depleting steadily.

Sophie felt Sean by her side.

'My God,' she said. 'They're leaving.'

Driven away by the Irishman's actions, the spirits retreated, thinning, vaporising, until they became nothing. Everything became still as the legion of wraiths dispersed. The last dregs lingered, wailing their outrage, but only for a moment; soon they too were little more than clouds of vapour.

Sean stared into the fog, his head buzzing, suddenly drained of energy.

'What was that powder?'

'A combination of angelica and salt from the Dead Sea,' the

exorcist said.

'Salt?'

'It isn't just a preservative or a seasoning. Traditions involving salt are legion. Throwing spilled salt over the left shoulder to keep the devil at bay. Its place in religion was established in biblical times from the covenant of salt that symbolised the eternal bond between God and Israel. With a universal sanctity, it has long since been an element of holy water.'

Sean listened, raking a hand through his hair.

'I mixed the salt with ground angelica,' Mallom went on. 'Root of the Holy Ghost, as it's sometimes known, is a powerful tool for warding off evil. When blended with salt it's extremely effective and can …'

The priest's words trailed off to the sound of distant music, instantly recognisable as coming from a squeezebox.

'I've heard that sound before,' Sean said.

'Where?' Sophie asked.

'At Brosswell College.'

A sense of realisation prickled him. 'The visions that caused my breakdown, the nightmares, the hallucinations, they're all linked to what's going on here. They weren't figments of my imagination or mental illness. Something was placing those thoughts in my head, something from this place.'

'Listen,' Mallom urged, as the lively tune continued.

Its hollow sound was joined by faint voices, which swelled and ebbed so that Sean had to listen intently to make out the words.

'We sailed in the morning when the sky turned black, it's hard to sail with the reaper at your back, run 'em through an' slice 'em up …'

He shuddered. The voices were wild, somehow impure, and with a grim hollowness.

'… follow our master through the seas of time …'

'Ah,' the Irishman spoke as the shanty faded. 'Now I understand.'

'Understand what?' Sean asked.

Mallom repeated the words. 'Follow our master through the seas of time. Do you see what they're saying? They're the crew of the *Gospall*, or should I say cohorts of Santia, their master.'

Sean stared back into the mist, desperately fighting the dispiriting chill, which threatened to envelop him. He barely noticed Sophie standing dangerously close to the boundary, or the small creature darting toward her. But he heard her startled cry and saw her stumble backwards, then fall away from them, breaching the perimeter of the circle.

Mallom called out a warning cry as the rat scurried past, but it was too late, the damage had been done. Fog invaded the circle. Tenuous drifts spun about them, weaving around their bodies until the mist covered them. It grew incredibly cold as the temperature plummeted.

Sean put a hand over his nose and mouth in disgust, but it took some time before they grew accustomed to the vile stench that now permeated the air. Eventually he lowered his hands from his face and coughed, clearing his throat. 'What the hell is that?'

Mallom gave a small shake of his head.

Vapours brushed against the Irishman's face. Their very existence exuded a malevolence that was frightening yet curiously fascinating.

The exorcist took a step forward and reeled back from the stale air; a few more steps and he almost disappeared from view.

Sean's eyes narrowed, but it was difficult to see the street ahead. He could only just make out the dim shape of Mallom, even though he was no more than a few metres away.

'Follow me,' the priest said. 'We can't stay here any longer.'

Sean moved forward slowly, searching the wall of sluggish mist for any signs of movement. He heard the shuffle of feet dragging along the road in a slow but deliberate manner. Sean peered into the murk, aware of a presence about him. At the limits of his vision, dark shapes stood a few feet apart.

'Who's there?' he said, as one of the figures came lumbering toward him with the sound of rasping breath, as though air were being sucked in through a rotted throat.

'Ridiculous! The dead can't return, not like this, not physically,' he found himself saying.

So why in God's name could he hear it?

He didn't want to confirm his suspicions that the things were empowered with extraordinary spiritual energy, nor did he want to accept that their corrupt spirits had begun to take physical forms.

Dear God Almighty. Could such a force breach the barrier between the spiritual and the physical world?

Sean felt a strong compulsion to turn away from the ghostly stalker, but he could not; the hypnotic grip was unbreakable. He was forced to watch something lumbering through the mist – *slowly – deliberately – coming for him* ... His senses tingled; another presence was close by. He desperately tried to refute what was in his imagination. *An ancient cadaver reaching out through the fog, its lifeless eyes on him.*

A hand clamped onto the young man's shoulder.

'Seamus,' he said, his nerves jangling. 'You scared the life out of me.'

'Sorry, Sean. There is something in the fog. I could see shadows moving around.'

The young man didn't reply, he just stared past the Irishman, his eyes focusing on a dark shape in the mist.

The figure emerging from the fog appeared to be a man, but its body was coated in a thick, dark crust, its face burnt beyond recognition. It shuffled forward from the cloaking mist, baring lipless teeth, its ghastly eyes fixed onto them.

Beyond the grotesque, more blackened heads came into view. Sean took a step backwards as he and Mallom turned their heads in the direction of more ghastly creatures. Some were partly burnt, others had flesh hanging like tattered rags as if they were in various stages of decomposition, but all had empty staring eyes.

The scorched cadavers changed, their charred flesh becoming less blackened, transforming into grey, bloodless skin. They were a parody of the human form, with rotting meat clinging to their bodies in the hope of becoming more. Others appeared like dried husks that were little more than mummified remains.

Sean was convinced that these things were part of the crew that had been destroyed on *Gospall* over a century ago. He stared into their dull grey faces, blank and expressionless, becoming more animated as they approached.

More cadavers advanced, holding antiquated swords and daggers in withered hands. Mallom had said he'd witnessed the pirates' cruelty on the Haitian island. These reanimated husks bore little semblance to their former selves; but, Sean wondered, could they still fight?

'Look out!' Sophie screamed at Sean.

A cutlass sliced through the air toward the side of his head. He reacted instinctively, chopping the inside of the pirate's wrist with the side of his hand. The sword fell to the floor, and Sean smacked the pirate's face, knocking the figure away from him and back into the fog.

Something struck Sean's arm, and he winced in pain as he pushed Sophie away from him, hoping she'd be safe. She cowered against a wall behind him. Another blow rained down on the top of his shoulder. He whirled around to face his assailant and thrust a kick into its stomach.

'Do something!' Sean shouted. He brushed a skeletal hand away from his face and grappled with another cadaver. Hideous white eyes stared back at him from its charcoaled head.

Mallom removed a slender, silver-tipped vial of holy water from beneath his cassock, and unscrewed the cap. The old man lifted the vial up, and the creature turned toward him. The exorcist started sprinkling.

Another splash of holy water caused the creature to stumble backwards and fall to the floor. The ancient husk erupted into flame as though doused in petrol, its thin, crisp flesh burning like paper. Engulfed in yellow flames, it writhed, its juiceless meat blazing. Sean coughed as a bony hand reached toward him. He jumped backwards, away from the stench, rich with fiery rot and decay

'Don't move,' he called out to Sophie, who was huddled on the floor with her back against a wall. 'Just stay there for now.'

More lumbering shapes approached. They moved slowly, shuffling rather than walking.

'Sean, stay behind me!' Mallom said.

Sean got behind the priest quickly, his eyes fixed on the charred mariners, who raised their swords high into the air, ready to strike. Mallom waited no longer. With a flick of the wrist he scattered holy water into the mist, its spray reaching far and wide. The mariners shrank away from him, back into the fog. Flames swiftly rose up their legs, enveloping their whole bodies in moments. Sean heard their groans and saw the blaze of bodies writhing in the fire of purification, their dark souls now relinquishing what little hold they had on life.

Sean helped Sophie to her feet. As she rose, he saw that she was visibly shaken and there was a fragility about her.

'We've got to get her away from here,' he whispered in the Irishman's ear.

Sean took Sophie by the elbow and pulled her onwards, keeping her upright. They made their way down Grime Street with a sense of urgency born out of fear. Sean slipped his arm around Sophie's waist, supporting her against his hip, while Mallom led from the front. The end of the street could not be far away, and that was enough to drive them on harder and faster.

The Irishman moved forward, a breeze sifting through his silver hair.

'Saints preserve us.'

Sean heard the old man's voice and raised his head.

It appeared in the blanket of fog as a huge shadow, without discernible form. It began to take on substance, emerging slowly from the gloom, its shape now unmistakable. Within those yellow vapours was the spectral outline of a ship.

'Oh, God. Sean!' Sophie's body was trembling against his.

Sean held her tightly, looking up at the vast structure. The maze of ropes and sails hung in tatters, while an icy wind funnelled skeins of fog along the main deck, carrying with it swirling mists that sighed like a host of wraiths.

Sean felt, rather than heard, the sob that came from Sophie, and she clung even tighter to him.

He surveyed the ship with dread. The tall windows of the Captain's cabin were encrusted with salt, and for a brief, uneasy moment an orange glow flickered through two of the stern windows.

'I've seen this ship before.'

Sophie looked at him in bewilderment. 'I don't understand.'

'In my nightmares.'

Incredibly the vessel seemed to float on a sea of rippling mist, and even though it appeared weatherworn, Sean could make out the lettering beneath the stern cabin window:

Gospall.

A thick cloudbank swept across their path, obscuring everything. He whispered words of reassurance into her ear, comforting her, but was wary of the threatening fog.

The shell that was *Gospall* came into view once more as they drew nearer, and for a few moments the haze around it thinned. Sean saw the bleak vessel stretching out across collapsed houses and rubble, which made it seem more forbidding, somehow more sinister.

'Stay back!' Mallom shouted. He held a hand up, warning the couple to stay put.

Sean kept his eyes on the wreck that loomed so close, its masts and upper sails lost in the fog, but something else caught his attention. A dark fluid oozed from the ancient scarred wood of *Gospall*, seeping from every fissure. Gradually it became an outpouring, running down the side of the ship as though she wept blood.

'In the name of the Father, Son and Holy Ghost,' Mallom cried, sprinkling holy water along the side of the ship. 'I command all evil to depart this vessel. Release those restless souls trapped within her, for I know there are some good souls here. Allow them safe passage, heavenly Father.'

A deep rumbling followed the old man's words, its ominous sound forcing Sean to look over his shoulder. The houses behind them began to rattle, and masonry smashed against ground. This wasn't an hallucination, it was real, and very dangerous. Roofing slates sliced through the air, easily capable of decapitating an unsuspecting victim, and the floor juddered. He felt the cold, its touch like ice. Streamers of mist brushed against his face, and he recoiled at the rumblings that shook the very foundations of Grime Street.

'This place is ripping itself apart,' Sophie screamed.

'I don't think it's over yet.'

Sean was pitched forward when the ground shook again, and amid the noise and billowing dust, he heard Sophie cry out as debris fell beside her.

'We need to make a run for it,' he shouted.

Sean grabbed Sophie's hand and pulled her along harshly. They scrambled across rubble near *Gospall,* breaking into a run when the way ahead was clearer.

Mallom continued, his head bowed in hushed prayer, as bricks showered down onto the road. Surprisingly the disturbance was short lived, stopping almost as soon as it had begun, aside from the odd tremor. After a few moments, even these had subsided.

Sean and Sophie stood, both breathing heavily, relieved by the sudden cessation of activity.

'You feel it too?' Sophie asked.

'Yes,' Sean replied. It was a momentary sense that the oppressive hatred had relented. Yet somehow this brought little comfort.

'Look.' Sophie was pointing toward *Gospall.*

It was only then that he noticed a steady stream of shimmering forms. Were these mutable apparitions the trapped souls Mallom had spoken of? Slowly they came into focus, like objects viewed through a telescope, becoming clearer and sharper; spirits of men, all differing in height, size and age. They wore breeches and shirts, some with waistcoats, others in blue frock coats, all untarnished by the flames that had consumed them in life. Heads tilted back, they stared upward and ascended from the deck of the ship into the sky. The sailors hovered, calling out to one another, laughing boisterously as they faded away.

There was a cold stillness in the crumbling walls of Grime Street as Sean glimpsed more movement. Another obscure shape paused just long enough for him to make out the blurry outline of a vaporous head and torso, before the last mariner was sucked upward into the black void.

38

Mallom raised his head once more. The young couple were a good distance from him and standing quite still among the debris, looking up at the ethereal vessel. Everything seemed to shimmer as if waves of intense heat rose from the hull. The vessel blurred, appeared to ripple and become little more than a mirage.

Then she was gone.

Mallom couldn't help but think of the unfortunate sailors who'd lost their lives in defence of their Captain, and the pirates who'd infested *Gospall* with their black-hearted hatred of all that was good. Murder, rape and violence were their legacy. He was sickened by the atrocities he had witnessed. Fatigue was catching up with him and he needed to rest, but he couldn't stop now.

Something emerged from the murk, another ancient figure, dressed mostly in black. Desiccated skin stretched over its charred head and ghastly eyes blazed from blackened cavities. The priest felt a shudder of disgust looking into that hideous face. The mariner's clothes had escaped the damage of the flames that had engulfed them in life. Its cloak swished this way and that over a dark jacket and cutlass, the hem reaching the tip of black leather sea boots.

Mallom took a step backwards, but it drew closer.

Shock, perhaps revulsion, caused the vial of holy water to slip from his fingers. It hit the cobblestones and shattered instantly. Despite the figure's ghastly appearance, Mallom had to force himself to remember that it had once been a man. The discoloured pendant that hung around its neck was familiar; he had seen it before in another time, another place.

Mallom took another step and felt suddenly drained of all

strength, as if the grotesque was sucking the energy from his body. It was using him. The thing was taking on form and definition. Its features became sharp: a prominent nose replaced the ruined face and a fine moustache arched over thin lips. But it was the eyes that Mallom recognised more than any other feature. They were incredibly dark and bristled with madness in the dim light. Long hair hung loosely onto his shoulders, casting the mariner's face in part shadow, but the priest knew the identity of the dark-clothed man.

'Francois Santia,' he said, with a resigned weariness in his voice, knowing that no rite of exorcism could drive a man's spirit from his own body.

The tall man grinned, gripping the exorcist by the throat and lifting him into the air, his legs kicking wildly. Mallom looked into Santia's eyes and saw the evil within. He felt the icy fingers squeezing tighter, cutting off what little oxygen was left. Even as his body grew weaker, he was conscious of the pirate's laughter, that same insane tone he'd heard before. He was going to die, nothing could stop that now; Santia was stronger than any human could be, and even though his feet drummed against the pirate's body in a futile attempt to break his attacker's hold, it was useless. Soon his vision began to swim, and as his consciousness ebbed away he saw a shadowy figure watching from the cloaking darkness.

'Get off him,' Sean screamed, running toward Santia. But as he rushed across the mist-covered wasteland his body sagged. He sank to his knees, drained, unaware that another being was using his energy for the purpose of materialisation.

A shimmering light appeared behind Santia, its appearance like thousands of diamonds emitting a tremendous brightness, yet it moved with the fluidity of water, its features melding into human form. Even as Mallom struggled, his strength and consciousness now all but gone, the shape began to solidify, to take on definition. The body, limbs and head evolved, the face becoming absolute.

Santia reacted angrily to the commotion, casting the priest aside. Mallom fell to the ground hard, but was uninjured. He rolled over onto his back, gasping for breath, his chest heaving. He sucked in a great lungful of air, and as he looked up he saw the other figure, now fully materialised.

39

The young man stood defiantly, his dress coat dark blue with one of the white lapels embellished by a decoration earned during his short career in life.

Although the Irishman was dazed and weak, his gaze focused on the face before him. The features were unmistakable; the thick blond hair drawn back into a tail, and those blue-grey eyes. Mallom recognised the man from his out-of-body experience and smiled weakly.

William Pike stood in the moonlight, its luminescence making him appear even younger than the priest remembered. He looked at the Irishman, his body whole again, pulsating with life, but his eyes full of infinite sadness.

As the exorcist slowly rose, he heard the stamp of feet. Santia was running toward Pike with murderous fury. The two men lunged at each other, becoming locked in a battle that had begun centuries ago. The pirate's hands closed around the young man's neck, but before he could form a grip, Pike brought his fist up into his stomach. It had little effect other than to tighten Santia's demented grin into a grimace. As they struggled, Pike grasped the marauder's lapels and drew him close, staring into his crazed face.

'It ends here,' Pike said.

'I'm going to kill you for good this time,' Santia retorted, then laughed as the violent struggle continued.

The exorcist felt totally useless. He tried to stand, but slumped to the ground, breathing heavily. He wondered if he and his young friends were being used as psychic catalysts to trigger this event. But as he lay there regaining composure, he remembered that the pendant Santia wore around his neck had been used on the Haitian island during the vodoun ritual. Santia had destroyed the Ioa, then stolen it. He knew that it was extremely powerful, and able, he guessed, to sustain the pirate between life and death. Once removed, surely he would lose his dark energy?

Mallom tried to call out but succeeded only in coughing. His throat ached; it was swollen and incredibly painful. He swallowed hard, then tried again.

'The amulet!' he shouted hoarsely. 'The amulet!'

This time his voice was heard.

'It's the source,' he spluttered, 'of Santia's power!'

Pike grasped the talisman, acknowledging the Irishman, and ripped it from the pirate's chest as though it were a beating heart.

Santia released an agonised cry.

Mallom pushed himself up onto one knee, his heart racing.

Santia screamed, yowling in agony, as his body began to decay. Without the amulet, the process of physical materialisation fell into reverse, and with it came unimaginable pain. The flesh of his skull began to sag and fall away, exposing muscle and discoloured bone. His eyes leaked from their cavities, slithering onto his ravaged face. Mercifully Santia's cloak concealed much of his withering body.

Mallom coughed as the deep stench of decay poured over him. He held his breath, afraid to take in the sickly odour. An icy mist brushed past him, surging toward Santia. It swirled around the pirate's legs, swelling and growing furiously. Within those swirling mists, dark shadows circled the pirate, taunting him with their cruel laughter.

Santia was outraged and in agony, screaming and bellowing at his tormentors. They had come for him, and their torture was ruthless. He lashed out, but they struck him, ripping the coat from his body along with the rotting flesh from his frame. Santia spun absurdly and released a maddened screech, but they did not relent.

The Irishman wondered if Santia finally understood what true fear really was. The pirate must have thought that he was in control, but without the protection of the amulet, he was rendered vulnerable to attack from the wraiths. His ambition, his wickedness and his abuse had unleashed forces beyond him. Had Santia only just now grasped the significance of his actions?

Pike was now no more than a fast dissolving blur. For one fleeting moment, the Irishman saw him raise a hand to the locket around his neck and touch it.

'*Rebecca,*' Mallom heard him say. Then he was gone.

The mutilated figure of Santia lay where he had fallen, his movements becoming weaker. Still, the wraiths hovered above him, their spectral fingers raking, pulling and tugging, eagerly exposing his ribs. He pleaded for mercy, his body flinching each time they struck, but the agony continued. Finally, the vengeful creatures had exacted their revenge.

Something dark slipped from the pirate's body and hovered over the carcass. It resembled his physical form but was dark and spectral. The wraiths closed in, and at first Santia didn't seem aware of them; his gaze was fixed on the rotting mass before him.

Mallom watched them steal the pirate's degenerate soul away, to be joined by more of their sort. A great gathering of phantoms surrounded the pirate. Santia's lips moved and he seemed to be pleading for help, but he was lost. His suffering would surely continue in another hellish place. He would be a plaything for the torturers' amusement in a world perpetuated by evil.

As the phantoms dissolved, fading into the whispering mists with their prize, Mallom shuddered.

'It's over,' the Irishman said, crossing himself. *But why didn't it feel that way?* He stood motionless, allowing the thudding in his chest to subside. He'd done everything he could. *Gospall* had been cleansed, Santia was gone and Pike and his crew had departed to a better place, so what else was left? *The amulet?* Mallom searched the ground, but the amulet too had been claimed by the mist, its power now useless. He wanted to heave a sigh of relief but could not. *Something was still wrong.*

A shadow, cast by the moon, fell over Santia's remains. Mallom traced it to its source. He peered into the patchy fog, shocked by something else. A figure stood, unmoving and silent, with an oppressive shroud of blackness surrounding its frame. Its domed head and lead-coloured face were pierced by terrible dark eyes that held a silvery glint.

It fixed its gaze on the Irishman and gave a wicked smile.

The exorcist summoned up all his courage. He'd seen this demon before in another time, and it had almost destroyed him. He'd had time to learn about it since it had claimed the life of poor Jacob. Exalted by legions of fallen spirits, this dark lord had once been an archangel, until he had been flung headlong from the heights of heaven.

'Methangalic.' He spoke the name without realising it.

Its ashen lips festered into a grin.

Mallom was more afraid of this than any other challenge he'd ever encountered. They had been nothing compared with this. His mind grappled with unanswered questions. *Why was the creature so silent, so still? And why did it have a triumphant grin on its face?*

Infernal forces had moved into the earthly realm, and this was controlling them. This being was too powerful for him to fight. He was just flesh and blood, and this entity had been around since the beginning of time. Mallom knew as much from the ancient occult texts he'd studied. This was truly the great enemy of mankind. Sitting on the right-hand side of Satan's throne, Methangalic ruled legions of demons.

The exorcist began to pray but was stunned into silence as Methangalic dissolved into the shifting mists.

A firm breeze swept along Grime Street, funnelling through the crumbling ruins that had once been homes, forcing the fog to retreat through the hollow-eyed windows and gaping doorways. Within moments the mist was driven away, its threads and drifts roaming the shattered street to find the mass, which was disappearing rapidly. Soon even those hazy vapours faded reluctantly into the night.

Mallom breathed deeply. The air was fresh, as if it had been cleansed. His body ached, and he felt incredibly tired, but it was over. The sound of footsteps heralded the approach of Sean and Sophie.

40

'What the hell was that?' Sean asked. They were breathing heavily, their clothes covered in a fine layer of dust.

'Methangalic.' The priest's reply sounded weary, his mind distracted. 'But something's not right.'

'What is it, Sean?' Sophie asked. 'What does he mean?

'It's over,' Sean said, trying to reassure her.

'Can you be so sure?' came Mallom's sombre reply. 'I don't think it is finished.'

The anxiety in the Irishman's voice roused nervousness in Sean.

'Methangalic has always been behind all of this,' Mallom said. 'But why?'

He ran a hand across his stubbly chin. 'You already know what happened on the Haitian island. But the Ioa, the fierce entity that possessed the young woman, was also a spirit of prophecy. Once summoned, it couldn't return, because Santia killed the host and removed the amulet from around her neck. With no body to inhabit, the Ioa was forced to use something else for its task.'

'What do you mean exactly?'

'Don't you see? Its psychic effluence possessed *Gospall*.'

Sean almost laughed aloud at the lunacy of the thought. It was impossible. Yet the thought persisted.

'It all sounds a bit …'

'Farfetched?' the Irishman's smile was humourless. 'Take a look around at what's just happened.'

'Before the fall of man,' the exorcist said, 'through the mists of time, thrice it shall come, a leprous vessel, the bringer of great evil and destruction to mankind.' Mallom's words were slow and deliberate, confusion giving way to an uneasy understanding. 'Heed the warning before my prophecy is fulfilled. Abbot Saul was right, the leprous vessel was *Gospall*.'

He turned to Sean. 'What were the dates of those newspapers you found in your mother's house?'

'1914 and 1939, but I don't …'

'That's what I was afraid of.'

'What's wrong?'

He fixed Sean with grim eyes. 'Do you remember the prophecies of Abbot Saul?' He paused for a moment before continuing. 'From a lowly soldier, he shall come to have supreme command, the great liar shall obtain dominion under the crescent moon.'

'What's that got to do with anything?'

'The date that brought us here tonight was scrawled across that prophecy in Saul's *A libri of oraculum*.'

'Yes, but …'

'You're familiar with what's going on in the Middle East and the recent terrorist attacks by Islamic extremists? My guess is that our Abbot was talking about Rafika, the new leader of Iraq. This is all part of a bigger picture. Think about it. Don't the dates of those newspapers mean anything to you?'

'Oh, God.'

The priest was staring at him intently.

'You're talking about the last two world wars.'

'I'm afraid I am.' Mallom looked away momentarily. 'That brings us to the present.' His penetrating gaze found Sean once more. 'In the new age, great lights shall descend from the sky. Fires shall rage, many people shall be burnt with heat and great cities shall be made desolate. Nothing will stop the world from dying.'

His gaze shifted to Sophie, then back to Sean.

'The ship was no more than an omen, a harbinger; and the dreams you experienced were a warning of what is about to happen.'

'No,' Sophie cried out. She was shaking her head, 'It can't be.'

'It is.' His reply was soft. 'I understand now why the demon was grinning. It has deceived us. The cryptic message I received earlier on my mirror warned of deception. *Gospall's* return couldn't have been prevented. Everything has been drawing us to this moment.'

Sophie continued to shake her head. 'No, it can't.'

Sean took her in his arms and held her firmly. 'It's all right.' He kissed her forehead and hugged her again.

Sophie stepped away from him. 'I'm afraid, so afraid.'

Sean brushed the glistening tears from her cheeks with a trembling hand.

'When, Seamus?' she asked.

'Soon, I would imagine,' he said sadly.

The grim acceptance on Mallom's face told him that the world was about to change forever.

The Irishman sank to his knees in prayer.

'I can't believe that this is the end, it just can't be.' Sophie's words faltered.

'Sophie.' As Sean opened his mouth again there was a searing flash in the distance. For a moment, it was like day instead of night. The young couple raised their hands against the intense brightness, and as Mallom turned toward the source of the flash there was a deafening explosion. A thundering whoosh of warm air brushed against them, and small particles of hot dust struck their bodies. More blast-waves reverberated about them, and Sean felt the ground tremble and heard the ear-busting roar that seemed to be going on forever, drowning out Sophie's screams. He was afraid to look, even when he thought it might be safe. He knew what the source of the explosion was. When he lowered his hand from his face, the reality of what he saw numbed his brain.

The entire area was an enormous ball of fire. London was a blazing inferno against the backdrop of a black velvet sky. They could no longer see any of the familiar historic structures in the distance, or any buildings at all. Everything had been flattened. The fire seemed to stretch for miles, like a panoramic view of hell. Billowing orange flames cascaded into deeper red fires. The debris drew itself together to form a huge mushroom shape, disturbingly awesome in its intensity as it ascended high into the sky.

Mallom looked heavenward, away from the carnage, and saw a small flickering light approaching fast. He closed his eyes again. This time Sean heard the Irishman whispering a prayer, imploring God for help. Although it was repeated over and over, no help was forthcoming. His prayer was answered by the faint hum of a missile as it closed in.

Sean felt his legs weaken, and he reached out for Sophie, wrapping his arms around her. As Sean stroked Sophie's hair and kissed the top of her head, the noise increased to a horrendous whining, and within a flesh-searing moment there was darkness.

About the Author

After many years of hard work I recently released my debut novel *The Haunting of Gospall* through Telos. My love of writing, and vivid imagination have ensured there is much more to come, with two more novels under my belt and a third underway.

My fascination with all things paranormal have definitely enhanced my ability to craft a terrifying tale. There is no substitute for experience. I have not only researched the phenomenon but have also been exposed to it since I was a child.

Having left school at sixteen to work as an apprentice hairdresser, and qualify, I progressed on to part time teaching. Although, I never really found my true vocation. I became self employed and began working in care homes for the elderly. It was a difficult job but incredibly rewarding. I enjoyed meeting and talking to the residents and made extra time for those who were very ill. I learned so much about myself during that time. But writing was always my passion. I graduated through Manchester University and attained a BA in Education which helped me pen my novels. After much soul searching I made the decision to follow my dream and become a full time writer.

Solomon Strange lives in Lancashire with his wife and two children.

Other Telos Horror and Steampunk Titles

STEPHEN LAWS
SPECTRE

RHYS HUGHES
CAPTAINS STUPENDOUS

HELEN MCCABE
THE PIPER TRILOGY
1: PIPER
2: THE PIERCING
3: THE CODEX

RAVEN DANE
THE MISADVENTURES OF CYRUS DARIAN
Steampunk Adventure Series
1: CYRUS DARIAN AND THE TECHNOMICRON
2: CYRUS DARIAN AND THE GHASTLY HORDE
3: CYRUS DARIAN AND THE DEMON (Forthcoming)

DEATH'S DARK WINGS
Alternative History Novel

ABSINTHE AND ARSENIC
Horror and Fantasy Short Story Collection

TELOS PUBLISHING
www.telos.co.uk

www.ingramcontent.com/pod-product-compliance
Lightning Source LLC
Chambersburg PA
CBHW071754190726
48292CB00003B/981